Finding Magic in Misfortune

NICOLE CAMPBELL

Finding Magic in Misfortune

NICOLE CAMPBELL

To all my witches: You *are* the magic.

-Nicole

Chapter 1: Sam

A *Work Happy Hour* was an oxymoron. I'd considered asking Hecate to encourage Chris's tie to venture closer to the tea light candle that was flickering on the table.

Stranger things have happened.

However, I hadn't worked with deities in years, and from experience, Hecate did not like being called upon willy-nilly. While unfortunate, Chris was going to stay char-free.

Asshole.

I stirred my third Long Island iced tea and ignored the chatter from the two other design assistants. They were new…ish. And I was not new. No, no. I'd been a graphic design *assistant* for almost two years. I'd been to forty-seven thousand happy hours, a billion and a half coffee runs, and I'd finally been taking lead on some campaigns with the promise of a junior designer role. I'd also slept with Chris about twelve times, but really four if I was only counting the ones where I got off, too.

Selfish fucking—his eyes snapped to mine from the end of the table, and I wondered if I'd said that last part out loud. No one else seemed disturbed, so I figured I was safe. The straw hit air at the bottom of my glass, and that was my cue to grab a cab, go home, and research an appropriate hex in response to him recommending someone else for the promotion.

I wobbled in my heels. *That's a bad sign.*

"Chris… have a *spectacular* evening," I ground out when I passed his chair.

He had the decency to look concerned and raked his hand through his bad haircut. I stopped and tuned into his energy. He was worried.

But about what…

I focused through the haze and followed his gaze flitting over to Melissa. I grinned despite the tears threatening to make an appearance after this shit-tastic day. Melissa was one of the new-ish assistants, and if the wave of fear I felt was any indication, he *really* didn't want me to tell her he'd been sleeping with me while flirting with her. I leaned toward him.

"Don't worry, your secret's safe. But Melissa probably isn't into guys who always finish first."

I shrugged, hoping I delivered that message in a menacing way. Chris' mouth hung open, and I felt like my chances of making it out of this bar in one piece were looking up.

"Sam!" a booming voice called as I attempted my getaway.

I groaned inwardly as David Carter, a senior graphic designer, and a garbage disposal of a human, waved me over. The only thought that sprang to mind when looking at him was how badly he wanted to be Harvey from *Suits*. He was *not* Harvey. He wasn't even Louis.

"David." I waved and turned to keep going.

"Oh, come on, come say hi. We haven't seen you all night."

You should have tried harder to reach Hecate, I scolded myself as I shuffled over to his side of the table, determined not to sway.

"Hi."

"You heading out already?"

"It would seem so."

My eyes shot to Chris, who was trying to look invested in something happening on his phone.

"Well, next time, you've gotta sit down here with us. You could be the most awesome assistant at this firm if you really got to know all the designers and their different styles." He grinned like he had just bestowed some wisdom worthy of Master Yoda.

Oh, for fuck's sake.

Of all the times for him to do this, it had to be when I was three Long Islands deep and already poised to hex someone's balls off. The white-hot anger that had been kept buried since the announcement that afternoon was no longer contained. It burned its way up my chest, and my fists clenched around the strap of my bag to brace myself for whatever was going to come out of my mouth.

"Well, David, thankfully, I don't give a rat's ass about being an *awesome* design *assistant*. I'm already an *awesome* fucking *designer*. I'm guessing that Chris here hasn't given me credit for my work on the Olive-Juice account, right? Or any of the others I've worked on this year, and no one else could be bothered to get their heads out of their asses long enough to notice. So why don't you both just fuck all the way off?"

I turned on my heel, not stopping to note any of their faces, and I welcomed the cool night air as it filled my lungs.

* * *

Fury carried me all the way home and into bed, so I didn't have any type of remorse about the events of the evening. That was my Taurus Mars talking. God, I fucking hated being condescended to, maybe more than anything else in the world. But at about two am, when the drinks came back to haunt me, my more rational Libra moon made an appearance. I started to wonder if perhaps I'd crossed a line.

Not more of a line than Chris crossed in sleeping with his design assistant, but of course, no one knows about that.

Ugh. I downed some ibuprofen and attempted to shut up my brain, at least until the sun had shown its face.

As it happened, life did not get any better at eight a.m. There were three missed calls from my HR manager and one email in my work inbox. On a Saturday. I closed one eye like viewing the email with the other one might make being written up at work easier to take.

Ms. Marsh,

Your employment with *Willow & Bark Graphic Design Co.* is hereby terminated immediately. The reasons for this termination of employment are:

a. *Insubordination:* According to Section IV of the handbook, all employees will conduct themselves professionally when representing the company.
b. *Harassment:* According to Section IV of the handbook, harassment is defined as offensive conduct that may include, but is not limited to, offensive jokes, slurs, or name-calling, physical assault,, intimidation, ridicule or mockery, insults, offensive pictures, and interference with work performance.

You will coordinate with Connie Carter, your HR representative, to arrange for the return of your keys, computer, and any other items belonging to the company, as well as receipt of your final compensation for work provided.

Respectfully,

John Matthews

John Matthews
CEO
Willow & Bark Graphic Design Co.

Well. Fuck.

Chapter 2: Jesse

"...two more…one more…and done. Good. Rest for two minutes. I'm gonna grab you some water."

Greg, my physical therapist, wisely left me alone after we finished too few side-step reps. I'd been stuck here for months, and my leg felt no stronger. I was making no progress. My knee ached, my hips were spasming all the time from over-compensating, and I was just fucking done.

I ripped off the resistance band with a satisfying snap and chucked it to the corner of the treatment area. Thankfully, the room was empty because I was either going to yell or cry, and I wasn't comfortable with either.

"Here you go, man," Greg said, handing me a cup of water.

I downed it on the off chance it helped. It didn't.

"I'm out, Greg. I can't do this anymore without feeling better. And I'm not blaming you or anything; I just can't."

My voice cracked on my last word, and I needed to get the hell out of there.

"I know it's frustrating to be stalled in your recovery, but you should—"

"What I *should* be doing is gearing up to be called to the majors, but instead, I'm here, in Emberwood, limping around because I can't do a fucking leg lift. Jesus Christ."

I blew out a breath and bit the inside of my cheek, hard, to try to settle the anger spewing out of me. Greg was quiet. He didn't look mad, but his pity was worse.

"I'm sorry, man. None of this is your fault… I'm just done for right now."

I grabbed my *Emberwood Dragons* hat and dragged my leg out of the office with as much dignity as I could muster.

Once the truck door closed, something between a yell and a

sob forced its way out of my throat. My hands shook, and my breath came in short bursts. I forced myself to take a few deep breaths and willed my heart to slow down.

You should not drive all the way home like this.

I needed a distraction.

JESSE: Hey, I'm gonna stop by the salon if that's cool
LAUR: Sure. Is everything okay?
JESSE: Peachy
LAUR: I'll have an ice pack ready.
JESSE: Thx

It wasn't the first time I'd hobbled over there after a PT session, so at least she didn't expect me to be in a cheery mood.

* * *

A tiny bell sounded when I opened the door to *The Dollhouse*, and Lauren was cashing out a customer. She had on some sort of sparkly dress that looked like it came straight out of 1985. It probably had; she liked to thrift. It was late enough that there was only one other stylist working and the place was ready for closing. My sister caught my eye and furrowed her brows at me, concerned, but I waved her off. She sauntered over with an ice pack wrapped in a paper towel when she was finished.

"Bad?"

"Bad enough I don't want to talk about it."

"'Kay. Do you wanna go next door and get a beer and not talk about it, or do you want me to cut your hair? It's a little past surfer dude and is entering the territory of maybe-he's-a-hippie."

She wrinkled her nose at that possibility, which earned at least a chuckle.

"No haircut today, but soon. It is about long enough to put into a ponytail, and I don't know if I can pull that off."

"You could, but you might need more tattoos and an earring. Maybe a bike and a bandana. We could do a whole makeover."

"Pass. Drinks are fine. I'll go grab a table."

She just nodded and went to clear her station.

The crowd was weeknight-light, so a table was easy to come by. I tried not to let my limp be noticeable even though I clearly had an ice pack strapped to my knee.

"Tell me you're not drinking alone, Jesse Garrett."

The server that came over was a girl I went to high school with, though she was probably two years younger than me. Jenny something. I tried to put on the grin of my former self.

"Ah, not tonight. My sister will be here in a sec. How've you been?"

Jenny prattled on about something until I heard, "...when do you think you'll be back to playing again? I loved going to the Mud Hens games when I was living in Toledo. I told everyone I knew you. Even in high school, we all knew you'd be in the majors someday."

She smiled, and I had no idea what my face looked like. The string tethering me to any type of social niceties was pulled too tight, and I could not deal with a trip down memory lane.

"Oh, uh, thanks. Not sure, still rehabbing the knee."

"Well, I'm sure you'll be back in no time. What are you drinking? First one's on me."

I gave what I hoped was a smile and not a grimace and ordered an IPA, cursing the misfortune of, well... my misfortune.

Thankfully, Jenny Something got the message that I didn't want to talk about the old days, brought my drink, and took Lauren's order.

"She asked about your knee, didn't she." Lauren didn't pose it as a question; she simply flipped her strawberry blond hair over her shoulder knowingly.

"She did."

"Damn it, Jesse, I can't let you go anywhere alone."

"It's been a while. I know people think it's reasonable to ask. Never in a million years did I think I'd be out this long, either. I probably *should* know what I'm doing by now."

"Sure. Anyway. Wanna hear about my bat-shit crazy client of the day?" Her green eyes widened, and I welcomed her ability to talk with no need for reciprocation.

"I thought you'd never ask."

I sat back and let her tell a story about some woman who wanted a cut without losing any length on her hair. I felt some of the day's anger leave my shoulders.

Perhaps I should see someone about that.

That being the anger that never quite dissipated. I imagined it wasn't healthy to carry it around *all* the time. For today, though, this was enough.

Chapter 3: Sam

Three months later: Summer

The sound that packing tape made while being stretched should have been used as a torture method by CIA spies. I didn't even have that much stuff, but my crystals and tarot cards alone took up too many boxes. Even though I only used one deck, I was still attached to all of them.

I had gone through *almost* all the stages of grief after losing my job. I just kind of missed the "acceptance" portion because I was still furious. There would be absolutely no forgiving and forgetting, but my rent payment and depleted savings decided I needed to get over stewing in my anger. I sat on the floor, using a box as a backrest, and angry tears sprang to the corners of my eyes. I let them fall this time. It was *just* an apartment and *just* a job, but they had been mine. I could go back to pretending I was fine tomorrow.

At least there is at least an end to the packing-tape symphony.

I took a break to shower before ordering takeout and packing my suitcase. My hair tumbled down my back after being released from a messy bun, and I attempted to brush through my curls. I was determined to avoid my own bloodshot blue eyes in my reflection. The girl in the mirror tended to be a judgy bitch sometimes, and I wasn't in the mood for her. While I tried to let the waterfall melt everything away, hot tears continued to spill over instead. They became part of the water until it ran cold. I turned them off along with the shower and resolved to make it through the one night I had left here.

I finished ordering from my favorite Chinese place, knowing it was going to be one of the things I missed most about Rockford.

That's a little sad.

But with no letter of recommendation and a sparse portfolio

(since I was told I could use none of the designs I worked on at the firm as an *assistant*), not a lot of employers were jumping at the chance to hire me. Freelancing kept me going for a couple of months, along with my savings, but now I had to face reality. Reality was the worst.

* * *

The sun was out and mocking me with its good vibes and vitamin D. I'd gotten up at the ass crack of dawn to finish loading the U-Haul and do a last sweep of my apartment. Reluctantly, I dropped my keys into the lockbox at the main office and got into my C-RV. I sent a quick request to my guides and the dragon that guarded my car to make sure I got to my destination safe and sound. I had six hours to get right with the idea that I was going back to Emberwood and that I had to be a big girl. I *hated* running to my aunt for help, and I hated telling my mother about it even more. Her holding back the words "I told you so" was worse than her just saying them.

I sighed.

You are an adult *now. Act like it.*

I focused instead on seeing my Aunt Zin. Nothing could seem all that bad if she was there.

I called her as I maneuvered the SUV and the trailer out of my apartment complex.

"Samantha," she answered warmly.

"Hi, Aunt Zin! I just wanted to let you know that I'm leaving Rockford. I should be there around three."

"I can't wait to see you. You have the dragon I sent you?"

I grinned despite my mood. Only with her would I discuss the importance of having one's dragon for travel safety. I looked down at the shimmery statue she'd sent me to represent my *actual* dragon in whatever realm dragons exist. "I've got her. Never leave home without Pearla." Yes, I named my dragon. It would have been rude

14

not to.

"Perfect. Then I'll see you this afternoon."

"See you—"

"Oh, also? Do not stop at the hamburger establishment. Drive safely!"

She hung up before I even thought about asking "What burger place?" but I'd learned to roll with it when she gave me vague predictions. Taking her word for it was better than getting food poisoning.

I listened to all the songs I'd had lined up for the first leg of the trip, but they were not enough of a distraction from the fact that my entire life had imploded in a matter of months.

Why did I have to go off on David like that? This thought plagued me often when I replayed all the dominoes that fell to land me here, but the answer I heard in my head every time was, "David was a dick." Okay, maybe the answer was typically, "Because you needed to leave," but I liked the first one better.

But I didn't WANT to leave, I thought back sharply. The thing about my guides, though, was that they didn't care. They were hilarious that way.

I chewed on my lip as I gave up trying to argue with my people. They were annoying me. The gas station up ahead beckoned for me to buy all the snacks for the four hours I had left. There *was*, in fact, a burger place next door, but I wasn't interested in testing my aunt. Gas station pizza would be safer. There was a gap in parking spaces that perfectly fit the car and trailer combo I was rocking, so I said thanks to Pearla for that. She was the best at finding parking. I pictured her curled up and looking smug on top of my car.

It had warmed up since I'd left Rockford, and I tugged on my jean shorts to cover my thighs as they rubbed together. I grabbed candy at random, a slice of who-knows-how-old pizza, and enough iced tea to keep me appropriately caffeinated.

Back in my car, pleasantly surprised at the freshness of said pizza, I tried to envision what living in Emberwood would be like.

Correction, staying in *Emberwood. 'Living' implies permanence.*

Not too many years ago, the idea of living there had been my whole daydream... until it wasn't. I hadn't been back since just before senior year of high school. Visiting my great-aunt was my most favorite summer tradition, at least until the end of that summer.

With effort, I tried to remember all the warm, homey feelings from before that, and my heart lurched. I did miss Aunt Zin's house and, even more so, her shop. I felt like I'd grown up in *Books and Broomsticks.* It was where I'd learned how to read tarot, read all kinds of books I shouldn't have, both witchcraft-related and not (Zin liked her pirate romance books near the register). But that place had felt more like *home* to me than my actual home for a lot of years.

You should have just gotten the soda; fake sweetener be damned. Water with pizza was not hitting the spot. I sighed and chewed.

Not that there was anything *wrong* with my parents or where I grew up in Indiana. My mom and dad just didn't quite *get* me. They loved me; I confused them. I was too strait-laced for my artist mother, who criticized my choice of graphic design instead of the "real arts." As she put it, graphic design was just creativity for capitalists.

Sue me for wanting health insurance.

I rolled my eyes despite the fact that no one could see me and took the last bite of pizza before heading back out onto the highway.

Me losing my job was probably the highlight of my mother's year. My dad was an accountant, and he didn't get any of my witchy "woo-woo" shit. No, they weren't still married, which was obviously shocking, but they were on friendly terms. Zinnia always acted as if everything I said and did made perfect sense.

I'm lucky to have her, I thought. There was some guilt creeping in about fighting so hard against moving to Emberwood. I could have been forced to crawl back home to one of my parents.

Horrifying.

I rolled down all of my windows and let the humid air swirl around me, my curls threatening to abandon my ponytail. I didn't care, I needed to clear out the negativity I'd brought to my car.

I decided that all of this reminiscing was serving a purpose; convincing me that I was doing the right thing by going there to lick my wounds. Start over.

Too late to second-guess now.

* * *

I pulled into the long gravel driveway of Aunt Zinnia's cottage outside of Emberwood proper, only grabbing my suitcase from the back—unpacking was not happening today. A smile couldn't help but appear at the jungle of a garden that overflowed onto the front walkway. The scent of the jasmine vines lifted my mood, and I knocked after traversing the terrain to the door.

"I'm offended that you knocked," Zinnia said as a greeting, pulling me into a fierce hug. We'd seen each other since I last visited, of course, but it wasn't the same as being together at her house. Tears sprang to my eyes when she didn't let go. I tried to tell myself it was her *Gold Dust Woman* perfume, the lingering scent of incense, or the sheer number of plants surrounding her house, but I didn't buy it.

"I missed you," I said, stepping back.

"Of course you did. The people in Rockford are boring, and you didn't belong there. Now come in already."

She practically glided across her hardwood floors, looking like Stevie Nicks' older sister, her collection of bangles chiming together, and I wondered if I'd ever be as effortlessly cool. Zinnia was one of those women whose age was difficult to determine. She had streaks of gray and silver that wove through her coarse, dark curls. She either had great skincare, or she was the sort of witch who stole youth from the town's children on Halloween.

I followed her into the kitchen, marveling at how her normal decor and witchy shit blended throughout the house. Crystals next to family photos, decks of tarot cards stacked next to her unopened mail, runes in the bowl with her shop keys. It all existed harmoniously.

"Are those margaritas?" I asked, looking at the full blender on the counter.

"Yes. Glasses are in the hutch."

"It's 3:30 in the afternoon."

"And time is a construct, so I don't care. The last time you visited, you were eighteen and couldn't drink, so consider this a makeup for lost fun." She arched a brow at me, daring me to argue, but I just shook my head and went to get the glasses.

She poured, and I relaxed. I was glad we'd already hashed out everything that had happened with work, so I didn't need to talk about it again. Zinnia had gone on a campaign to get me to come stay with her as soon as I told her about losing my job. I'd pushed back. Hard. It had already knocked the wind out of me to admit to my mother that I couldn't cut it in corporate America, or the "capitalist hellscape," as she called it. I'd tried to explain to my aunt that I wanted to fix my own mistakes, but she simply continued to act as if it were an irrefutable fact that I'd be staying with her. I couldn't decide if me being there now was a testament to her psychic abilities, her manifestation abilities, or a little of both.

"Who's manning the shop if you're here?" I asked, noting the time.

"No one. It's closed. Closing periodically without warning only adds to the mystique of the store."

I laughed through my nose at that. Her shop didn't need any more mystique, but that's what kept the tourists coming, so I guessed she knew what she was doing. "Well, whenever you want to put me to work, I'm ready. I need to unpack and return the U-Haul, but other than that." I was going to at least be useful while I stayed there and attempted to figure out the rest of my life.

"Oh yes, actually, I asked Shelly, you know my neighbor? To send her sons over to bring your boxes to the guest house around five. So don't worry about that."

"Aunt Zin, that's not necessary—"

She interrupted me with a wave. "I told her the same, but I took care of an… issue, we'll call it, with her now ex-husband a few months back. She's been intent on repaying me since then."

I raised an eyebrow at her this time. "Do I even want to know? Or is this like a 'he-was-never-seen-again' situation?"

"Don't be ridiculous, he's in Columbus. I just helped get him there faster. And with less money than he wanted." I had to laugh at that.

"Fine, fine, they can unload the U-Haul."

"Good. Glad that's settled. We can talk about the shop later. After more margaritas. Go check out the guest house; it's changed a bit since you were last here. Relax, change, and then we'll have dinner. I know you said you decided against hexing your former employer, but we can at least put him in the freezer, no?" She gave me an innocent smile before shooing me out the back door toward the tiny guest house.

I shuffled down the gravel path with my suitcase. I tamped down the little spark of comfort I got at being taken care of. Getting too comfortable was the opposite of the purpose of my time here. *Recover and move on*— that was the only goal.

Chapter 4: Jesse

I couldn't decide if it annoyed me that my therapist's waiting room had such cliché elements, like an essential oil diffuser, watercolor landscapes, and a white noise machine, or if it annoyed me that they actually did make me feel calmer.

It was only my fourth or fifth session since my mom coerced me into coming to therapy. For my mental state rather than my knee, that is. I had been considering it anyway, but seeing my mom cry because she was worried about me was enough to make me do just about whatever she wanted. The armor of anger that had been so prevalent in the past year was starting to come down. I was scared shitless to think about what would be left once all of it was gone.

In the middle of that uplifting thought, Dr. Merrill came to get me. I sank into the pale green armchair across from her and accepted a water bottle.

"Did you do your homework?" she asked.

"Ah, so we're jumping right in then." My throat became suddenly in need of that water.

"Would you rather talk about the weather first? It is unseasonably warm, even for the end of July, yes?"

"Point taken. Yeah, I did my homework." I pulled out some sheets of paper I had folded in my pocket and smoothed them out. "This was…a lot harder than I thought it would be."

Dr. Merrill nodded. She had asked me to write out four versions of my future. The best-case and worst-case scenarios of each possibility: being able to go back to baseball and, well, not.

"It had seemed like getting back to my team was the only good outcome for so long that I couldn't think about what might be bad about it. But when I had to write it down, it was… difficult."

"How so? What is the worst thing that could come out of

returning to baseball?"

I took a purposeful inhale. The essential oil diffuser was going to have its work cut out for it today.

"I guess I always assumed I'd return because I would recover completely. I never thought about returning if I just recovered *partially*. I could re-injure my knee to where I'd never walk without a cane or some other support again. I could keep playing but never get back to the same level and never move on from Triple-A ball. I could be second string or lower and rarely even see the field. I— I don't know how to explain it. But the worst-case scenario would be going back, but it being like an alternate universe where I'm not the same."

"So, it sounds like the sport itself isn't the thing you want to get back to. It's the version of you from a year ago, at the top of your game, that you miss."

The sound of her pen sliding along her notepad used to make me anxious, but I'd gotten over it. I didn't particularly care what she was writing anymore as long as I was feeling better.

"Yeah. It wouldn't feel like home if I'm not the same player. Writing it all down was helpful, even though I thought this whole exercise was kind of ridiculous before I started. Ridiculous because I don't think I'm going to have a choice. Not really, anyway."

My voice grew thick, and I willed my throat to relax and let me just get through this without breaking down.

"Sorry, I haven't said this part out loud to anyone yet."

"You know the only rule I have. No apologizing for having emotions. Take your time."

God, why is this so hard? Just spit it out.

"I'm not going back. My rehab has been stalled for a while, no matter how hard I work. My doctor says it's likely that this is as healed as it will get. While I'm a lot stronger than I was after surgery, it's nowhere near where I was, and definitely not good enough to play professionally. So. I'm out. I am no longer a shortstop, baseball player, athlete, whatever."

Dr. Merrill was quiet for a moment, which felt appropriate. Those words were like lead coming out of my mouth. I sucked down what was left of the water, welcoming the cold sensation along my throat.

"Okay. It sounds like you've accepted this as the outcome. Before we get into some of that, can I ask about your best and worst cases for *this* path? For not returning?" Her eyes were soft, and I knew I didn't have to share them if I didn't want to.

What else is therapy for?

"Can I just give you the highlights?" I asked, knowing I wouldn't get through reading what I'd written without losing it.

She just nodded again and waited.

"The best thing I could think of would be to find something that makes me feel even half as good as being on the field, like I'm where I'm supposed to be. Having people in my life that support the new version of me instead of people who only saw me as a player, or people who are waiting for me to go back to 'normal,' whatever that is."

"I think those are both really important things to find for yourself."

I nodded, almost embarrassed at being complimented on the pretend life I'd created. The other details would have been even harder to share, though.

She doesn't need to hear about how your girlfriend and your teammates stopped answering your calls and texts once you were off the roster.

"And the worst thing would be to just continue on where I am now. I am... floating down a river without a paddle, and it feels like people are just watching me and rolling their eyes, asking why I can't steer the damn boat. Not everyone, obviously. I've got my parents and my sister and a couple of friends. Maybe I should be more grateful than I am. I just... I feel like I'm not me, and that's something I've never felt before."

I ran a hand over the stubble that was threatening to turn into more of a beard from the last week of me not caring enough to shave.

"The craziest thing is that I've been doing *well* running my dad's business. A lot of it sort of came intuitively for me, and maybe I should feel good about it and lean into it. But that sound's awful."

"There's nothing wrong with you for feeling like you do. You're allowed to be angry and grieve the loss of the life you thought you'd have. It doesn't matter if other people have it worse. Because your life and your experiences are yours, and theirs are theirs. You don't have to fit your loss or disappointment on some sort of scale to see where it fits with everyone else's."

I breathed out, some of the weight leaving my chest. A lot of well-meaning people would remind me I still had my family, still had my health, or at least I got to live my dream for a little while. And absolutely none of that shit made me feel better *at all*.

"Okay. That helps. So, where do I go from here?"

Chapter 5: Sam

She wasn't kidding when she said the guest house had changed, but the feeling that I could do anything, be anything in that space hadn't changed at all. I couldn't remember its exact origin story, but I thought my Great-Uncle Linden built it for her to use as an apothecary slash library. Years later, she'd have herbs harvested from her garden all somewhere in the drying process, tons of books and journals, art supplies, easels, whatever. It was magical to be allowed in there as a kid. Once she had the shop, it became more of just an art studio. Zin was not an artist the way my mother was—Zin's art was whimsical and fun and maybe not *technically* great, but that's what made the energy of her space more fun.

But now… it was light and airy with soft white bedding and a beautiful rug full of pinks and golden yellows. She'd put in a chandelier where each bulb sat in a different vintage teacup and saucer. The bookshelves were mostly empty for my own things, though there was a brand-new set of notebooks and fancy pens waiting for me on the nightstand. The small bathroom smelled like handmade soap, and I couldn't wait to shower off the road trip later. There was never a reason for a kitchenette before, but Zinnia had put in a mini-fridge, a toaster oven, and an electric kettle on a little cart along the back wall.

How has she made this space feel more like me *than my own apartment?*

I put my suitcase next to the little wardrobe cabinet and started hanging up my clothes. I'd changed into a soft, oversized pink t-shirt and a pair of wide-leg pants when I saw two high-school-aged kids carrying boxes toward the room.

"Go on up to the house, Samantha. I'll make sure they get everything settled," Zinnia assured me.

I nodded, thanked the two kids, and made my way back toward the main house.

Tacos.

A giant platter of tacos and rice and beans and chips and salsa sat in the middle of the butcher block island, and my mouth watered. There was almost nothing in this world that couldn't be improved by adding tacos. I hesitated an entire three seconds before deciding that my loving aunt would not want me to wait when all I'd eaten was a piece of gas station pizza.

I took one bite of delicious fried tortilla when my phone buzzed in my pocket. I tried to take it out without getting grease everywhere, but sometimes sacrifices were necessary. I pressed the answer-call button with my pinky and put it on speaker.

"Hey, Laur!" I said, trying to sound like I did not have a mouth full of food.

She squealed in response at a decibel usually reserved for dolphins, but it made me laugh anyway.

"I was originally calling to ask if you'd made it to town and politely see when you wanted to hang out, but in fact, I've already driven by your aunt's house once and saw that your car is there, and I'm now circling back around because I think we should hang out now unless you have a convincing reason we should not."

Lauren spit out this information without taking a breath, and I was walking to unlock the front door before she finished.

"Come in, you crazy stalker. Aunt Zin ordered six thousand tacos."

"I get to see you, AND there are TACOS? I'll be there momentarily. Love you byeeee!"

I shook my head at how she hadn't changed at all. Lauren and I were "summer best friends" the whole time we were kids, and that evolved into just normal best friends as we grew up. She was one of my favorite people on the planet, and I had to admit that living near her was a check in the "pro" column for moving. No one ever quite gets you the way your childhood best friend does.

A minute later, I heard the creak of the front door and freakishly fast footsteps coming toward the kitchen. Her strawberry blond ponytail trailed behind her as she ran, and she looked as cute as ever in a cropped Care Bears t-shirt and bright green shorts.

"I can't believe you're actually here!" Lauren yelled, practically knocking me over with a hug.

"I can't either, though I don't think our disbelief comes from quite the same place," I said, laughing.

"Don't even get me started on your slug-slime ex-boss. I'm here for celebratory tacos. Where's Zin?"

"Overseeing the neighbor kids as they unpack the U-Haul. Don't ask why the neighbor owed her a favor."

"Oh, I don't need to ask. That lady's husband came into The Bar all the time when I used to bartend. Total dick. His quick exit had Zin's name written all over it." She grinned widely, making me huff out a laugh.

"I need to go there now that I'm well over 21."

"You'll be disappointed if you're expecting something charming. But I'll come with. They still give me free drinks sometimes."

More than anything, I loved that whenever I saw Lauren, it was like no time had passed since we last hung out. She was a low-maintenance friend. When I called her, hysterical, after losing my job, she drove up to do absolutely nothing but hang out and eat trash food. She was the best.

"Well, in that case, I'm buying," I joked. "But really, I owe you for coming up to Rockford. I'll take you to dinner, anywhere you want, once I get my first check from the shop."

"Sorry, offer declined."

"You would decline free dinner with me?!"

"One, I'm currently eating a free dinner with you. And two, you're not 'paying me back' for coming to see you. You're dumb." She raised her eyebrows, daring me to fight her, and once she determined I wouldn't, chomped down on a taco.

The back door swung open, and Zinnia glided in, satisfied that my things had all been moved.

"Lauren, dear, so happy you're here. Margarita?"

"As if you have to ask," Lauren answered, happily accepting a glass.

The sun sank down, and the full moon rose high in the sky as we ate and drank and chatted. I caught myself forgetting that I was there to repair the life I'd burnt to the ground, and that slap back to reality was less than pleasant. At least Aunt Zin kept us entertained by giving us our horoscopes for the next month—my life would be looking up if I could get over myself. As a Scorpio sun, it was unlikely. I had the feeling that was her opinion and had nothing to do with my actual chart, though. Before the day caught up with me, my aunt also made me put the name of my ex-boss and a few others on pieces of paper so we could stick them in a bag of water in the freezer. It wasn't a hex, but it felt good to put them on ice.

Both Lauren and I also set out jars of moon water in the back garden. Zin made us promise to let go of all the things that were holding us back and send them to the lovely moon. I didn't quite know how to let go of "everything" because it felt like it was my entire life that was holding me back, but I tried anyway. Maybe I'd take shots of the moon water tomorrow and all would be fixed. A girl could hope.

Chapter 6: Jesse

Despite the mountain of responsibilities I'd taken over at Garrett's Hardware, I didn't know that it would ever feel like *my* store. Maybe it would always be my dad's because I was only inheriting his dream.

And tarnishing its reputation daily, I thought, if I believed my father's grumbling.

I opened the back entrance and disabled the alarm, hoping to get started on some invoices before opening.

I poked my head out of the office when Heather arrived to make sure all was well, and then I went back to the task at hand. Mostly. I also may have checked scores from last night's games to see how my favorite teams were looking. I hadn't tried to *watch* a game in a long time. It felt like viewing my future in an alternate universe where I'd never get to exist, and I couldn't do it yet. But checking the scores at least made me feel like I had some connection to that world.

When I forced myself to focus on my actual job, I went to check on Heather and our new hire, who was training with her today. There wasn't any worry; Heather had worked there longer than I'd been alive, probably, but it seemed like something a boss should do.

"Hey, Garrett Jr.," Heather said, looking up from where she was working with Bryan at the cash register. She had called me that since I was a kid, so it felt wrong to correct her now, even though it felt un-boss-like.

"Hey, how's it going? Bryan, are you getting the hang of things okay?"

"Yeah, everything seems straightforward. I have to learn the difference between a lot of different sizes of screws." He shrugged, and I laughed a little. He wasn't wrong.

"Well, let me know if I can assist. We have a couple of shipments coming in this afternoon, and you can help me with that. That is, if Heather's done with you."

"Sure thing, kid."

Again, with the 'kid.' I sighed. I didn't know if it was worth worrying about.

"And before you grab lunch, make sure you stop by the breakroom!" she called after me. I headed toward the back of the store to check on any lacking inventory on the floor.

"Will do." I meandered through the aisles, straightening sale signs and returning misplaced merchandise. I said "hey" to Danny, our resident fix-everything-guy, and decided I'd pop into the breakroom before heading to the cafe for lunch. My eyes widened at the bunches of balloons and a small banner that read "Happy Anniversary!" There was a round cake on the table that said "Happy One Year" with a card next to it signed by all our employees.

"Took you long enough to get over here!" Heather said from behind me, making me jump a little. "We all wanted to show our appreciation for you stepping up for your dad. This store is home for a lot of us, and you've done a great job, Jesse. I know your dad is proud of you, even if he's too grumpy to say it." She shot me a knowing smile. "Cut yourself some cake, kid! I wouldn't let Bryan or Danny have any until you did."

She winked at me and left to go back up to her trainee, and I stared at the cake. I had been essentially running the store for a *year*. Obviously, my dad and Heather had to help me through almost everything because what the hell did a twenty-four-year-old with a history degree know about running a hardware store? I'd only ever worked there sporadically around my baseball schedule. But I hadn't bankrupted us or lost an employee yet. Was I *good* at this? Did I *want* to be good at this? The break room was now oppressively tiny.

I popped off the lid to the cake container and cut a piece for the sake of Bryan and Danny, but I took my plate and the card to the office. My office. I flipped open the card and read through the brief messages from the staff. They were nice; it was validating to be appreciated, I guessed?

Would Dad have sold the business if I hadn't been here? I wondered, still feeling claustrophobic.

I hadn't thought about it at the time because my head was so fucked up from my injury and surgery and PT… and then my dad having a massive heart attack at 55. I did what was asked of me, but I didn't think about what would have happened had I not. Or what would happen if I didn't want to do this forever. Would people like Heather and Danny be out of jobs? That was a bigger weight than I knew I'd been carrying around, and I now felt every ounce of it.

I grabbed my jacket and my *Emberwood Dragons* hat and headed out.

"Hey, I realized I have some deliveries I need to make, so I won't be able to help with the shipments today. I can do them tomorrow, or Danny can show Bryan the ropes. Sorry, it slipped my mind. Thanks for the cake, Heather. It was unnecessary but appreciated." I nodded as she waved me off, and I hurried out to my truck.

The sun was still warm on my face, and I tried to soak it in, knowing the fall chill would be here soon enough. I started the pickup and pulled out of the lot. There was not a single delivery scheduled that day; I needed to escape.

There wasn't a particular destination in mind, but I ended up parked across from the Little League fields at the Emberwood Park. It was one thing to acknowledge that I wouldn't be playing in the majors. It was another to dedicate my life to my father's hardware store without even realizing it. I sat there for a long time with the windows down, remembering how it felt when I first fell in love with the game. I could forget everything when I was on the diamond. The only thing that mattered was the trajectory of the ball and my ability to anticipate it. Life stress, relationship stress—it never followed me there, and I was *excellent* at what I did. I really, *really* missed being excellent at something. Anything. Even in my head, that sounded conceited, but it was the truth. I *missed* being who I was on that field and knowing that everyone knew I was great at what I did. Being not-terrible at running Garrett's Hardware was not the same. I wished it was, but it wasn't.

Maybe this is how life is, though, for most people. Maybe I should be grateful that I can still walk and have a job and an apartment. My therapist would tell me not to qualify my feelings that way, but it was hard not to. I tried the breathing techniques and even the tapping technique on my pressure points to calm down, though that last one felt like it was a made-up thing. My heart still raced at the thought of *this* being my forever.

"What the hell am I going to do with my life?" I asked aloud to myself as the sun sank lower in the sky. Unfortunately, no one answered.

Chapter 7: Sam

Sunlight spilled into the tiny guest cottage, and I stretched until my toes curled. I didn't need to see my reflection to know that my hair would be in a bun today, the frizzy curls tickling the back of my neck. I sucked down a full glass of water before pulling on some yoga pants and a tank top, assuming I'd be doing inventory and unpacking boxes all day. I looked in the full-length mirror on the front of the wardrobe and squashed my inner pessimist's urge to criticize my appearance. Instead, I began my ritual of saying nice things to myself first thing in the morning. I read something that said people could train their brains to be more positive by saying things out loud, even if they didn't mean them. I figured it was bullshit, but I was nothing if not dedicated to proving things wrong. Unfortunately, I did feel better at the beginning of every day, and now I talk to myself in the mirror each morning like a lunatic.

"Your hair is very healthy and looks whimsical in a messy bun."

No, it doesn't. I gritted my teeth.

"Your belly is cute. Handsome, non-douchebag-type-men are attracted to your curves."

What men? Where are these men?

"You are absolutely getting your life together, and today is the first day of the new chapter." I smiled to trick my brain into happiness and didn't roll my eyes until I'd walked away from the mirror. I already felt the little dopamine hit from my pep talk.

Annoying.

"Good morning," Zinnia called without looking up from the paper. She had a platter of fruit and bagels out, and nothing had ever sounded better.

"So, I'm ready to work today! Whatever you need me to get started on is fine. Laur even said she'd come by later and help."

"Oh, perfect. You'll be doing all the boring things I hate to do and have, therefore, put off for months and months." She grinned unapologetically at me before going back to the paper.

"Happy to do it."

"You say that now. But you haven't seen the shipments sitting in boxes taking up almost all of the back area."

I shrugged; it really didn't matter. I loved the shop; she needed help, and I needed a job. Swallowing down the shame of needing said job was becoming a more familiar feeling, even if it wasn't getting easier. I finished eating while she got ready, and we headed to *Books and Broomsticks* together. Walking in from the back parking lot into the office and storage space was like traveling in a time machine. It still smelled of the incense and essential oils and soaps that it always had, and the scent wrapped around me in a hug. I threw my bag onto the office desk, cringing at the natural disaster of invoices and receipts strewn about, but that was how I'd help. Zinnia was a genius at creating an aesthetic, stocking the coolest stuff, and keeping people interested. The paperwork to make all that happen? Not so much.

After vaguely gesturing to a mountain of boxes and handing me a spiral notebook with handwritten inventory numbers in it, it sunk in how much work lay before me. But for now, I would roll with her non-existent system and at least get shit unpacked so we could tag it and sell it. Mabon and Samhain, or the Golden Harvest Festival and Halloween to non-witch-people, were coming up in September and October, and those were two of the biggest tourist-attracting events to the shop. Zin went to the storefront and lit her candles, dusted, put on some Fleetwood Mac, and switched the sign to 'Open.' As for me, I sighed and grabbed the box cutter.

* * *

"Were you planning to help go through any of this inventory? Or just gaze at your own face in your phone?"

I shot an almost manic smile at Lauren, who looked quite comfortable sitting on the one folding chair in the storage area. I, on the other hand, was covered in dust and opening what felt like my twelfth box of crystal balls, which were *heavy*.

"Listen, I know we're in the middle of dealing with your existential crisis, and I'm with you, but this app is making me wonder if I need bangs again. Like they look *sexy* here."

She flashed her phone screen my way. I blinked, trying to remember why I'd agreed to her coming to 'help' in the first place. Her face stared back at me from whatever app she was in, but her long red hair had a set of wispy bangs in the image.

"You hate bangs because they always touch the tops of your glasses when you wear them. Now start counting candles."

"Oh my GOD, I *do* hate that. This is why you're my best friend. And yes, counting candles, going now!" She grabbed the notebook from the ground and shuffled toward the other end of the back room. "But turn on music, please! You know I can't work in silence."

I grinned at that and flipped on the radio on the ancient boom box. It helped boost morale. I finished with the crystal balls and placed the last box on one of the shelves I'd cleared off for ready-to-tag items. It was slowly looking like there was a rhyme or reason to the piles of stuff I'd found in every corner of this room.

"There are one billion candles," Lauren deadpanned, pulling her hair up into a high pony.

"I know. That's why I got you to come count them."

"Rude."

I laughed in response. "Let's try to count boxes rather than individual candles for the colored tapers and skinny spell candles for now. We will only count the large charm candles on their own." We got to work listing products, making tallies, and filling up the cleared shelves. After the crystal balls, candles, herb bundles, and only a small portion of the crystals, it was almost six o'clock.

"Did you eat today?" Lauren asked as I shut off the lights and locked the doors.

"Shit. Not since this morning, I don't think. Well, there was the lollipop I found in my purse, but I don't think that counts."

"Right. I'm going to grab food from The Bar, and then we can eat at my place?" Lauren asked.

"You're amazing. But can we go to Zin's? I wanna hop in the shower and change to get the whole day's worth of dust off of me. It's going to be permanently stuck in my hair."

"You got it."

She gave me a cheesy finger-gun motion and set off toward The Bar. Its actual legal name was "The Bar." It was the only one in town for decades, and I didn't think it had an official name back then. When the town grew and other places popped up, they just slapped on a big sign that said *The Bar*, and that was that. I'd sent Zinnia home earlier but stayed so I could clear at least one corner of the storage room. I let myself sink into the green velvet chair in the front of the store, feeling the soreness in my muscles from packing and unpacking the boxes of my life and at the store. Life had changed a lot in a very short period. I wasn't sure if I was failing or succeeding, but I was doing *something* anyway.

I took out my bun and shook out whatever dust I could from the waves before double-checking that everything was ready for us to open tomorrow. If Lauren wasn't coming over, I might have just gone home and fallen into bed, dirty or not. But when she returned with burgers, wings, and beer, I rallied.

I hopped in the shower to de-dust-ify myself, and my brain was swirling with questions about how I was going to work on my portfolio, find another job, and make sure I was working enough for Zin to repay her for taking me in. Did I even want to stay in graphic design if I had to start all over again as an assistant to someone? Could I be okay with freelancing and the uncertainty of where my next job would come from? I forced deep breaths into my lungs. For tonight, I decided to let the water and steam absolve me of any more adult-y thoughts.

Just for now.

I wanted greasy food, cheap alcohol, and a rom-com.

A pair of sweats and an old t-shirt brought me to the promised food and Lauren—already on her second beer.

"Pace yourself. We have a plethora of movie possibilities. Most of them starring Matthew McConaughey."

"I will not. You catch up," Lauren replied, pushing a drink into my hand and a plate full of food across the little round table in my makeshift kitchenette. "And it is interesting how many romantic comedies he managed to star in within a span of, like, five years."

"Agreed. And thank you for dinner. I didn't know how hungry I was," I explained while shoving fries in my face."

"Girl, same."

We ate in silence for the three and a half minutes it took to consume an unholy amount of food, but my brain was functioning again. I resolved to fix that with several more drinks.

My face was fluffy and warm from the alcohol, and my body had become one with the bed. It wasn't the worst way to feel, especially after the past few weeks.

"What am I going to do with my life, Laur?" I mused between movies.

She only sighed. "You're going to find something that you're wildly excited about, meet an adorable man who worships you, and it will be fantastic. Obviously."

"Easy as that, huh? I guess I have plenty to keep me busy at the shop. But I might have to find help to figure out what software I need and how to bring Zin's business practices into this century." I groaned. I had hoped my brain would shut off, but here it was, chugging along like a goddamned choo-choo train.

Lauren sat straight up with a gasp. "Sam!"

"Oh my god, don't DO that. You scared the shit out of me."

"Sorry, sorry, just, I have the exact solution to that problem!" I stared at her, and yet no words came out. "You're going to *hate* the solution. But before you say no, recognize that it *is* a solution."

"Okay? Why would I hate it if it solves this problem?" My eyebrows pinched together.

She ignored my question. "I know someone who's great with the computer and business-y stuff but needs graphic design help to modernize his logo, branding, whatever. You could do that in your sleep."

She was right, I could. "What's the catch?"

"Ummmmmmm. It's my brother?" She smiled her most winning smile as my face fell.

"You're right. I do hate that solution. I am *not* working for *Jesse* under any circumstances." My stomach twisted at the inevitability of seeing Jesse. I had accepted it as a byproduct of having Lauren as my best friend, but the idea of sitting down *alone* with him was something else. The thought of it had me blinking far too quickly and warmth creeping up my neck. "I didn't even know he was living in Emberwood! I assumed he was in Toledo."

"Oh, well, that's kind of a longer story. But you wouldn't even have to *see* him. Not really, anyway. It could all be done over email, mostly! And you could get the help in exchange for the designs, and it wouldn't cost Zin anything."

I glared at her. "I don't even want his energy to be allowed in my inbox." She was sneaky. Lauren knew I'd do almost anything for my aunt's benefit. But this was too much.

"I know. I also know that I'm right. And you will, too, once you think about it long enough." She cleaned up plates and napkins. "I'm gonna go home and crash. I'll leave you to come up with reasons why you can't possibly be in the same room as my brother before eventually deciding it's still the best solution."

"I *am* thinking of reasons. *Good* reasons. Mostly about how awful it would be," I called after her on her way to grab her bag and leftovers. I reached blindly next to me for the remote to shut off *The Wedding Planner*. The whole idea of the happily ever after was now making me want to vomit. *Jesse* fucking *Garrett*.

Chapter 8: Jesse

My heart leapt into my throat immediately when my phone rang around midnight, interrupting my late-night rewatch of *Buffy*.

"Laur—what's wrong?" I asked immediately, pulling on my hair and bracing for bad news.

"Nothing, nothing. I'm sorry; I should have texted. I know, the phone calls are the worst." Ever since our dad had a heart attack shortly after my injury, any middle-of-the-night phone call was cause for panic.

I blew out a breath, annoyed and so fucking relieved. "What could you possibly need at almost one a.m. on a Monday?" *Shit. I should be asleep.* Sleep had been difficult to come by since I stopped working toward returning to the game. Lying quietly while alone with my thoughts was an issue.

"Well, you know how Sam moved in with Zin?" I tensed at that. Of course I knew. Laur never stopped talking about it, but I had been avoiding it, too.

"Oh? That's so weird; you haven't mentioned it, like, at all."

"You're hilarious. When you're done crafting your new comedy special, Sam needs help, like, bringing the shop into the modern era—an inventory program, online booking capability on the website."

"Okay… not seeing what this has to do with me, Laur. And I'm exhaus—"

"*You* can help her, idiot."

A lump immediately appeared in my throat, and I swallowed it down. "She does not want my help. I can guarantee that."

The other end of the line was quiet for a moment. "Well, you're not wrong. *But* I think she knows she needs it. *And* she could do the new logo and help you with the shirt designs in exchange. It's seriously the perfect arrangement."

Lauren's optimism was a lot to take in the middle of the night. I rolled my eyes even though she couldn't see me.

"I mean, I guess? But Laur, I'm not in the mood to have someone… just, I'm not looking for drama. And Sam never even took my calls after that summer. I doubt the way you're picturing some reunion in your mind is how things would go."

"It was *six* years ago. The two of you must move past it because she is my best friend, and somehow, you and I are one of those weird pairs of siblings who hang out voluntarily now. It has to happen, and you might as well help each other while you do it. Go to the store tomorrow afternoon when you have time. Don't question it, byeeeee."

And then she was gone, and I was even further from sleep than I'd been before. My history with my sister's best friend was one of those things that made my head hurt if I thought about it for too long. Lauren claimed Sam would hardly talk to her after whatever we had sort of blew up. I didn't understand exactly what I'd done to wreck everything, and eventually, I'd given up trying. Not because I'd wanted to, but it seemed like that's what she wanted. I shook my head, trying not to let my mind wander too far down memory lane. There would be no 'dropping by the shop.' I was not putting myself in the line of fire for another person to tell me how I'd disappointed them. Sam Marsh would just have to wait her turn.

That's what I told myself for a whole hour while I attempted to go to sleep. But every time I closed my eyes, I was right back in the summer before senior year. It had been the type of summer people make nostalgic movies about—all memories of late nights and laughing and dipping toes in the lake. It was far better than it had any right to be after Christy broke up with me for some college guy. Sam… she'd made things so easy. Taking the leap from friends to something more should have been awkward, but it was just like we fell into step. I hated that the longer I lay there in my bare room in my generic apartment, all I felt was a flicker of excitement about the possibility of seeing her again. An audible groan forced its way from my chest.

You are a glutton for punishment. I knew she probably hated me…
but that feeling when her big blue eyes used to light up at seeing
me—like I was someone important even though she'd never once
seen me play ball? That was something I hadn't experienced with
anyone else, and I'd do just about anything for the chance to prove
I was still the guy who deserved it.

Well. It looked like I was going to be Sam Marsh's completely
unqualified business consultant on the off chance she agreed to
it—and I was going to make it hard for her to refuse.

Chapter 9: Sam

There was tossing, and there was turning, but there was not sleeping. I turned on my white noise machine, opened one window just a crack, drank water, read a chapter from a book on the shelf—nothing was enough to scrub my brain of the thought of sitting down with Jesse and just talking to him casually about fucking websites or something.

Should I pretend that I'd never even thought about him again since whatever we had dissolved into nothing? Should I address the six-year-old elephant in the room immediately and ask him why he'd bothered to use me to get over his ex and then just gone right back to said ex? Should I try to set up the perfect moment where I would lean over to brush something off his shoulder so that he could look into my eyes and obviously notice how beautiful they are and slowly lean in until his lips are just hovering above mine, asking silently to kiss me?

I despised that my stomach flip-flopped even thinking about that last idea because there would so obviously never be anything between Jesse and me again, but it was hard not to wonder "what if."

Or recognize that you should be over all of this by now.

I karate-chopped my pillow and gave up. My mini-fridge contained nothing appetizing, so I threw on my robe to raid Zin's fridge instead. The almost-fall air was cool on my bare legs as I hurried up the path to the main house. It didn't matter that I was 24. The dark was a little scary. The door creaked slightly when I let myself in, but the trek was worth it when I found Peanut Butter M&M's sitting in a bowl on the counter. I settled into one of the wooden barstools and popped one in my mouth, trying to think of a way I could get Lauren to leave this idea alone, or conversely, how I could go through with it without it being obvious how much a meaningless little fling still bothered me.

"I couldn't sleep either," Zin's voice sounded from behind me. I jumped and almost spilled the M&M's.

"Don't *do* that!"

"I'm sorry to have scared you. I was just up and heard you come in. Are you sharing the candy?" she asked, glancing at the bowl.

"I suppose." She first put on the kettle and then glided over to the counter in her green botanical satin robe and sat down, her silver hair braided down her back. We sat in silence for a bit, but I could feel the energy building.

"You know this is a five-year for you, yes?"

That was not anything close to what I expected her to say, but then again, few things often were. "A five-year?"

"Mhm. Your personal year in numerology. A five is the hardest year for many people because change is hard, simply put. But you have to do it because it's the only way to align with who you are and what you are meant to do."

The kettle whistled at that moment and Zin got up to make a cup of herbal tea for each of us. I didn't try too hard to decipher what she meant; I knew she'd have plenty more to say if I'd just wait. She placed the teacup and saucer in front of me and raised a brow to question whether she should continue, and I just nodded.

"Maybe I should have pushed you harder when you were first released from that horrible job. We could be so much further along by now, but I also know you have to do it in your own way. That's hard for me. I'm old, and my patience is thin." She grinned at that and steeped her tea.

"So, my life falling apart is just what the universe ordered?" I tried to add some levity to the conversation, but my tone still held bitterness. My aunt smiled apologetically.

"I know it feels like that. But from this side, it just looks like your not-right-for-you life set you free. Your five-year is about change, certainly, but it's really about freedom."

I didn't feel free. I felt more dependent on everyone around me than I had in a long time. But I also couldn't lie. I felt like I finally had room to breathe, whatever that said about me.

"What did you mean, 'we could be further along'? Further along in what?" My brain was only now processing everything she'd said before.

Zinnia side-eyed me in a way that only a witchy great aunt could, like she knew infinitely more than me about everything. It wasn't a condescending look, just one that said she was determining how much of the curtain to pull back during our little midnight chat. "Your magic, your intuition. We could be further along in getting you back to it."

I shook my head, confused. "Aunt Zin, you know I read tarot and talk to my guides and do all kinds of witchy shit, right? Like I haven't forsaken the old ways or anything."

She almost snorted at my exaggeration, but I had to infuse some humor somehow, or I was going to start biting my nails.

"You, my dear, have been a witch since the day you were born, and no one can convince me otherwise. Let me try to explain this in a way that makes sense in today's lexicon."

She set her teacup down and clasped her fingers together. I sincerely felt like she was about to share with me the secrets of the universe, ao leaned forward.

"Most people out there are spiritually operating in analog. You are operating in dial-up. Certainly, a different world than most, but you *could* be operating in high-speed internet, or whatever fancy thing they haven't invented yet that will come after. Your clairvoyance is a thing of wonder, Samantha. I could connect with you in a meditative state before you could talk; you were doing protection work when you were five, activating sigils at eight, and your tarot readings are the only ones I trust besides my own. You do not know how powerful you can be if you let yourself."

I felt my shoulders creeping higher the longer she talked from…I didn't even know. Embarrassment? Inferiority? Zin was an artist, and she always painted me in far too good a light. I *wished*

I could be the person she described because that bitch sounded amazing. But *I* was a failed graphic designer living in her aunt's guesthouse.

"I do want to get better at practicing my craft while I'm here. I've maybe… drifted for a while. But as always, you make me sound much cooler than I am." I sipped my tea and tried not to make eye contact. I'd taken all the undeserved praise I could in one sitting.

Zinnia seemed to understand this and simply gave me an encouraging smile. We sipped in silence for a bit before she cleared our teacups. I murmured a quick goodnight before I hurried back down the path to my room. Sleep still took its sweet time getting there as I imagined and reimagined what I was going to do if I had to meet with Jesse, but finally, my brain relented.

* * *

A groan forced its way out of my mouth when the incessant buzzing woke me up far too few hours later.

"You had better be dead. Or else I'm going to kill you," I rasped, now on the hunt for my water.

"Yeah, yeah. You're such a scary witch; you'll hex me; you'll curse my bloodline, whatever. Have you thought of any reasons that mean anything?" Lauren asked.

"I have absolutely no idea what you're talking about. I was unconscious seven seconds ago."

"Jesse. You. Getting help with the shop and not being a stubborn ass about it. Remember?"

I swallowed. "No comment."

Truthfully, I hadn't gotten past daydreaming about the different ways things *could* go if I *did* see Jesse again. Some of them were not suitable for casual conversation. Others involved kneeing him in the dick. I hadn't decided, and it was honestly a gamble.

"Good. I should probably mention, then, that I think Jesse is going to swing by the shop this afternoon. So, use this time to get pissed off or whatever you're gonna do, but he can help you with the 'how to run a business' stuff. He's pretty much taken over—"

"Laurennnnnnn," I practically growled. None of my imagined scenarios took place *today*. "I am not nearly caffeinated enough for this information, and I told you I am not working with Jesse! He's just… it's too much, and I know you have to love him because he's your brother and all but—"

"I'll stop you there. I do love Jesse, and not because I have to, but because we're friends, Sam. And can we just agree that your senior year was a long time ago?" Her voice was a little softer now. "He's not the same person any more than you and I are the same as we were at eighteen."

I just blinked and let out a sigh. It was rare that Lauren shut me down that hard.

When did she and Jesse become actual friends?

My heart contracted at the knowledge that I wasn't there for her nearly enough after her dad's heart attack, and my obstinance crumbled.

"It really doesn't sit well with me when you're being all reasonable. Kind of rude, actually."

I *wanted* to let it go. All that talk with Zin about a five-year and being free had weighed on my mind last night. I *wanted* to laugh and say 'Omg, remember that summer we hooked up and I let myself absolutely fall for you, and you absolutely *didn't* fall for me? What a *hoot*.' But it was *not* a hoot to me yet. It was hootless.

"I make no apologies for my maturity and reasonable-ness. And also? Cinderella didn't complain to her fairy godmother that her wish-granting wasn't enough. You said you needed help. I provided help. So bippity-boppity-do-what-I-say."

I snorted in a very ladylike fashion. "Except that she *did* complain about not having a dress. After the poor woman went and expended all that magic to make her a horse-drawn carriage. She was probably exhausted."

"That wasn't a complaint; it was just her explaining—you know what? I am not arguing with you about this. Make coffee, get dressed, and put on your big girl pants so you can run that shop like a goddamn boss."

The conversation was over, being that she hung up on me. Never mind the fact that I was an employee at the shop, and I didn't do anything close to running it 'like a boss.' At least I'd annoyed her enough that I wasn't the only one in a bad mood already this morning. This would not go well, but I took an extra few minutes to really lay on the bullshit in the mirror during my morning affirmations.

* * *

The bell above the door chimed when I unlocked *Books and Broomsticks* for customers and propped the door open to let fresh air in. The store did, in fact, house both books and broomsticks, though she only carried romance novels. She claimed they were the key to happiness. Upon skimming through her inventory that week, however, I vowed to convince her to order more titles from this century. The fancy broomsticks with crystals and herbs woven into them? Those were exactly right. I took a deep breath and grounded myself in the space before I let the to-do list take over my mind. Aunt Zinnia spent decades curating a very specific "neighborhood witch" vibe in the store, and she was trusting me to infuse it with something as mundane as organization and technology without fucking up that magic. I didn't take it lightly.

Besides allowing the cool morning air into the shop to clear out any stagnant energy from yesterday's customers, Zin had given me other magical homework. Apparently, the pretty notebook and pens she'd left for me in the guesthouse were for me to struggle through a list of shadow work questions. I glanced through said questions, and that sounded like the worst thing ever. A deep dive into my relationship with my mother and my hidden insecurities did not entice me, so I would not be doing that.

Not yet, anyway.

I had at least agreed to meditate in the mornings and connect with my guides more intentionally instead of just when I was in the middle of a crisis.

So, there I sat, cross-legged on the rolling chair behind the check-out counter, with juniper and sweetgrass lit in the bowl beside me. I was attempting to clear my mind of all the cobwebs of self-doubt and fear until I could find myself comfortably in my favorite spot—a single-room cottage not completely unlike Zin's guesthouse, though the one in my mind was tucked back in a forest next to a clear blue stream. In this space, my guides often came to the door as visitors, and I called for them to come in. Today, they didn't try to bring me any information; it was more of a feeling of relief that I was letting them in to simply sit with me so we could all be present together.

My guides appeared more as wavelengths of light than *people*, but it was easier to describe them as my people. Breath rushed out of my lungs, and I felt more relaxed and safer than I had since well before I lost my job. Time was kind of wonky when I meditated, but when I felt like our visit had reached its conclusion, I reluctantly said my goodbyes, buttoned up the cottage, and slowly came back into my body. It was honestly annoying how much better I felt after just doing what my aunt told me to do. I sighed, stretched, and moved on to the physical tasks on the to-do list now that the metaphysical ones were taken care of.

* * *

The bell jingled again when Lauren arrived, entering like a tornado of strawberry blond hair and floral perfume. I didn't so much *see* auras like some people did, but I could sort of feel them. It was how walking into a dentist's office always feels the same way, or how the sun feels on the first warm day of spring—

people's energies triggered sensations like that for me when I let them. Lauren almost always felt like the moment of anticipation before going out with friends, all good vibes and fun makeup. Today was no different, and that feeling made it hard to be mad at her.

"I come bearing gifts," she stated, with a very large iced-coffee and what looked to be a bagel sandwich in hand.

"Hmmm. If that's turkey on an everything bagel with sundried tomato paste, then I almost forgive you for inviting your brother here."

I took the coffee greedily. Emberwood Cafe had the best coffee anywhere on the planet. I didn't need to visit everywhere on the planet to know this, I just did.

Lauren rolled her eyes, *hard*.

"I have a client in twenty minutes, or I would stay and harass you until I was satisfied you wouldn't throw coffee in Jesse's face, but I did make sure it was iced so at least you won't permanently scar him. Also, you are adorable, and your boobs look fantastic in that top. Have a great day bye!" She was gone again without even bothering to glance back at the glare I sent her.

I had been *very* deliberate in picking out something to make it seem like I was not trying too hard, but that also wasn't the oversized t-shirt and leggings I'd been wearing every day to clean out the back room. I'd settled on a fluttery royal-blue tank top and my favorite pair of jeans. I pulled up the deep-v neckline to ensure I wasn't giving a free show. Then I pulled it back down again because fuck him; I did have nice boobs.

Chapter 10: Jesse

I'd been idling in the pharmacy parking lot across the street from *Books and Broomsticks* for a few minutes. Lauren had called again that morning to "make sure" I was going to swing by Zin's shop. This meant that she was prepared to coerce me. Luckily for her, she didn't have to dig into her bag of creative threats because I still felt more anticipation than dread about seeing Sam when I woke up. I was not quite as confident as my middle-of-the-night self, but I was prepared to at least satisfy my curiosity about what it would feel like to see her again.

And get the logo done. Of course, all of this is for the business, right?

I grabbed my Emberwood Dragons hat from the passenger seat and put it on, already feeling a little more like myself.

Here goes nothing.

She was dusting one of the crystal displays toward the back of the store when I walked in. The scent of whatever candles or incense she had burning took me back to eighteen almost immediately. I never really had a reason to come to her aunt's store except to see her, and I half expected a teenaged Sam to run up to me and covertly thread her fingers through mine.

That's because she didn't hate you then.

She walked toward me, feather duster in hand, and her eyes met mine too briefly for me to figure out how this was going to go. I adjusted my hat as I took her in. She still looked like the girl I had imprinted in my memory—but like now she existed in HD. Her dark curly hair was longer, and while she had the same big blue eyes and heart-shaped face, her body was now that of a modern-day pin-up girl. She had always been curvy, but *Jesus*. My breath tried to choke me when my eyes roamed over the rest of her.

And she's apparently trying to kill me.

I had thought she might be mad, but murder didn't really cross my mind. Her shirt dipped down low enough to show an unfortunate amount of cleavage. Only unfortunate because the memories flashing back now were far less appropriate, and I hadn't even spoken to her yet. I had a desire to stick a hoodie on her, but I just tightened my grip around my bag instead, hoping my knuckles weren't white.

"Hey, Sam. It's good to see you."

Chapter 11: Sam

It didn't feel awful that his eyes almost fell out of his head when he not-at-all-subtly checked me out. It would have felt *better* if he'd somehow devolved into a troll or something over the past six years. I looked him over quickly, taking my own inventory, and my nails dug into my palm of their own accord when I took in the addition of his tattoos.

The rest of him just looked so much *bigger* than I remembered. He still had shaggy blond hair, ocean-blue eyes, and the perfect summer tan, but he was all man-like now and decidedly not an eighteen-year-old boy. I didn't know exactly what had happened with his baseball career, but just the muscles that were visible through his shirt were ridiculous.

Not that I *cared*. It was just an observation. He shifted his weight, almost looking uncomfortable, but I didn't feel the need to be too covert in my assessment after his display.

"Jesse, how've you been?" My voice sounded abnormally light, but that's how I'd practiced it that morning.

This is going swimmingly.

"Fine. Good." I thought he might continue this super fun back-and-forth, but he seemed to decide against it and cleared his throat. "I'm not sure how much Laur told you about my situation or what exactly you needed my help with, so I just brought my laptop and figured I could be better prepared next time."

Kind of a big assumption that there will be a next time. But fine, we'd get right to it.

He looked around silently to ask where we should set up shop. It made the most sense for us to go to Zin's office, but I also remembered vividly the one and only time we were in that office together, and I could feel the pink splotches creep up my neck.

I might spontaneously combust in there.

His hands reached up to rub the back of his neck, and I could *feel* the same memory playing in his head. *Damn it.*

"Um, I still need to be up here if there are customers, so... let's just clear one of these." I started clumsily taking down Zin's romance novel display from one of the small round tables, and he went to grab two of the mismatched chairs scattered around the shop before helping with the books. He chuckled softly as he skimmed the titles.

"*Destiny's Captive* and *Lord of the Privateers.*" I ignored him and continued to stack books on other shelves. "Which one of these is your favorite?" he asked, his tone serious but his face alight with *something.*

Was he seriously teasing me? Or worse, *flirting* with me? I simply stared at him blankly, hoping it would put the kibosh on whatever little game he was playing. He cleared his throat again, seeming to take a step back.

"I never noticed they are all shirtless," he declared, bringing the conversation back from the edge.

What in the actual fuck is he trying to do here?

I pondered possible answers, none clicking with my gut, when I realized I'd been simply staring at him for far too long.

Shit.

"Oh. Romance covers? Yeah, they like their shirtless men," I agreed, tossing him a book with a half-naked pirate on the cover. "This one's good. It's on the house."

And what are YOU *doing?!*

My skin prickled with the delight of having shocked him, though. His crystal blue eyes looked up at me from his chair, his hands gripping the stupid pirate book like I'd just thrown him a life preserver.

"Thanks, I'll get right on it. We can have book club when I'm done."

And just like that, he's back on top. I sighed at the loss of my brief victory.

"Right. Anyway. We can get started."

I pulled my hair up into a ponytail before plopping down in the chair, and I tried not to react to feeling his eyes linger on my neck as he scooted his seat closer to mine. I pulled my energy shield tighter around me, knowing that if I felt the same aura around him I used to, I wouldn't be able to maintain whatever semblance of professionalism I was managing. Whether that meant I would rip him a new one or climb into his lap was unclear.

"Right. So, um, Lauren said you'd be up for doing some design work for help setting up new software and an appointment booking platform on the website?"

"Yeah. Just tell me what you picture." His eyes snapped up, and I was quite concerned that my own might fall out of my goddamned head. I wanted to swallow the words back up and start again. Those were some of the last words I ever spoke to him before it all burnt to the ground. I could practically see them hanging in the air above our heads now, threatening to fall and pop whatever precarious, polite little bubble we were in. His eyes remained on me, his gaze dropping to my lips and making me want to shift in my seat.

"In terms of the design. What you picture for the design, I mean." I spit it out as quickly as I could, wondering if I would ever recover from that moment or if I should just crawl into a hole now.

"Right."

He at least had the decency to camouflage his shock by biting the inside of his cheek, but the shift in the air was tangible.

Awesome. Way to keep control of the situation.

"Anyway, you know I took over at Garrett's Hardware a little over a year ago?"

I nodded like that made complete sense, but I knew I looked confused. I knew his dad had a heart attack, so I guess it made sense that he needed to take over. But he went to college on a baseball scholarship and studied… I couldn't remember.

Good. Unimportant. I filed those questions in a drawer labeled "Things I Don't Need to Know About Jesse Garrett."

"I never really planned to be in the hardware store business, but this is where I am, and well, Dad needed to step back, so I thought I could at least try to do it my way. Or something." He shrugged, his voice flat.

That drawer of questions was trying to open, but I locked it in my mind.

"We needed to expand our reach beyond resident remodels here in Emberwood, so I started offering delivery to job sites in four surrounding towns within a ten-mile radius. That turned out to be a bigger sales bump than I thought—it seems contractors forget tools and run out of supplies kind of regularly. So, I tried to come up with ways to get even more tradespeople to use the service."

"That's actually a really smart idea," I murmured. My mind was already turning, wondering how I could adapt that idea to the shop.

He leaned in and grazed my shoulder with his own. "I do have those sometimes."

His breath ghosted down my neck and froze me in place. I may have been able to block out his energy, but his physical scent was the same. I'd once snuck into his and Lauren's bathroom to see what kind of soap he used. It was called something dumb like "oak and amber," which meant nothing, but it was woodsy and slightly sweet, and it sent a wave of nostalgia through the synapses in my brain.

"Sorry," he muttered. He'd replaced the gap between us immediately upon me having some sort of fit like a Victorian damsel. Teasing had always been his go-to form of communication with me, but I didn't think it would still be that way.

It isn't. *It isn't the same, and he* should *be sorry.*

But fuck it all, nothing in my brain felt angry. I forced the generic smile of professionalism to click back into place. The only option I had was to pretend it never happened.

"So. How does this connect with graphic design?" I leaned away from him and rested my cheek on my fist, desperately trying to project casual indifference.

"Oh, right. I would have gotten there, eventually." He grinned, and I tried to glare so that he'd stop. "Patience, Sam."

I rolled my eyes, annoyed with his ability to recover so much faster than me at this clusterfuck of awkwardness.

"Anyway, the contractors and trades I was working with were mostly dudes, and I wanted a way to get our name out there without having to spend a ton on advertising, so I figured if I gave out some shirts that the guys could wear on the job site that had the store name, word might spread faster. I started with just shirts with our logo, but then I kind of ventured into… other things?" He raised his eyebrows in what I thought was a sheepish expression.

"Okay? What kinds of things?"

"Like… t-shirts with some *mildly* suggestive sayings."

I narrowed my gaze. "Like…?"

He rubbed his hand over his face and let out something between a sigh and a laugh. "Do you promise not to punch me?"

I only tilted my head. "I'm a big girl. I think I can handle your t-shirts."

His look said, *you asked for it.* He reached down to the bag he'd carried in and pulled out several shirts. He held up the first one, and it read **OUR TOOLS ARE HANDLED AT GARRETT'S HARDWARE** in black block lettering. The next ones read **MY TOOL COMES QUICK WITH GARRETT'S HARDWARE DELIVERY** and **ALL MY TOOL NEEDS ARE MET AT GARRETT'S HARDWARE**.

I read over them slowly before letting a genuine laugh escape. I didn't *want* to bolster his ego, but the shirts were genius.

"Okay, then. I understand what you mean now." That *professional* ice was thinning just a bit, and I didn't know if I cared enough to re-freeze it.

"I know they're stupid, but I got more new delivery customers in the two months after sending out these shirts with orders than

I did in the eight months prior. So, there's something there, even if they're ridiculous." He shrugged at me with apparently nothing else to say on the matter. "But this is where you come in."

"I'm somewhat intrigued." It wasn't even a lie. This was the sort of project I loved.

"So, my request is really three things. One, I want a new logo that's not so 1980s. I still want it to be prominent that it's a family-owned business, but it just needs, I don't know…"

"To still show that it's an established company, but also like you didn't make the logo on the first edition of Print Shop."

He laughed at that, and it made me wonder if their logo really had been made that way.

"Exactly. That would be excellent. The second thing is that I want these sayings that I already have to look a little more professionally designed versus just black letters on a white shirt. Nothing too detailed. It should be a work shirt, just like it was put together by someone who knows what they're doing." I pointed at myself, and he just nodded. "And last, I want to make at least one shirt option for women. I've met some female electricians and contractors, and I want to expand my business the same way with them. I was thinking **I DON'T NEED YOUR TOOL. I'VE GOT MY OWN FROM GARRETT'S HARDWARE.**"

I found myself laughing again, and a hesitant grin spread across Jesse's face. "I like it. Honestly, it's really good."

"Yeah? Thanks. It's, uh, kind of cool having someone to bounce ideas off of that doesn't think I'm 'tarnishing the Garrett brand.'"

His voice deepened into an amusing impression of his father, but I could tell he was a little bothered by it. I tried to think about how it would feel if Zin openly disapproved of something I tried to do at the shop, and I realized Jesse was probably more than just a little bothered.

"Hey—" I started, feeling the need to reassure him he was doing a good job.

He just raised his brows at me, and I chickened out. That was a more serious turn than I had planned on taking, and it shook me that he so easily made me forget my goal of *detached and aloof.*

"I…I can work with that and come up with some mock-ups to see if we're on the same page. It'll take me like a week?" I steered right back on course; glad I had said nothing else. But his eyes glinted with what might have been disappointment.

"That works. I'll bring lunch next week, same day, same time?"

"Oh, um, that's not… or I can email them to—"

"Sam. You have to eat, and so do I. It's fine. Plus, we need to discuss the book." He waved the romance novel at me tauntingly. My eyes rolled, hard, but he'd lightened the mood.

"Sure, right. Whatever works." I shook my head in disbelief that I was agreeing to this. "But I haven't read that one—just heard positive things. So, you'll just have to give me a book report instead." That was an abject lie. I'd devoured that novel at an age when it was not appropriate.

He stared at me with half-squinted eyes for a moment.

"If I didn't know better, Sam Marsh, I would swear you were lying to me to get out of discussing the literary merits of… *Pirates of Desire.* But that's fine because I'm going to give you the most detailed book report you can imagine. You might want to pop some popcorn."

"Oh, good god," I groaned, face falling in my hands.

"Love the enthusiasm. It's a date." My head snapped back to attention. "So now walk me through what kind of stuff you're hoping to update so I know how to help."

What an asshole. Just throwing that stupid date comment in there before a legitimate work question.

I scowled at him but gave a bullet-pointed version of the inventory clusterfuck that was my aunt's notebook system, my want for the website to have some sort of sales platform, online booking, and questions about creating a community mailer.

"Okay, yeah, I can help with all that stuff. I'll start with the program I use for inventory—it's connected to our payment platform, so anything we scan and sell comes automatically out of the inventory list."

"Wait. Are you telling me I'll be able to take credit cards without using that gods-forsaken carbon paper machine?"

He just huffed a laugh in disbelief. I got it. This store was like a relic of ancient retail lore. "Yes, that is what I'm saying. You'll need just a basic computer, nothing super expensive."

"Yeah, Zin ordered the one I told her to get. It should be here this weekend to replace the dinosaur." I gestured to what was maybe the very first home computer ever sold that sat behind the counter.

"Great," he said, standing. "Well, I'll get out of your way, but I think this is going to be good, Sam. I…"

You what…I thought, holding my breath.

Instead of finishing that thought, he cleared his throat. Again.

"Thanks for the help. I'll see you next week."

The bell jingled in what I was certain was a mocking tone, and then he was gone.

Chapter 12: Jesse

It could have gone worse. I mean, it could have gone better, but I was willing to take the W in the fact she looked at me like I was the same guy she knew before. There were no pity-eyes. She also didn't yell, *and* I made her laugh, so two more points for the winning side.

I was going to have to work harder to remind her that she actually did like me.

At least she did at one time.

I didn't even know what my goal was. That morning, I'd just wanted to satisfy my curiosity in seeing her again, but this little venture into being around someone who really *knew* me and didn't give half a shit about baseball had me craving more.

Sam had always been the person who said whatever popped into her head, whether it was ridiculous or harsh or out of left field, but she hadn't said one word about the last time we'd seen each other, at least not intentionally. She certainly seemed even more shocked than me when she let that question slip about needing to know what I pictured.

I had paced the night before after I talked to Lauren. Literally paced back and forth, ignoring that my knee was swollen from doing a workout that was absolutely not PT approved, and thought about what I'd say or how I'd ask why she completely shut me out. It had not occurred to me that she'd ignore it and act like we were just old acquaintances meeting to talk about a website. The whole thing threw me, but not in a bad way.

Maybe she was trying to start us with a clean slate.

Lauren was a master at laying the guilt trip that we needed to bury the hatchet and get along for her sake, and if I knew Sam, she'd do almost anything for my sister.

Okay, then. I'd try the whole new leaf thing, too. I wouldn't be

"Jesse, the former baseball player." I'd just be "Jesse, a guy she knew growing up," and we were reconnecting to help each other with a work thing. That was a perfectly reasonable way to go about all of it, and maybe Sam had just put all the other shit in the past where it belonged. Easy.

Except for the part where she turned to stone when you touched her.

I hadn't yet decided if that response was a tally under winning or losing. It didn't feel like she was angry or horrified that I'd touched her… but it was a strong reaction. I decided just to let things play out and see if there was even a reason to find out what it meant before I let it take up too much brain space.

I pulled into the lot of the townhouses one of my clients was building for a major development project. I took a deep breath and resolved to stick with my first instinct, which was to take the win, even if it was messy. Grabbing the saw blades and caulk and the buckets of primer, I made my way to the trailer to see the foreman. The thoughts about how hard it was not to smile when she gave a genuine laugh or how stupidly sexy she was in that shirt would have to wait. *Tools. Just deliver the tools.*

Chapter 13: Sam

The last hour kept playing on a reel in my head. I didn't know if I should congratulate myself for keeping his energy from overwhelming me or scold myself for still letting him affect me at all. Him and his stupid blond hair that fell in his face and the sparkling blue eyes and the *I-never-even-needed-braces* smile.

Such a fucking Leo rising.

I'd sworn to *all* the gods multiple times during that meeting. He had a tattoo that took up his entire right forearm. It could have been a skull. I was trying not to stare at it every time his muscles flexed.

Okay, it was absolutely a skull that had stitches across the top like a baseball, and it fanned out into flames at his elbow and wrist, and now I needed to know in exact detail what other tattoos he had because I had the flimsiest of all resolve in the entire universe. Oh, *"I'll just be reserved and professional."* Until I fucking parroted the words I'd said to him the night everything imploded. I couldn't have made things more awkward if I had planned it ahead of time.

"And what a sneaky little bitch," I voiced aloud.

He did *not* just create a lunch date where there didn't need to be one. I could do all the design stuff over email, but no. Now, I had to think about *that* for an entire week on top of everything else. I aggressively re-did the romance novel display on the table we had used, trying to tamp down the excitement I felt at getting to redesign the Garrett logo and have fun with those t-shirts.

This is not a cute little collaboration. You will do them begrudgingly or not at all, I told myself.

It didn't matter that the shirts were genuinely perfect from a marketing standpoint or that I'd forgotten to hate him the more we talked. I remembered what it was like to be the focus of Jesse Garrett's attention, and it was just a lot. Even blocking out his energy, the brush of his gods damned *shoulder* still set off a host of swirly, fluttery things that I had no business feeling.

Super smooth recovery on that, by the way. He definitely didn't notice that you turned into an ice sculpture the moment he dared to brush your arm.

I finished the display and blew out a breath, now lost because I had nothing to do with my hands or my brain.

This simply will not do. Stomping, I made my way to the bathroom in the back and stared at myself in the mirror. If I could build myself up with my fake words of affirmation, it stood to reason that I could admonish my subconscious as well.

"You are a grown-ass woman. You can be a professional and do good design work and ignore his fucking forearms."

Or just turn the AC down so low that he will be forced to wear a jacket, I added silently.

I could almost feel my guides rolling their eyes at me now that my energy shields were long forgotten.

"No amount of flirtatious little murmured quips can make you forget how long you cried about him."

I shivered involuntarily. That moment he'd practically whispered in my ear had brought forth memories of all the softly spoken compliments and the near permanent goosebumps I'd had whenever we'd been together.

The increase in my heart rate was certainly unrelated to me slinking away from the mirror and flopping back down into the soft green chair to recall in perfect detail the first time I'd ever hung out with Jesse alone.

Reliving it is obviously the only way you'll remember why it's a terrible idea to have any sort of warm and fuzzy feelings toward him. The memory is for science. You can't argue with science.

Right.

I curbed my car in front of their house, even though I'd successfully parked there a thousand times that summer. Shit. I rested my forehead on my steering wheel, trying to be careful of my makeup. I was going to throw up. This is a sign that you shouldn't be here. You know it, your guides know it, the universe knows it. *Shit shit shit. I hadn't even bothered to pull any cards that morning because I simply didn't want to know.*

Wiping the sweat from my palms on my skirt, I shook out my hair, determined to make my waves bouncy and alive like the products I used all said, instead of flat and clumpy like the persistent humidity of Emberwood thought they should be.

I knocked twice at the Garrett's front door, the familiar scent of honeysuckle from the vines on their porch helping calm me a bit. Jesse answered, clearly at the tail end of pulling a t-shirt over his head. I waited for him to brush his blond hair out of his eyes and focus on me. The grin that lit up his face made me mentally stick out my tongue at my guides because that smile was enough to get over all the reasons I should have stayed home that morning.

"Hey, you came." His blue eyes subtly took in my outfit, which was perhaps chosen with more care than my usual tank top and jean shorts.

"Such a keen observer."

"Yeah, yeah, shut up." He rolled his eyes a little but moved over to let me into the house. It was so weird to be there without Lauren. I had spent every vacation in this house for the last seven years with her, ever since the summer before my fifth grade and her fourth-grade school year when we bonded over our hatred of the swim test at the Y. Because having that many people watch to see if you were going to drown was not a wonderful summer camp memory.

I'd never been at their house with Jesse, at least not with Jesse, and I felt like I didn't know where to go or sit. I still couldn't believe he'd asked me to hang out, secretively in a note on folded notebook paper even.

"Do you want something to drink, or... I guess you know where everything is," he let out, running his hand through his hair.

My stomach dropped, realizing that maybe the awkwardness of us trying to test the waters between friends and something else might be too much. If this were the swim test at the Y, we'd both be stuck in the shallow end. I wanted to be fine with it if that was the case, but my fear was that I would absolutely not be fine.

"This is weird, right? Is it too weird, though? Should I go? Or..."

Jesse laughed and licked his lips before answering. "We're just going to dive right in, then?"

"Apparently?" I said sheepishly. I was just never good at trying to beat around the bush.

"Okay then, direct it is."

He stepped closer to me, so I was trapped between him and the kitchen counter. The only words in my brain were "holy shit," because I'd convinced myself this little back-and-forth banter thing we'd had going on all summer was only flirting on my side.

"The only thing that's 'too weird' right now is that I'm trying not to kiss you, and all I can think about is kissing you."

My brain almost imploded at his words.

"Oh my god, that's such a cheesy rom-com thing to—"

He kissed me to shut me up, and it was extremely effective. His thumb traced my jaw and down my neck to my collarbone, and I just held on to his belt loops for dear life because I was drowning, fully in the deep end, and I absolutely didn't want to be rescued. I sank into the kiss and let myself forget he was my best friend's brother. And that he had just broken up with his longtime girlfriend. And that I had to go home at the end of summer. None of it mattered when he kissed me like he'd been thinking about doing it for as long as I had.

He pulled back slightly, his thumbs now resting above the band of my skirt.

"Cheesy romance movies are fan favorites for a reason, Sam." I didn't even have a witty retort for him because my brain was only static by then.

"Mhm," I managed. Jesse just smirked and tugged on my hand.

"C'mon, let's go watch an episode of Buffy or Charmed or one of those other witchy shows you and Lauren record, and you can talk about how the magic is right or wrong or whatever."

My heart almost flew out of my chest, and I felt a smile take over my entire face as I followed him.

"Why are you smiling like that? It's weird. Put your normal eye-roll back on your face."

"Nope! You know my shows."

"Yes, because you insist on watching them at my house repeatedly. What was it you called me earlier? A 'keen observer'?"

I sighed happily as we sank into their oversized sofa.

"Buffy, please."

I just continued to grin, but I was kissing him again by the time the theme song ended, and he'd pulled me onto his lap before the end of the first episode.

"That storyline was just mind-blowing. I totally get why you like this show," he deadpanned.

His hands had found their way to my ribcage, and I hoped he couldn't feel how fast my heart was beating. I was floating.

"It's a classic, yes."

"Erm, my mom and Lauren will be home from the gym soon, just in case you didn't want to explain... well, this to her."

"Ah, yeah. You're probably right." I hadn't really thought about what this looked like for Jesse and me beyond this morning. Telling Lauren about it was an entirely different problem.

"I don't mean to, like, kick you out or anything. I'm more than happy to keep you right here for the rest of the day." He flashed me a grin and planted a kiss under my ear.

"Well, I'll likely be back in a bit to hang out with Laur, but I assume the agenda will look a little different."

"Come back tomorrow morning. They're doing some sort of boot camp class all week long." The pragmatic part of my brain told me not to be too available, that it wasn't attractive. But I felt his fingers shift beneath the clasp of my bra, and my arms and legs broke out in goosebumps.

"Mmkay." I let him kiss me again before sliding off his lap and pushing myself off the couch. "I'll see you later."

"Hey, Sam?"

"Yeah?"

"I'm really glad today happened." He shot me another smile that made me want to melt.

"Yeah? Me too."

I didn't remember the drive back to my aunt's house, but there was nothing else about that morning that I would ever forget.

I cursed inwardly as I let the memory play itself out because, damn it all, I could still feel his hands on me and how his words buzzed over my skin and made me want to giggle and kick my feet. I *hated* that I was ever naïve enough to think that the *friends-to-lovers* or *falling-for-my-best- friends-brother* tropes were meant for me when they so clearly were not. I also hated that I couldn't even see myself in a happily-ever-after anymore. As time went on, it was clear that I was more of a minor character in someone else's romantic plot.

Or someone at the office you use to pass the time. We could call it lovers-to-enemies, I thought bitterly.

I wished there was a spell I could do to make it so that I could be the first choice. I was so tired of always being second—in relationships, in line for a promotion—it was exhausting.

I wasn't surprised that my cheeks were wet. The tears really had little to do with Jesse, if I was being honest, though blaming him would have been easier. I'd probably needed a good cry since I got to town, and I had been flitting around like a bee on a mission instead of feeling the weight of everything.

Ugh. I was going to have to double the affirmations to get my brain out of this downward spiral. With a shaky breath, I decided that 4:30 was close enough to the end of the day to lock up and head home. I would burn extra herbs tomorrow to clear out whatever bullshit energy this was—I was *not* a fan.

Chapter 14: Jesse

My phone buzzed on my drive back to Emberwood to close up.

JER: The Bar later? I'm completely spent but I can still beat you at pool.
JESSE: Yeah, yeah. I'll be done closing in an hour. See you at six.
JER: I take cash or free food and beverages. Just as a reference for when you lose.

I rolled my eyes, but playing pool with Jer was a better way to end today than going home and trying not to text Sam something innocuous to get her to talk to me. Even if I did have to buy him fries, because he would absolutely beat me at pool.

* * *

"Beer or cheese fries?" I asked, after the first round I lost.

"The night is young. I'll take a beer, dealer's choice." Jeremy answered, racking the balls for the next game.

I stuck my hat in my back pocket and leaned on the bar until Jackie made her way over. We'd known each other since elementary school, and she sometimes comped drinks on my tab. I didn't hate that.

"Jesse," she greeted.

"Jackie, a pleasure to see you as always. Two of whatever you feel like that's on tap." I slid my card onto the bar top while she went to fill the pints.

"Try to stay out of trouble, Garrett," Jackie said, tracing one of her fingers up my forearm.

I typically enjoyed being shamelessly flirted with, but for whatever reason, Sam popped into my mind. I just nodded and pulled back from Jackie before she helped the next customer. I started back toward Jer, drinks in hand, when I stopped short of running someone over, beer sloshing over the sides of the glasses. Looking up, ready to apologize, I saw two familiar green eyes glaring up at me.

"What the *fuck* did you do, Jesse?" Lauren shot off, her arms crossed, giving me flashbacks of her threatening to tell our mom something stupid I'd done.

"Hi Laur. So good to see you." I started to walk around her but heard her stomp after me anyway.

"Little Garrett!" Jeremy called when he saw Lauren coming up behind me.

"Jer," she answered curtly, her eyes still lasered in on me.

"Ohhhhhh, what'd you do, man?" Jeremy asked, taking his beer. He looked far too pleased, his hazel eyes practically beaming at Lauren.

"Your guess is as good as mine." I shrugged, grabbing my pool cue.

"What did you say to Sam?" she demanded, her eyes narrowing even further.

"Um, that I needed a logo and some shirt designs. Is that not exactly what you told me to go talk to her about?" I was already wracking my brain for something I did that would have come across as offensive.

"Wait, who's Sam?" Jeremy asked, leaning in and clearly far too invested.

"You remember Sam. She was my summer-best-friend through junior high and high school and is now just my regular best friend. Honestly. You can't be part of the group if you insist on not remembering important shit."

Ha, at least he gets some of her wrath. He looked sufficiently admonished. "Wait, wait. Cute little curvy brunette, huge—"

"Watch how you finish that sentence, Jer," I warned, my voice tight.

"—*hair?*" he finished. "Curly hair? Lots of volume?"

"Yes," Lauren answered, a smile playing on her lips. "She has great boobs too. It's fine."

"See?!" Jeremy practically shouted. "It's a compliment. Jesus."

"Everyone shut up. What exactly is it you think I did, Laur?" Guilt was crawling up my spine for absolutely no fucking reason. "I only followed Sam's lead, and I did exactly what you asked me to do. I played nice, and everything seemed fine. We're meeting again next week."

"Then why is she canceling plans with me tonight and *obviously* post-crying? Did you say something fucking stupid about that summer?"

"I said nothing! Wait, what? She was crying?" I started replaying our interaction for the forty-seventh time, and I couldn't think of anything specifically *wrong*—

"So, you went in, and you asked her for a logo, talked about software, and you left." She still sounded accusatory. I ran my hands through my hair just as a nervous habit.

"Yes! Laur, I swear to god, I said nothing."

"This is riveting," Jeremy added, resting his chin in his hands as he leaned on the pool table.

"Oh, fuck off," Laur and I said in unison.

"I love this family," he responded, still grinning.

"I swear to god, Jesse, if you have made her regret coming here with *one* meeting, I will disown you."

"I don't think you can—"

"FIX IT, Jesse." Her voice rose at least an octave, her eyes grew far too large for her face, and she stormed out of The Bar.

"When did Lauren get that *feisty?*" Jer asked, his eyes following my sister out the door.

"Don't say another word, or I *will* kill you." That only made him smile wider, and my fist clenched at my side, my mind still racing at the idea of Sam crying and it being my fault.

"Break." I glared at him and grabbed the pool cue again,

thinking briefly that I might suggest he shove one up his ass if he said anything about my sister or Sam again.

How am I supposed to fix something when I don't know how I broke it?

Chapter 15: Sam

I felt bad canceling plans with Lauren. I really was tired, but less in the way that I needed to sleep and more in the sense that I felt like any type of personal growth I'd been proud of in the past six years was just erased because I was, in fact, the same ridiculous teenager who very much cared what people thought of her. Trying to figure out a way to make that *not* true in my head was fucking exhausting. I just wanted a pair of sweats and an episode or ten of *Buffy*, and that would be great.

The sweats were not a problem. But as soon as I'd washed my face and began preparing for a *Buffy* marathon, a knock sounded at my door. I knew that as soon as I answered it, Zin would read me like an open book, and I'd have to talk about my stupid feelings. I just didn't want to do it. But this was also her house, so *not* answering the door was not an option.

"Hey, Aunt Zin," I said in what was hopefully a cheerful tone. "I was just going to get to bed early; I think the move and everything is catching up with me."

At least it's not an outright lie. All of it is *catching up with me.*

"Samantha."

"Yes?" I asked sheepishly.

"You are welcome to do whatever you want. But lying about it is useless. Your energy gets… twisty."

I sighed, but I didn't argue about it.

"I brought you food. You don't have to talk… yet. But the day after tomorrow is a tarot event at the shop, and I have readings booked for almost the entire evening, meaning I won't be able to take walk-ins. *You* will, though." She grinned at that and waited for my acceptance.

"Zin… I haven't read for strangers in years. I don't want to screw up for your clients or mess something up—"

"One, you're an exceptional reader—*far* better than I was at twenty-four. Two, I wasn't *technically* asking because you're *technically* my employee. *But,* because I am a kind and benevolent employer, you can just read for me tomorrow, be the charming salesperson you always are, and you can take over some readings for the next one. Fair?"

"Fair," I grumbled.

"Excellent. Unpack your decks and pick whichever one you want to use tomorrow. And here." She thrust a large tray of cheeses, crackers, salami, and grapes into my hands and glided back toward the main house before I could rebut her points. *I guess I'm jumping into commercial tarot reading.*

* * *

On tarot days, Zin always made the shop a little extra witchy. She'd make a simmer pot in her slow cooker at the front of the store so the smell of citrus and rosemary wafted throughout the space. She had turned on all the twinkle lights that were wrapped around most of the bookshelves and display cases. There was some kind of ethereal music playing lightly on the speakers. I brought with me the happiest looking deck I owned. No, it didn't technically make a difference because the cards were the cards… but when The Tower was in rainbow colors, it looked a little less menacing. My aunt was in the back getting her own deck and the decor for her table, which left me alone trying to keep out the memory of one of the last times Zin did an impromptu reading for me. I was failing spectacularly.

Zinnia was sitting in her front garden with a cup of tea when I got back from that first morning with Jesse. There was a contemplative expression on her face, but she didn't ask questions. The next morning, it was the same look over a latte at her shop when I showed up to help create a new crystal display. The third morning, it became apparent that she had something to say after another round of raised eyebrows and a "good morning" that sounded more like a question than a greeting.

"Yes, Aunt Zin, it is a good morning."

I couldn't have stopped smiling if someone had paid me. Being with Jesse made me feel bubbly in a way that was completely foreign. Another raised brow. She wasn't going to have any forehead left if she kept it up.

"You, my dear, have been bouncing around for days, energy coming off of you in waves."

"And?" I grinned.

"I'm not one to pry—"

"Aunt Zin, that's literally all you do is pry. Into everything. And you don't even have to wait for me to give you the answers to any of your questions because if you wanna know, you've already pulled cards about it and read my energy and—"

She held up the hand that wasn't holding her teacup to stop me, and her lips pressed together, trying to hold back her smile.

"Fine, I'll pry. You've convinced me," she said sarcastically. "This boy likes you. And you like him."

"This is not the best showcase of your psychic abilities, Auntie. Very vague," I teased because I knew she was only getting started.

I tried to tamp down the hesitation in my stomach, telling me I didn't want to hear what she had to say. Couldn't I just be infatuated with Jesse and enjoy it?

"Ah, maybe not. But sometimes, knowing things isn't the important part. Knowing people is. And I assume that if you wanted to see what choices lay before you, you would have read them for yourself or asked, yes?"

"Probably. I don't know. I… well, I just want to keep feeling like this, and I know if I pull a Tower or a whole mess of swords out of my deck, I'll have to brace myself for things that I don't want to think about. Do you think that's dumb?"

I bit my lip, really wishing I didn't sound so uncertain.

"I never think anything you say is dumb," she said sincerely. "Except when you asked me why people were called 'human beans' and animals weren't called 'animal beans'."

"Oh my god, I was seven, and it sounds like beans! You're never going to let me forget that, are you?"

"Definitely not. I'm going to put in my will that you have to include something about it in the eulogy at my funeral."

"Sure, sure. We all know you're immortal. It's in the tea, I suspect, some mixture of the tears of men who've wronged you and herbs bathed in the beams of the 7th full moon of the year."

"Shhh, don't say those things out loud." She grinned, her gray-green eyes squinting at me from across the table. "Enjoy the lightness of summer, and this boy, and all of it. But remember that you draw people to you, not the other way around, Samantha."

She paused like she was trying to collect her words, tapping a long nail on her coffee cup.

"What I mean to say is that I sense you feel lucky that you have Jesse's attention, and you're wrong. He is lucky to have yours. You're as magical as they come."

She seemed satisfied with that, and I knew I was free to walk away to dust the bookshelves at the shop, but I stayed with her in comfortable silence, sipping my coffee for a while longer before heading to get the cleaning supplies. I considered what she said, and I couldn't help but feel like she was wrong. Whoever this strong girl…er, woman was that she described? I just didn't see it when I looked in the mirror.

It didn't take long for my mind to drift to Jesse and that brew of worry and excitement and absolute shock to bubble up in my stomach. I could still feel a leftover buzz on my skin where his hands had wandered while we were not watching Buffy that morning. Because I was avoiding reality, I still hadn't broached the subject with Lauren, and it felt wrong. I knew I'd have to soon if we kept doing… whatever we were doing. A sigh escaped my chest. Things were on the verge of being far too real and complicated, so I vowed to wait just one more day to deal with any of it.

"Pick out whatever crystals you want for your reading, dear," Aunt Zin said, making her way from the back, carrying a large basket of fabric, candles, and crystals. She shook me out of my memory, and I thought my brain may not be fully present yet when I looked at her.

"*What* are you wearing?" I asked, not bothering to keep the laugh out of my voice.

She had on a bona fide witch hat. It looked to be a handmade witch hat, made of suede with ivory lace detailing. But never once in my life had I seen my aunt wearing a witch hat.

"You laugh now… but that's only because you haven't seen the one I have for you." She shot me a gleeful smile and pulled another hat from deeper in the basket. It looked like hers, but the lace was purple.

"You're completely serious right now?" I asked, taking it from her. It was surprisingly heavy. "You're not going to tell me that this is commercialization of the craft?" Zin had always been very against anything that made witches seem silly—certain movies, shows, Halloween costumes, etc. *This* was a departure.

"Sadly, it *is* the commercialization of the craft. But it's also a little fun, and I look magical in this hat. I may have calmed down a bit in my old age."

I put the hat on and turned toward the mirror. She wasn't wrong. The hats *were* fun. Wearing one even made me feel like I was kind of a badass witch. I followed her to the little tarot table to pick my crystals.

* * *

It felt exciting to have my cards flying through my fingers. It had been a while since I read for someone other than myself, or occasionally Lauren if she was having a man conundrum. My Rockford friends weren't into anything witchy.

Maybe they were *boring*, I thought, recalling Zin's words when I'd arrived.

I put out my standard protection and guidance request to the universe before I finished shuffling, already feeling grounded in the space.

"Okay, hit me," I told my aunt, who was looking smug before I'd even done the reading.

"What does the next year look like for the shop?"

I laid down my go-to six-card spread and rolled my eyes slightly.

"Someone is going to come in and help you with the day-to-day in the shop so you can… be free? Those are the words I hear in my head, anyway. The image I get is canvases and paint, or even being a student? Or a teacher. I can't tell. Anyway, this… helper-person is a good choice for you, for the shop."

I refused to acknowledge *myself* as the "helper-person" because it would give her far too much satisfaction that she was right in pushing me to come back to Emberwood.

"Well, we shall have to find this helper person immediately and thank her." She gave me an incredulous stare and smoothed the lace on her hat.

"We certainly will. What else've you got?"

"Mr. Jack Henry."

I raised a brow. Zin dated, but since her husband passed decades ago, she'd never lived with another man or seemed like she wanted to remarry or anything. I laid down the cards.

"Genuine, kind," I said as the King of Cups showed up with The Star. "I don't know why, but he feels temporary, though? Not in a bad way, like he would disappear, just like there's a timer set to go off at some point."

Zin just grinned at me. "He is a dashing gentleman who is here for six months doing an artist-in-residence course at the college. I've agreed to dinner."

"How is even your dating life more exciting than mine?" I protested.

"Because I accept that I am exceptional, and it is normal for people to appreciate me. Honestly, Samantha, it's very simple."

"Super simple. Of course." I widened my eyes in annoyance at her and she laughed. "Anything else?"

"Should I let this new 'helper-person' take over ordering new titles for the store?"

"No cards needed. Yes." I grinned. I laid down three cards to confirm, but all of my pentacles backed me up. *Give me alllll the books.*

"I didn't need the cards for that one either," she agreed. "We'll go over the process once the new inventory system is set up."

I just nodded excitedly. I'd been dying to revamp her book selection forever, and I was already making a mental list of romance novels we *needed* to have on display. A breath caught in my chest when I realized I was getting ahead of myself. It wasn't *my* store; it was just a project. I needed to slow my roll.

"And now it's your turn."

I sighed, resigned to her reading whether or not I wanted to hear it. I closed my session and put my cards away as she got hers out and shuffled. Her deck was gorgeous but much more traditional than mine.

"Do you have a question, or do you just want me to see what comes up?"

"Fire away," I answered.

Zin read differently than I did. I *could* just lay down cards, I supposed, but it made me nervous not to have a guiding question. She preferred to go into it blind, like opening a book without reading the blurb.

She laid down a much more complex spread of cards while I waited. I couldn't quite decide if I was dying to hear what she had to say or if I wished we could skip the whole thing.

"My darling girl, you have to be kinder to yourself."

"What do you mean?" I couldn't possibly do *more* ridiculous affirmations.

"I mean, you seem to take any course correction in your life as a setback or a misstep that deserves blame… or for you to punish yourself." She paused, and I recognized the look of waiting for the words to come to her. "But it's like you're too focused on the road in front of you instead of seeing the map of the entire trip. Just because you missed one turn doesn't mean the trip is ruined; it just means you'll get there a different way—perhaps a better way. But you're so angry at yourself for missing the turn that instead, you're missing all the amazing things on your alternative route. I promise I'll stop with the road trip metaphor; that's just how it's being shown to me."

I took a breath and wished it wasn't so shaky. This was why I was afraid of her reading; Zin was a master of her craft. Those words were like a punch to the gut because they were true. My throat tightened at the cutting analysis. I didn't want to miss out on things. It was why I did the stupid morning mirror talks. I wanted to make myself see the positive because I knew I had so many amazing things surrounding me. It just didn't feel like *I* was one of those good things.

"I can't see the destination, Zin. And I feel directionless." I didn't want to get into this with her, or with anyone, but her energy was so safe.

"The destination is for you to be comfortable in your own skin, to be surrounded by people who love and support you, and to be focused on doing something that fulfills you. There are a million different ways you can get there, Samantha. It's not a job, an apartment, a boyfriend. It's just you."

She paused, looking back at her cards. "To be fair, that last part wasn't from the cards or anything. That was just my life experience being packaged up into something that sounds like wisdom."

I chuckled at that, my throat relaxing slightly. "That's okay. I'll take your wisdom, too. Anything else I should know?"

"Just… they really want me to hit home that you're probably going to keep making detours, and your focus needs to be on how you handle them and move on, not trying to be perfect and never make another one as long as you live. This makes sense?"

"Yeah. Yes. I think, anyway. Are we *sure* I can't just do life correctly from here on out, though? Like, get a little life GPS if my people are so keen on road trip metaphors.”

“They’re pretty sure that would be boring. I don’t know how many times I need to tell you that you’re not a boring person, Samantha.”

There was a question about Jesse on the tip of my tongue—if I should work with him or figure out a different way to get help, but customers started arriving for the event just then, effectively ending our heart-to-heart.

Just as well, I thought.

My little…fling, or whatever it was, with Jesse, had simply been a detour in my life, so I needed to leave it behind me and look ahead, like she said. I put on my best salesperson smile and readjusted my new hat, determined to live up to the title of “helper person” I’d so eloquently given myself.

Chapter 16: Jesse

The follow-up meeting with Sam wasn't until early next week, but Lauren's demand that I "fix it" was bothering me more than it should, considering I didn't do anything wrong.

Sam had said the new computer would be there days ago, so it seemed reasonable that I might stop by and set up the inventory software now so that I could just teach her how to use it next week.

Completely reasonable.

It was this sequence of events that had me standing outside of *Books and Broomsticks,* hands shoved in my pockets, during what was apparently a "Tarot Night." The shop was livelier than I'd ever seen it during the day, and my once *completely reasonable* offer of installing software seemed not at all well-timed. I could see Sam inside, helping a woman looking at some crystals. Her smile was relaxed, and she was in her element.

I let out a breath and accepted that my presence might make her less happy, and that kind of sucked, to be honest, but this obviously would not be the casual drop-in I'd imagined. As I turned to walk back to my truck, the shop bell chimed when a customer exited. Sam looked up through the door and caught my eye before I could try to disappear down the street.

Shit.

Now, I looked like a stalker lurking outside of her workplace. Leaving at this point would be worse than going in and explaining myself, so I caught the door as it was closing and shuffled inside.

The store was very… twinkly. And Sam was wearing some kind of fancy witch's hat, but she looked cute.

She always looks cute.

"Jesse…" she greeted warily, stepping away from the customer she was helping.

"Hey, I, uh, well, I came by to maybe get a head start on loading the software so that we didn't need to take that time when we met…but I didn't expect a party?" I gripped the back of my neck, hoping she didn't think I was a creeper.

"Ah, gotcha. Well, to be perfectly honest, the only thing I've had time to do is turn the computer on once to make sure it worked. So, I can't say whether or not it is ready for software." She shrugged apologetically.

"Okay, that's no problem. We can just take care of it next week."

I had accomplished nothing I'd set out to by coming here. No software, and I highly doubted this conversation counted as fixing anything. She didn't seem as cautious as she did during the first meeting, though, so that was something.

"I also like your hat," I added, grinning at her.

"Oh god, I forgot I was wearing it."

She reached up to take it off, and I instinctively stepped forward to grab her wrist. Sam stopped moving almost immediately, and her eyes locked on mine.

"I was serious. Keep the hat, it's cute."

I brushed my thumb across the palm of her hand before dropping her wrist, but I stayed in my new, closer position. Surprisingly, she didn't step away either. I reached to straighten the hat just a bit, and Sam opened her mouth to say something. Before any words came out, a customer interrupted with a question about a specific tarot deck, dowsing that moment. I stepped back then, resisting the urge to clear my throat, and I watched her switch back into her sales persona, happily chatting with the older lady. Although I'd counted this as a bust before it even began, now I was invested. Because *that*? It wasn't anger. I leaned onto the checkout counter to wait for her to have another second, an idea already forming in the back of my mind.

The customer apparently decided on a deck to buy, and they both turned toward the check-out. I didn't miss Sam's step falter just slightly when she realized I'd waited for her. She rang up the purchase, wished the woman a good night, and then turned her gaze on me.

"What are you still doing here?" She seemed genuinely curious.

"Well, Sam, it's Tarot Night, and I would like a reading."

She laughed in response. "Well, sadly, Zin is booked up for the evening, but I'm happy to put you on the schedule for the next one if you'd like." Her smile held a challenge, which only made me want to press harder.

"Unfortunately, I *really* need a reading tonight. I seem to remember that you have read for Lauren a bunch of times in the past. So how about it?"

"I'm not reading tonight. I don't even have my deck—"

"Ahem," her aunt voiced from behind her. Sam's eyes fluttered closed, and she almost grimaced. I was about to get my way.

"Hi, Ms. Crawford. Nice to see you again," I greeted.

"Mr. Garrett," she replied. "Now, Samantha, what is this I am hearing about you not having your deck?" Her aunt reached for the electric kettle and poured herself a cup of tea.

"Thanks for that reminder, Aunt Zin. I *do*, in fact, have my deck, but I'm not reading tonight. I need to man the register and do sales-y things, you know."

I glanced around, the store having mostly cleared out within the past fifteen minutes.

"You know, Sam, I'm getting the impression you don't *want* to do a tarot reading for me. I'm truly wounded."

"It *would* be good practice. I believe it was you who said you hadn't read for strangers in too long, and well, Mr. Garrett here isn't even a stranger. That seems rather serendipitous, doesn't it?" The older woman smiled over her teacup and made her way back to her waiting client.

"I dislike her very much," Sam grumbled after her aunt was out of earshot.

"But you have the hat on and everything, and I really don't want that to go to waste. I'm doing you a favor, Marsh. It has to, like, enhance your powers or something, right?"

"I hope you get all swords and The Tower in your reading." She glared at me and dug a tarot deck out of her bag under the counter. I had no idea what that meant, but I assumed it was an insult. I didn't care. If me trying to be cordial and professional had made her upset, then I was going to be friendly, bordering on flirtatious, and see how that went instead.

Chapter 17: Sam

He had fucking snuck up on me, and I had no time to block out his energy or do anything to keep him from getting under my skin. Jesse Garrett's energy felt like the excited shiver of your crush offering you his hoodie when the air gets chilly. It's all butterflies and cool summer nights, and it was *the worst*.

I was so angry shuffling my deck, I almost lost control of my cards more than once and sent them flying. *"Oh, how serendipitous, Samantha!"* I was going to kill my aunt. She *knew* some of my history with Jesse, the meddling witch. I stayed behind the counter for this; it was safer with the large piece of furniture between us.

It didn't help that Jesse's eyes were practically lit up like a Christmas tree. I silently threw out my protection request to the universe and leveled Jesse with a stare. I *really* hoped I could pull some cards that would at least show him being inconvenienced.

"Okay, I don't really know how this works. Do I just ask a question?"

"That would be the gist of it, yeah."

"Let's see… how will my dad feel about the new t-shirt designs?" He clearly asked it as a joke, but the amusement in his eyes died down a little.

I laid down six cards and sighed. Why did he have to make me feel bad right off the bat? He was obviously struggling with his dad's approval.

"Well, Jesse, he will not love them any more than he loved the old ones, even though my designs will obviously be phenomenal." I tried to lighten up the answer with that. "*But* he thinks you're doing a great job. Like, this clearly shows that he's proud, even if he doesn't really *get* you."

"Maybe I should have started with a less loaded question?" he asked, his voice noticeably tighter.

"Sorry. Fire away."

He waved off my apology before refocusing. I was trying to ignore any extra insight outside of the cards because I already felt too much being this close to him. I didn't need a more intuitive connection. But his people were persistent.

"Ummm, is Heather secretly planning to stage a coup and take my job?"

I snuffed out a laugh at that. Heather Samuels was about as malicious as a butterfly, so this one should have at least lightened the mood. But the cards didn't say what I thought they would. Not that she was going to take his job. Obviously, the store was called *Garrett's Hardware*, just that there were more emotions at play than on the surface of his question. I looked up and let my eyes go out of focus. I found I could better grasp the information that way. His people were adamant that he stop *looking* for his way out because then a path would appear directly in front of him. And if Heather needed to step up, then, she would.

"Interesting."

"Oh my god, is she really going to mutiny?!" he asked more loudly than before.

"Inside voice!" I admonished. "No, of course not. She'll only take over parts of your job if you want her to. And they keep showing me taking weight off your shoulders and putting it on multiple other people to carry. And that it's fine to do that. They show it as you holding on to all of it really tightly."

"Who are 'they'?" he asked, more curious than concerned.

"That's a question for another time. You can have one more; then I need to start to clean up."

He looked up thoughtfully. "Can I just ask a general, like, *what the hell is going on* type of question?"

I smiled a little because I couldn't count how many times I'd asked exactly that.

"Sure."

I laid down a past, present, and future spread, and my heart sank a little at the recent past. There was so much hurt there. The present showed more uncertainty than pain, but the future became brighter.

"I know this is such a cliché answer… but it's just part of the journey. You can't skip where you are now to get to the good part any more than you could have gotten here without going through the last year and a half of your life. But it does… get better, I mean."

I laid down three more cards just to clarify the Two of Cups I got in the future. When up popped The Lovers, the Queen of Wands, and The Star, I felt heat rise in my chest and then immediate irritation with myself.

You cannot be jealous of the possibility of some future woman from a tarot reading. You don't even know him anymore.

And yet, I didn't feel the need to tell him there was a love interest that might be 'the one' for him if I even believed such a thing existed. That would be his punishment for ambushing me tonight.

"Just… again, this sounds so unhelpful, but let things unfold. You don't have to search so hard for where you're supposed to go or what you're supposed to do because it will just kind of fall into your lap. Does that make sense?"

Jesse let out a long breath and pushed his hair out of his eyes.

"Yeah. It does. And I have to tell you that you should probably get paid at least as much as my therapist." He shot me a grin that didn't quite reach his eyes. "Thanks for the reading, Marsh. I'll see you on Tuesday. With lunch."

He *winked* at me before getting up and heading toward the exit. I didn't know that anyone had ever legitimately winked at me before, or if they had, it wasn't memorable.

Wait, did he say he had a therapist?

I bit the inside of my cheek, trying to reconcile the version of Jesse that lived in my head with the real-life one who had just left. This was a concerning development.

* * *

Trying to work on the Garrett Hardware logo while trying *not* to think about Jesse Garrett was problematic, at best. I'd gone with sort of a vintage label look that might have been found on an old milk crate back in the day, but I made the font super clean and used a more modern navy and orange color palette to pay homage to the Emberwood Dragons, which I thought Jesse would appreciate.

See? Problematic.

I had three mock-ups to show him, anyway, and my stomach was not at all experiencing turbulence at the thought of seeing him.

My phone buzzed, and I smiled when I saw Lauren's name. She'd forgiven me for canceling our plans last week, but she'd had some sort of stylist trade show out of town over the weekend (however, this also made me realize it would be an okay idea to make a couple more friends to have as backups).

LAUREN: I'll be there in 5. Have out wine and snacks thx.
SAM: I even bought fudge-striped cookies and marshmallows just for you.
LAUREN: You really DO love me

"I brought you swag from the trade show," she said without so much as a greeting and plopped a gift bag down on my miniature table.

I immediately handed her a glass of Riesling and dug in. I oohed and ahhed appropriately at the expensive shampoo samples and hair masks.

"Thank you. I should probably start using hair products that aren't from the grocery store."

"Please, don't tell me those things, Sam. I'll buy you some decent stuff. Promise me you'll pour out whatever you have."

"Done." I grinned, getting out cookies and marshmallows along with regular-person snacks.

"So, what did you do without me?"

"I actually finished the logo mock-ups for what's-his-name."

"Don't think we aren't coming back to the fact that my brother is now nameless, but let me seeeeeee them." I grabbed my laptop to let her scroll through the samples, and she clapped. "These are so so perfect. Jesse and my dad will both love love love them. Seriously, you're a genius."

I felt some pink creep into my cheeks at the compliment. "It's just a logo. It's fine."

She glared at me. "And I *just* do hair. Except I'm fantastic at it, and I make people feel pretty, and that's awesome. And you help businesses and brands feel pretty and get noticed. It's the same. Anyway, do you want to talk about Jesse before you see him tomorrow? Or explain why he is now nameless to you?"

I gave in to her comparison and let it go. She really was a genius with people's hair and always had been. "Nope," I replied, letting the "p" pop loudly before I took another gulp of my wine.

"You're infuriating. Okay, just tell me this then—is the problem that you see him, and it brings up negative feelings? Like, is he being an ass? Or is the problem that you see him, and it brings up not-so-negative feelings, and you don't want to deal with that?"

"Yes." I didn't have it in me to sort through the things that swirled around in my brain about that man.

"Fine, I can work with that. But we can talk about something else. And make fudge-striped s'mores." She hopped up to microwave our treats and left me to stew.

I let out a breath, grateful she was going to let it go for the moment.

After our next couple of meetings, it will be a non-issue anyway, I thought.

It wasn't like he *had* to be around me after that, so all the swirly feelings could go right down the drain. There was no point in fixating on them now. At least, that's what I'd been telling myself all week as I worked on his designs. I could exchange goods and services and not let my Taurus Mars or my Cancer Venus run away with my brain in either anger or infatuation and let it go. I could take this as a quick detour where I have to deal with it, and then I could move on. No big deal. I was fully committed to the road trip metaphor now.

"Tonight, we will go back even further in time to enjoy the classic: *Clueless*," I informed Lauren as we settled in.

"How does Paul Rudd look exactly the same as he did then?"

"Superb genes or a vampire," I declared.

"Def-ly uh vmper" Lauren tried to get out with a mouth full of marshmallow. I just laughed and tried to forget about the inevitability of tomorrow's lunch and whatever awkwardness that would bring.

* * *

I was checking the clock for the six thousandth time at the shop that morning and almost dropped my phone when it buzzed in my hand.

JESSE: Hey, I just wanted to see if a bagel sandwich is acceptable for lunch. I asked Lauren what you liked but let me know if you want something else. See you in a bit.

I had to wait at least three and a half minutes before responding, and I hid my phone in a drawer behind the counter for a reason that I didn't even understand. I walked to the back of the store twice before finally texting back.

SAM: That sounds good thx

Inspired reply. That was absolutely worth the pacing.

I knew I was being ridiculous—I just couldn't stop. I was momentarily grateful that I'd updated my phone several times in six years because none of his old texts popped up with this one. That was not a trip I wanted to take.

In a moment of confidence after my affirmations that morning, I'd put on a rose-colored wrap dress that hugged my waist. The ruffled hem made me feel a little like a fairy, but now that I was here, I was second-guessing all of it. I almost called Zin to bring me jeans and a t-shirt, but I didn't think she'd get here in time, anyway. I put my hair up and took it down and then put it back up again before a customer came in to save me from myself. After ringing her up, I saw Jesse's truck pull up outside.

Just look busy.

I concentrated on logging the sale into the notorious notebook system and was putting it back into the drawer when he walked in. Panic rose in my throat when I realized I hadn't bothered to work on any type of shielding or grounding this morning, and his energy filled my senses…*again.* I cursed the goosebumps that appeared on my arms and tried to fix my face into something that read *nonchalance.*

"Hey," he said, looking at me quizzically.

I assumed that meant my face was full of *chalance,* whatever the hell that was.

I tried smiling instead.

"Hey!" *Too loud, calm the fuck down.* "Um, thanks for bringing lunch. We can set up at the same spot," I directed, gesturing to the table I'd already cleared.

Jesse got out the food, and he also set a comically large iced coffee down with my sandwich, so it could have been a worse start. I came out from behind the counter with my laptop and went to sit down, hoping we could just work while we ate and be on with our day.

"You're wearing a dress," Jesse said.

"Impressive detective work, Garrett."

He let out something between a sigh and a laugh and licked his stupid lips.

"Right, sorry. You look nice." He held my gaze for a moment too long, and I willed the heat creeping up my neck to *not* turn into a splotchy mess.

"Thanks," I said quickly, swallowing. "Are you ready to see the logos?"

Chapter 18: Jesse

She was adorable. That wasn't a word I could ever remember using for someone I was interested in. In college, it was always, *"she's so hot."* And Sam was stupidly hot. But right now, there were blotches of pink appearing on her collarbone and up her neck, and her moving her hair to cover it was *adorable* and I wanted to reach for her hand to—

"Yes… no?" she asked. "Did you want to eat first or something?"

"Oh, no, yeah yeah yeah, I want to see them. Obviously."

Smooth.

I unwrapped my sandwich while she turned her laptop toward me. The design that was on the screen made my throat tighten, which was not a sensation I'd expected to have while looking at logos.

"There are a few more options… you know, if you scroll," she said. My sandwich forgotten, I scrolled through several variations, and I honestly liked each one better than the last.

"These are fantastic, Sam. Like, exactly what I wanted, but I didn't know how to explain it."

"Oh, good. Your silence was a little concerning." She took a deep breath and pulled the laptop back toward her.

I knew what happened with Sam's job back in Rockford from Lauren, and I could have kicked myself for making her think I was judging her designs in any type of negative way.

"Hey," I said firmly, my hand reaching for her wrist this time. Her eyes lifted to mine, and I traced over her pulse point with my thumb. It should have been awkward to touch her that way after six years, but it was the opposite. "These are amazing. I was busy imagining how much better our ads are going to look, which was the reason for the silence. Honestly, I'm blown away."

"Okay, okay, they're amazing," she replied, rolling her eyes slightly. I stared at her pointedly to hit it home that she was ridiculously talented.

"Thanks," she added more seriously.

My thumb was still tracing light circles on her wrist and up to her palm until she shifted slightly, and I sat back.

"Why don't I load the software onto the computer? It should be done by the time we're finished eating, and I can show you how to enter all your inventory."

"That sounds like a hellacious amount of work," she groaned.

"Oh, it absolutely will be. Have a blast with that."

That earned me a full eyeroll, and I almost felt like I was talking to the girl I'd known at eighteen.

We ended up choosing my favorite logo, and she said she'd finalize it and then do the t-shirts to complement the design. I felt like I had a buzz from the whole thing. It was the first official thing to do with the business that was mine, and not something I'd inherited. Sam seemed to loosen up and at least be willing to banter with me. I didn't know if I could call it flirting yet, but it was definitely a far cry from our first stiff, awkward meeting.

"Well, even though you've now given me 87 thousand hours of work to do putting all our stuff into this system, I think I get how it works. It will be super helpful once it's up and going."

"It will, I swear. Better than 'the notebook,' anyway." She grimaced, and I laughed. "And I brought you a present to help with the 87 thousand hours of work."

"A present?" A smile tugged at her lips.

"Don't get too excited; it's small," I warned her, reaching into the bag I'd brought. I handed her the box, and she ripped it open with a legitimate gasp.

"Is this like a beep-y scanner gun thing?!" She immediately took it out, pointed it at me, and pulled the trigger.

"Yeah, I'm pretty sure that's the industry term for it," I teased.

"Like at the library, and they scan the barcodes, and it makes that satisfying beep sound—I am now in possession of one of these?"

"You are, yes. You seem a lot more excited about it than I thought you'd be."

"Well, I take it you never played library with your friends growing up and pretended that your mom's spatula was one of these bad boys."

"I can say that I did not have that experience. There's a barcode printer in the box, too." I was laughing in earnest by then as she dove back into the box and gave an only slightly less enthusiastic reception to the sticker printer. "You just print out the barcodes for each item entry, and then you can scan one of them with this and enter the total number you have, so you don't have to enter or scan them all individually. And then obviously you just scan again on the sales screen when someone buys one."

"What if I *want* to scan them all individually?"

"Then you can. Whatever floats your boat, Marsh." She grinned somewhat manically at me. "Just let me know once you've gotten everything in, and then we can work on what you want to do with a website as far as just doing in-store pickup orders or if you want to ship places. You'll be able to do all of it; this is just sort of the foundational piece."

"That sounds utterly fantastic now that I have this special gun. I'll also have the t-shirt files for you then too. And lunch is on me next time." She shot me a smile that surprised me, and my eyebrows raised at the suggestion that we do this again.

"It's a date. I might even be finished with the pirate book by then and have my report ready. I *can* tell you I was woefully under-prepared for what the content of this book would be. You've expanded my horizons." I smirked at her, loving the pink on her cheeks, and packed up my laptop.

Happily, I walked to my truck, feeling more like myself than I had in a long time. I didn't know what *this* was, whether friendship or at least acquaintanceship.

Or something else? I dared to ask in my head.

That was a dangerous idea with much heavier consequences. But that thought alone was enough to catapult me back to one highlight of my adolescent life, in which Sam had a starring role.

By the Friday of that first week, we didn't pretend we were going to watch TV. We'd seen each other every morning, exchanged stupidly obvious glances every afternoon when she came to hang out with Lauren, and I had come by the store whenever she was there bearing gifts of coffee. I wanted to be in her orbit all the time.

"Sam," I got out between kissing her lips and her neck.

We'd simply gone straight to my bedroom that morning, and I felt like I was going to explode with how much I wanted her.

"Jesse," she breathed back, grinning against my lips.

"I want you. Like all of you. So, so very much. You are... So.Unbelievably. Hot."

I dug my fingers gently into the soft part of her hips, and I wanted to figure out how to explain to her it was my new favorite part of her body. I kissed her stomach and pulled her black tank top over her head. She was wearing a lacy purple bra, and I ran my fingers along the band before she pulled me back up to kiss her lips. She tasted like Wintergreen Lifesavers.

I'd only had sex with one person before, and I didn't think she had ever. I didn't even know if that's what was happening here. I just knew that I did not want to stop kissing her. She'd been quiet since I'd confessed how badly I wanted her, and my brain caught up to that fact as I drew circles on that new favorite body part.

"I'm sorry," I murmured, willing my thoughts to stop racing so I didn't freak her out. "I didn't mean to pressure you or anything. Is it too fast?" I slowed, intertwining our fingers and pulling hers up to my mouth to kiss lightly. I looked at her to see if I could gauge where her head was. "Is this okay? We don't have to do anything. I don't know if you've ever... or if you even want to."

"Jesse. Don't get me started on how virginity is a concept of the patriarchy, or we will be here all day, okay? Do you have condoms?" she asked, and I

think my eyeballs almost fell out of my head.

I sat back slightly, searching her face for any sign of uncertainty. My brain didn't even have a response to the virginity comment, and I fell over my words.

"I... yeah. Yeah. Absolutely. Are you sure? I want you to be sure. Like I want you to be out-of-your-mind sure because I am losing it thinking about being with you."

She laughed at my declaration. "I'm out-of-my-mind sure, yes."

I captured her mouth again, and she moved her hand to my chest, trailing it down my body until it rested exactly where I wanted it. She squeezed hesitantly, forcing a fuck *to fall from my mouth. I pulled away to rummage through a drawer for a condom before I turned around and fumbled with the buttons on her jean shorts, exposing her matching purple underwear.*

God, she is perfect. *I traced new paths on her body, judging her reactions.*

"Is this okay?" I asked, not wanting to rely only on her breathing to figure out what she liked.

"So okay, yes." I took a breath, intent on keeping myself in control. My hand found its way between her thighs, and I watched her intently to try to figure her out. Her eyes met mine, and her gaze was intense. I met the expression right back.

"You're so... beautiful," I murmured into her hair.

I should have had a better word for what she was. I felt high as she pressed her body into me and pulled me back to her lips. The way she grazed her teeth against my tongue was enough to almost finish me before I got started. I felt like my mind might never re-enter my body.

Her fingers tugged lightly at the roots of my hair, and I moved to her neck, letting her guide my actions. "Are you sure sure? Out-of-your-mind sure?" I asked against her ear.

"So so so so very sure," she answered.

I sat back on my heels to tear open the condom package and roll it on. My hands were shaking, and I couldn't decide if it was nerves or absolute wanting, but it didn't really matter. I leaned back over her and kissed her bottom lip gently, then the top.

"Tell me if I'm hurting you, and I'll stop," I said softly. She just nodded

and kissed me in response.

I pushed into her slowly, kissing her at the same pace until our bodies were perfectly molded together.

"Jesus, Sam."

I had no idea how long I was going to last, but I assumed a shockingly short time. "Are you okay? Do you want me to—"

"I am perfect," she answered, her blue eyes gazing into mine.

Every part of her was touching every part of me, and I was on fire in the best way possible. I felt her hands in my hair, her mouth pressed against mine, and her thighs wrapped around me. I never wanted to stop any of it.

"You are… fuck*" I said as I began to lose hold of my control.*

I kissed her harder, wanting to stay connected, and my hand traveled to where we were joined. I needed to make sure she was taken care of. Her fingers brushed over my skin while I moved, and all at once I felt her body let go of all the tension, and she gasped against my mouth. Any semblance of reality ended at that moment, and I followed her over the edge wordlessly.

I rested my forehead against hers and tried not to crush her. I kissed her temple, her cheek, her nose, her lips, and she grinned against me.

Reluctantly, I left her to go to the bathroom, and also to get rid of the condom very far away in a trash can my mother wouldn't be emptying, ever. I grabbed us both some water, and I relished seeing her looking comfortable in my bed when I came back.

"Are you okay? Good?" I asked cautiously, snuggling up against her back and letting one arm fall comfortably over her stomach like it belonged there.

"I am better than good. Excellent," she murmured.

"I am also excellent." I smiled into her skin, pulling her closer to me, her curly hair tickling my bare chest. My fingers were tracing a path up her thigh when the telltale rumble of the garage door sounded from the other side of the house.

"Oh, shit!"

She jumped up, scrambling for her clothes, and pulled on her shorts as quickly as possible, running her fingers through her hair. She looked like she was thinking about jumping out my second-story window. I would have laughed if she didn't seem so panicked.

"Sam, it's okay," I said slowly, pulling on my own clothes.

"How is this okay!? I haven't told... just, it's not okay."

She hurled herself toward my bedroom door and flung it open, making her way to the hall bathroom and closing the door while I went toward the kitchen. I became very involved in filling up a glass of water when my mom and Lauren came in.

"Is Sam here?" Lauren asked immediately, obviously having seen her car out front.

"Hello to you, sister. Yeah, she just got here a bit ago, and I told her she could wait for you. I think she's in the bathroom."

As if on cue, Sam exited the bathroom, her hair pulled into a giant ponytail and a smile on her face as if we hadn't just takne a flying leap from having fun to something much more serious.

Lauren was droning on about baking cookies or something, but I couldn't take my eyes off of Sam.

She seems okay, right?

I hated that any type of conversation got cut short by the damned garage door. I should have planned better. She couldn't leave without me being able to tell her how amazing she was.

I took a long drink of my water and grinned at her before heading back toward my room. I heard Lauren complete her baking plans and say she was going to take a shower.

Thank god, I thought.

"Hey." I stepped out and caught Sam by the waist in the hallway on her way to Lauren's room. She jumped, and her eyes still held a bit of panic in them. I wanted to take it away.

"Don't sneak up on someone like that!"

"In my house... where I live?" I smirked.

"Yes!"

"Everything is fine, Sam. I can talk to Lauren if you want. Or be with you. Or we don't have to tell her at all. That's not really my concern, but I know it is for you. Just... I didn't want this morning to end that way."

She was avoiding eye contact, and I reached for her face to encourage her to look at me.

"Can I kiss you?" I stepped toward her and rubbed my hands up and down her arms. I felt her relax slightly.

"Mhm," she answered.

I leaned down and brushed her lips with mine.

"This morning was, like, incredible. I'm sorry it was interrupted, but it doesn't make it not incredible. Okay?"

"Okay, you're right. Yeah."

I placed one more light kiss on her lips before heading back toward my room, just in time for me to hear the water shut off in the bathroom.

It killed me to walk away from her while she was smiling at me like that, but I made it back to my room and fell into my bed that now smelled like her shampoo. I felt like I could kick a door off its hinges at that moment.

I didn't remember driving back to *Garrett's Hardware*, but I found myself idling in the parking lot, grinning like an idiot.

Chapter 19: Sam

"And lunch is on me next time," I mocked myself in my head. He gave me one fucking compliment about my work, and suddenly, I'm Suzy-Flirts-A-Lot.

But the beep-y gun!

Admittedly, the barcode scanner thing was maybe my favorite gift since my Barbie motorhome in second grade. It'd become a *witchy* Barbie motorhome, but that just made it even better. I tried to meditate because I'd been slacking on my homework, but I couldn't reach a Zen space. I just kept replaying the epic abandonment of my boundaries.

I plugged in the scanner as soon as he left and started printing out barcodes on the little sticker-printer. This was like a real twenty-first-century business.

Amazing.

I was dying for a customer to buy something I'd already stuck a barcode on just so I could scan it. They didn't, but the shop was busier than usual that afternoon, thanks to tourists arriving for the upcoming Golden Harvest Festival. I'd suggested to Zin that we get a booth space at the fair rather than relying on customers to make their way to the shop. Thankfully, whoever oversaw renting out booths owed Zin a favor and got us a prime spot, even though the event was less than two weeks away. I didn't ask about the favor. I spent the rest of the afternoon pulling likely-to-sell items for the booth—sparkly crystals, wire-wrapped jewelry, spell candles. I only wondered if I could take the beep-y gun with me to the fair.

* * *

"Dear, have you even set up an altar since you've been here?"

Zin asked abruptly at dinner that night.

"Not yet. I need to figure out where to put it."

"On the altar table I got for you. Obviously."

I looked up at her quizzically, and she disappeared into the living room for a moment. When she came back, she was carrying a long, thin wooden table.

"Handmade using locally sourced oak. It should fit nicely at the foot of the bed."

She set it on the counter so I could look more closely. The warm wood had an energy that grounded me immediately.

"This is gorgeous. Are you sure you don't want it for yourself?"

"My altar table was handmade by my Linden, so I've no need for a new one. This one's for you."

It was smooth beneath my fingertips as I ran them along the top. I was already picturing which crystals and candles I wanted to set out for the equinox.

"Well, thank you so much. You do too much for me."

"Hmmmm. Well then, you can do something for me."

"What's that?" I asked warily.

"Tell me how your meeting went earlier." She innocently sipped her glass of wine, and I narrowed my eyes.

"It was fine." I sipped my wine right back at her.

We sat in silence for a full minute, and my jaw got tighter.

"He brought me lunch. And a present. And it wasn't a horrible meeting. He liked the logos."

"Well, at least we know he has some degree of intelligence. The logos were excellent. What kind of present?"

I launched into a monologue about the scanning gun, and my aunt didn't even try to hide her smugness.

"I blame most of this on you and your little tarot scheme from the other night. It is absolutely your fault I'm all in my head about him. Again. And only a little tiny bit my fault for forgetting to block out his energy during this meeting. And maybe the previous one too."

"Oh, *honestly*, Samantha."

"What?! It happens!"

"Does it? Would you *forget* to shield yourself if your mother walked into the shop unexpectedly?" She smiled her smug smile again.

"I don't know why you would even put that scenario out into the universe, frankly."

"Would you 'forget'?"

"*No.*"

Only a satisfied "Hmm" came from Zinnia after that. She loved my mother, but their relationship was not the same as ours. My grandmother, Zinnia's sister Dahlia, had died only months after I was born. Zinnia took on the role of grandmother from that point forward, saying she knew her sister would never forgive her if I wasn't absolutely spoiled at every moment. My mother loved Aunt Zin for it, but the two didn't see eye to eye on everything.

"You're incorrigible, by the way. I thought you were going to be helping me move through the detours and get where I'm supposed to be going, not pulling me off on side quests to see the nation's biggest ball of yarn or something! Jesse is a very complicated ball of yarn. Full of knots. I don't have time for that."

"It's possible, dear, that you and I have different ideas about what makes up a detour and what does not."

With that, she cleared her place at the table, said goodnight, and left me sitting in the kitchen, my head filling with very confused thoughts about Jesse and yarn and road trips.

* * *

I knocked twice with the little bumble bee knocker on the front door of Lauren's townhouse. I felt bad I hadn't been there other than to drop her off; I'd been making her come to Zin's for weeks.

"Hello, and welcome to my not-at-all-humble-abode," she answered, swinging the door wide open.

Her hair was in the highest ponytail imaginable, and she was wearing what looked to be a Rainbow Bright nightgown altered into a mini-dress with bright red tights underneath.

"Can you just be my personal stylist? Hair, clothes, living space, whatever? How much does that cost?"

I was certain my mouth was hanging open while looking around her space. It was so full of color that it should have been overwhelming, but it just made me happy instead. A bright blue wall against an orange velvet sofa and a pink tufted chair with more house plants than I could count filled the living room.

"You absolutely could not afford me. Luckily, you get my best friend rate, which is free. So, we'll shop soon." A smile lit up her face as she set down a comically large tray full of snacks down on the coffee table.

"You're my favorite."

"I know. Speaking of being ridiculously talented, Jesse sent me the final logo plus the images of the new bags and signs he's ordering with them, and they look ah-mazing. I wonder who had the idea for such a fantastic partnership?" She blinked her big eyes at me and took a sip of her rosé.

"You're less of my favorite when you gloat." This only made her grin bigger.

"That's okay. I might be your least favorite in a second when I tell you that you're coming with Jesse and me to The Bar on Friday. The two of you should be comfy cozy now, so we can hang out."

"That sounds like a hard pass, but thanks so much for the invite." I sipped my wine and glared at her over the top of my glass, wondering how one tiny woman could cause such chaos.

"You're so silly. It isn't an invitation; it's a demand. Friday about five. We'll shop for something cute tomorrow when I'm off."

"Mmmmmm. I'm working tomorrow."

"You won't be when I text Zin and tell her you need a cute outfit to wear out. So, what movie are we watching tonight? Your expression is suggesting *Drive Me Crazy* or *10 Things I Hate About You*. Both classics, excellent choices, Sam."

She could hardly even contain her giggles at how amusing she found herself. And it was even more annoying because she was right, and Zin would forbid me from coming to work if Lauren texted her.

"*Drive Me Crazy* feels very appropriate right now." I sighed in defeat while she started the movie even though there were a few sparkles floating around in my chest at the thought of buying something pretty and going out with Jesse.

Going out with Lauren *where Jesse will also happen to be present.*

It would be really fucking helpful to my stupid Cancer Venus if he would *stop* calling everything a date. I'd all but completely given up my grudge, and that never ever ever happened. I was a seasoned grudge-holder. A black belt. A sensei. I could hold it for.ev.er. But Jesse Garrett and his stupid funny marketing t-shirts and the beep-y scanner gun and the forearm tattoos and the *therapy*. Never in any stretch of my imagination would I have said that a man going to therapy was a turn on but *damn it*.

I was so very screwed.

Chapter 20: Jesse

Today, the essential oils and the landscape paintings did little to calm me down, but I wasn't angry. In fact, today was the first session I was *excited* to tell the doc something. Nothing monumental had changed since my last appointment, but all the small things seemed to come together to create a shift. I couldn't stop my good knee from bouncing while I waited.

Finally, the door opened after the previous client left, and I practically jumped out of my waiting room chair.

"Am I imagining things, or are you in a pleasant mood?" Dr. Merrill asked.

"I think I am in a good mood. A great mood even. Though, I don't know if I should be. But I am. I guess. You know?"

She just smiled at me and took out her notebook. "Let's unpack that, shall we?"

The little *click-click* of her pen after that phrase could have been a commercial for therapy. I had no idea how to start, but after I got through the initial explanation of who Sam was and a *very* glossed-over history, the words just came tumbling out.

"I don't know. I feel more like myself with Sam than anyone else I know. And I haven't seen her in six years. I'm not trying to knock any of my friends or family; there's just something… comforting about the fact that she knew the old me, before the injury, and she wasn't here to see me hit rock bottom. I'm so grateful for the people who were, but they don't look at me the same now. I guess I wouldn't either. But she didn't see that… there aren't the *pity eyes* that we've talked about. She doesn't talk to me like she's afraid I'll spiral if she says the word *baseball*. She also doesn't give a shit about baseball, so that's helpful."

I shrugged, realizing that I'd been talking for a very long time. Longer than I'd ever spoken at a session.

"I hear you saying that you're feeling excited about new possibilities in your life instead of only focusing on the lost chances because of your injury. Would you agree with that?"

"Yes. It feels possible to get the things I said I wanted when we talked about best and worst-case scenarios. But if I feel like I can have it… that also means I can lose it. And that, I think, is what's holding me back from doing anything real, with Sam, I mean."

"Ah. Well, I wish I had special therapist wisdom that would make it so there was no chance of experiencing loss again. But I don't. The goal is not to have everything go perfectly from here on out, though that would be nice. The goal is that you have a support system and coping strategies to know that you'll make it through whatever rough patch you hit."

I nodded at that. It oddly made me feel less freaked out… just admitting that I couldn't control what happened. I could only control how I tried to handle it.

"What does it mean to do something *real* with Sam?"

"I guess it could be a lot of things. But doing more than just flirting. Asking her out. Giving her the chance to reject me. Talking about what happened six years ago because I don't feel like that can just disappear. But you're the professional… can we just ignore our history and move on?" I asked, mostly as a joke.

"I don't need to be a professional to answer that. I could be a Magic 8 Ball and still say "*Outlook Not So Good.*" But, since you're my patient, I'll give you my professional answer, which is that leaving any type of big emotion buried beneath the surface is a great way to ensure a shaky foundation for anything you're trying to build on top of it."

"Right. So… rip off the band-aid?"

"Maybe gently take off the band-aid. There's not a prize for doing it the fastest."

I exhaled. My thoughts stopped racing once we were done, so I knew everything Dr. Merrill suggested was sound advice. I wanted to build something with Sam—whatever she'd let me, really. And I wanted to make sure it was built on solid ground. It was helpful that this session was directly before I met her and Laur at the bar. It would hopefully keep me from doing something impulsive.

Chapter 21: Sam

I was there early, but that was by design. I'd gotten into a decent meditation before I left work; however, the only wisdom I'd gained from my guides and my subconscious was to follow my intuition. Not that it was terrible advice; it just helped me prepare very little since I did not know how I felt or what I wanted. I at least needed time to get my bearings before I had to sit across from Jesse.

This whole thing was probably a bad idea. Flirting with him, letting him dissolve my grudge… now the only thing my stupid brain would allow me to picture, think about, or imagine was him winking at me or his thumb making circles on my wrist. I shook out my hair and smoothed my pink and purple moon phases skirt of some invisible wrinkles. My eyes had *actual* make-up that contained some type of very fine pink glitter, and I loved it. I grabbed the happy hour menu to see what looked good.

I felt eyes on me before I saw him. I tried to put out a very forceful *leave-me-the-fuck-alone* energy, but unfortunately, drunk men didn't tend to respond to subtle energetic shifts. Shocking.

"Hey, there," his voice slurred, closer to me now.

Jesus, it's barely five. How long has this dude been drinking on a weekday?

I looked up to see what might have been a good-looking guy under different circumstances. He had a medium build and a scruffy five o'clock shadow, deep brown eyes, and dark hair that barely curled at the ends. I just raised my eyebrows in response. His eyes were glassy as he leaned onto my table clumsily.

"Aw, don't be rude. I gave you a compliment. Come and dance with me."

While there *was* technically a small dance floor, there was no music because some type of sporting event was on the one TV in the bar.

"I'm good, thanks." I scanned The Bar for Lauren or Jesse or *anyone* who might come and interrupt this little scene.

"It's one dance," he stated, his voice turning harsher. "I don't bite. Unless you want."

He grinned at his little cliché innuendo that sounded like it came directly out of a bad porn.

"Oh, but *I* do. *Hard.* Whether you want me to or not." I stared pointedly at his crotch, hoping it might shock him enough to leave me the hell alone. I clenched my fist, ready to beeline for the door if it didn't work.

"I mean, if you like it rough—"

"What the fuck are you doing, man?"

Jesse was beside me out of nowhere, his voice tight. His energy felt like trying to open a locked door. It was borderline panicky.

"Heyyyyy, it's Garrett, everybody's favorite has-been." Jesse flinched next to me, though it was almost imperceptible. This was going to be a whole thing. *Fuck.*

"Go have another shot, *bro.* If your liver can handle it, anyway. You don't look great."

The guy stood up taller, taking a step back from the table, and I relaxed slightly until his eyes snapped back to me.

"Simmer down, Garrett. All in good fun. I didn't know she was your girl—she's not your normal type."

He made a sad attempt to create an hourglass shape with his hands. I assumed to point out that Jesse normally dated skinny women. "Are you even cleared to lift that much on your knee?"

Assumption confirmed.

He laughed like he had really hit one out of the park. It was disappointing how predictable these men were to go from complimentary to insulting as soon as a woman turned them down.

"The *fuck* did you just—"

Jesse started toward the other side of the table, and I caught his elbow. They were both built similarly, though Jesse had a few extra inches, and the drunk idiot probably had an extra twenty pounds of beer gut. I was wholly uninterested in seeing a National-

Geographic-type-display of masculinity, however.

Jesse looked at where I'd touched him and shot me a questioning look, his anger rolling off him in waves. The asshole laughed again to himself before he turned to walk away. I should have let him go, but I couldn't help myself. It was a gray area, maybe, to read a stranger without being asked.

But didn't he ask for it, though? A little? I thought.

His people were practically shouting at me anyway, so I opened the line of communication. I closed my eyes and let the information come to me.

"If I could… Michael—no, Mike? *Mitchell*, right? Can I call you Mitch? Great."

I could see his shoulders start to creep up towards his jaw, and I knew I'd at least gotten his attention. Jesse also widened his eyes at me. I raked my fingers through my curls and dropped my shoulders because now I was in my element. My anger lessened slightly while his people bombarded me with details because it was obvious he was struggling. I tried to pick out the most complete information so that I could get this done quickly.

"I'm not going to let my friend hit you because I get that you're having a rough time, and I don't think it would help."

"Who the hell is this bitch?" Mitchell asked Jesse accusingly like he'd somehow set this up.

"I'm Sam, your friendly neighborhood witch. Anyway, you should know that your wife is about one late night away from filing for divorce. And she will, in fact, get the house and full custody of… Flynn? Finley?" My eyes searched his to see if I was getting there.

"Finn." Mitchell's gulp was audible.

Bingo.

"Thanks. Finn. So, my suggestion to you is that you take your ass home and beg for forgiveness. You'll still have a long road ahead of you to get there, but it's a start. Then get yourself a therapist, Mitch, to deal with your daddy issues so that Finn doesn't end up with the same ones, yeah?"

My voice was softer when I ended my impromptu reading because apparently, Mitch's dad had done a real number on him. But at some point, he had to want to heal that wound.

"What the actual fuck?" Mitchell almost whispered, shaking his head and wandering away from our table.

Jesse's expression looked like it might be permanently stuck, so I waved my hand in front of his face.

"You still in there?" He ran his hand through his warm blond hair, and I admired the way his green t-shirt stretched across his chest.

"How did you know that about him? Did I say his name earlier? He was several years ahead of me in school, but I don't think I said—"

"His people told me."

"His *people*. That sounds like he has a PR team. Who are his people?"

"His guides. Spirit-type entities. Whatever."

"So, his *people* just told you all that shit about him. While we were all standing here."

"It's really not such a huge thing, and I'd really like a drink because that was a lot of energy."

"I will get you ten drinks if you want them because you're a little scary, Sam Marsh. But then, you explain the people, okay?"

He raised his eyebrows at me for reassurance, and I just sighed and nodded. The ten drinks might have been overkill, though. I tried to hide a smile a few minutes later when I saw Mitchell getting into the passenger side of a minivan in the parking lot.

"I'm here!" Lauren said, falling onto the barstool next to me just as Jesse got back with our drinks. Mine was something pretty and purple, and it looked delightful.

"It's called a Witch's Brew, so you needed it," he said, grinning at me but then shooting a slightly annoyed glance at Lauren for interrupting his expected TedTalk on my intuitive abilities.

"Oh, I might want one too," she said. "What'd I miss?" Jesse and I made eye contact, and I just barely shook my head at him. He just mouthed *later* to me, letting me know I wasn't off the hook.

"Not a lot. Just got here, really."

"Perfect. Also, I invited Jeremy. He'll be here in a minute."

"Where were you that you invited Jer?" Jesse asked, a slightly suspicious edge creeping into his voice.

"I cut his hair this afternoon. Calm down." She rolled her eyes at her brother, but I saw the slight blush appear on her cheeks and knew it wasn't just a haircut. I pocketed that information for later. "Also, killer skirt. Obsessed," Lauren added, even though she'd been the one to pick it out yesterday.

"You do look pretty," Jesse said. "I got sidetracked before."

His mouth quirked slightly, and we both relaxed. Despite its rocky beginning, the night was looking up.

* * *

Because I was secretly an 80-year-old woman, I was ready to head out by nine and get into my pajamas to watch *Buffy*. I was halfway through season two, which was one of my favorites.

"Fine, fine. But *lame*," Lauren whined when I said I was going to get going.

"*You* are free to bar hop to your heart's content, Laur. In fact, you and Jeremy should most definitely go to that new wine bar, Crescent Moon. I hear it's great." I shot her my most innocent smile, and she gave me crazy eyes.

"You *hear* it's great? From whom, Sam? Everyone you know is here."

"My many customers. They are chatty. Now, go and let me be boring."

"Sam, a pleasure," Jeremy said, looking pleased before he followed Lauren to go close their tabs.

"Why must you encourage that?" Jesse sighed.

"Because it's a good thing. Promise."

"I guess I have no choice but to believe you now. Did Jer's *people* tell you that?" he teased lightly.

"*No*, my eyes told me that. Plus, I don't read people unless they ask. So, Mitchell earlier… that was probably not the most ethical thing I've ever done. But to be fair…"

"He was a dick."

"Right," I agreed, scrunching my nose and hopping off the barstool to pay my tab.

"I already got you." I stopped to look at him, but he wouldn't make eye contact.

Instead, his hand brushed the small of my back to guide me toward the door and out of the low-key buzz of a small-town Friday night. I loved the fall chill in the air, but a jacket instead of a cardigan probably would have been a better idea.

Before I'd even completed the thought, Jesse's zip-up hoodie was being held out in front of me. It was one of the new ones with the logo I'd designed on the front. He must have rush-ordered them to get them that fast. A flicker of static made its way from my heart to my throat because this was the *exact* feeling his usual energy gave me, and having it happen outside of my mind was making my brain fuzzy.

"Sweet hoodie," I said, admiring the logo as we stood in front of The Bar.

"Thanks. I scammed this super-talented designer into working with me in exchange for installing some software on her computer. It was criminal how much better my end of the deal was." He smirked down at me, and I bumped him with my hip.

"Can I drive you home?" His tone was hopeful, and while I felt okay, that Witch's Brew had been stronger than I expected.

"Yeah, actually, that would be great."

Just a ride. It's not like you're inviting him in.

I felt the pressure of his fingertips at my lower back again as he gestured to where he was parked, and I shivered, pulling the hoodie tighter around me to play it off like it was the cold. He opened the passenger side door without even a trace of irony before he got in and started on the way to my aunt's.

"So… what you did at the bar with Mitchell…" This conversation was going to kill my buzz.

"Is there a question hidden in there that I'm supposed to decipher?" I asked, hoping my joke might take the slightly awed look off of Jesse's face.

When people first saw what I could do… *actually* do, not just making moon water or carving things into candles, they tended to either want to know everything, which was a little exhausting, or immediately close up and be afraid I'd read their mind at any moment.

"Sorry. I don't know. It was kind of surprising. Even though I know you are a witch, and you do witchy things. I've never seen you do *that*. Can you just read everyone that way?"

I expected that question, but he sounded genuinely curious and not afraid I'd hear all his thoughts.

"Am I *capable* of reading most people that way? If they let me, probably. It's not like Snape in *Harry Potter*, where I can just *legilimens* my way into someone's mind. Someone's *people* can give me information that is in their best interest to know. Their guides or ancestors or whoever is hanging around wouldn't tell me something to the detriment of the person, if that makes sense. It is only to help."

Jesse nodded and opened his mouth like he was ready to spit out more questions, but I held up my hand gently. This wasn't my first rodeo, and I wanted to give my standard spiel to cut down on the back and forth.

"In public, I shield myself from other people's energy most of the time just as a necessary habit, and even if I didn't, most people have a *vibe* if they aren't open to any type of energy work. So no, I don't walk around bombarded with information about strangers." I shifted in the seat of the truck, hoping we could just let this go with a summary.

"That's… that's fucking cool, Sam. I wish I had a more eloquent way to say it. Honestly, I felt like time stopped when you were telling him all that stuff in the bar. I don't want to play twenty questions or anything. Well, I do, but I don't want you to have to answer twenty questions," he added, shooting me an apologetic glance. "But I would love to know more about… well, just you, I guess. Sometime. Not all right now. I want to give you a chance to make a slideshow or some sort of posters, visual aids."

I laughed, amazed at the way he could diffuse just about any amount of tension. The way he'd been looking at me before had raised the temperature in the truck about fifteen degrees.

"Thank you… for not playing twenty questions. I'll think about the visual aids. Those might be helpful—a pamphlet or brochure. And thanks for the ride home."

I put my hand on the door to escape the car because it was becoming difficult to ignore the *something* between us, and I just couldn't. His door opened, and he was around to my side, holding out a hand to help me down from the cab and shutting the door behind me. He was close enough for me to see the stubble along his jawline and feel the warmth coming off his body.

He pressed even closer, my back now up against his truck, the metal a sharp contrast in temperature against my skin.

"About what Mitchell said at the bar… before you turned his world upside down."

This is not *what I want to be talking about with you this close to me, you complete idiot.*

"You really don't need to say anything, Jesse. Honestly, it's a tale as old as time- girl rejects man, man angry, man insults girl… it's a whole cliché."

"Mmmm, I get that. And I know you know you're gorgeous. Though, if you need to hear it more, I'll tell you." His voice had dropped the playful tone I'd gotten used to over the past couple of weeks. I felt literally weak in the knees as he spoke. "However, I meant what he said about *me*, not about you."

I wracked my brain for what the guy had said about Jesse and somehow missed him leaning down and caging me in. All other sounds died out except for my now stuttering heartbeat and his voice low in my ear.

"I can assure you that regardless of my knee, I am perfectly capable of throwing you over my shoulder and taking you back to the captain's quarters aboard my pirate ship. Just as well as any of those shirtless men in—"

"Oh my god," I groaned loudly, my brain slowly clearing the fog from him being that close to comprehend that he was going on about that *stupid* pirate book.

He was laughing, but he hadn't stepped away from me, and I could feel the vibrations of it in my chest. I was going to punch him. "Good *NIGHT*, Jesse," I said, scowling and attempting to duck under his arm, prepared to stomp my way to the guest house.

His reflexes were faster than mine, though, his hand dropping to my hip to stop me. I looked up at him, annoyed but also trying to breathe normally after the rollercoaster he'd just put me through. His free hand reached up, his thumb first tracing down my jaw, fingers now resting wide across my neck, and all intake of oxygen ceased.

"I was not supposed to do anything impulsive tonight, Sam," he murmured, his lips barely an inch from mine. I still couldn't breathe. This moment was hanging on by a thread, and even a slight exhale might prove too much.

"Are you going to, anyway?" I whispered.

He only hesitated for a second, searching my eyes—for what? I wasn't sure, but it seemed like he found it. In the next breath, his lips crashed to mine, his hand moving from my neck to tangle itself in my hair. With purpose, his tongue traced my bottom lip, and I hurriedly let him in. His kiss felt desperate, and I didn't care. I skimmed my fingers up the muscles of his back and pulled him in even tighter, needing to feel him pressed against me. He hummed slightly against my mouth at that, and I responded by pulling his lip between my teeth. His hands were everywhere, and my skin was on fire—his thumb traced my ribs, his fingers dug into my love handles like they were the very literal definition of that term. I never wanted him to stop touching me. He pressed open-mouthed kisses below my ear and down my neck to my collarbone, and I tried to take in a steadying breath.

The porch light outside of Zin's front door suddenly blazed to life, snapping me out of the haze that was kissing Jesse Garrett.

"Shit," I muttered.

The light was on a timer for 9:30, and I wasn't worried about my aunt "catching" me, anyway. It was just enough of a shift for me to press pause.

He pulled back after I'd sworn, a mixture of desire and fear swirling around in his eyes.

"I'm sorry…I should have asked if this was okay—"

"Jesse, you're fine. This is… better than fine. Just, the light came on, and I realized we're standing outside my aunt's house, and I don't know what is… I just don't know. I need a minute."

My hands were gripping his biceps by this time, and I had to force each of my fingers to let go, when what I really wanted was to tighten my hold and pull him back into me.

Chapter 22: Jesse

Her fingers flexed and re-gripped my biceps multiple times as she tried to convince me, or herself, I honestly wasn't sure, that we needed to pause and go home for the night. I would have done anything she asked in that moment, but I was terrified to let her walk away. My heart was still thumping far too loudly in my chest. Her curves felt so soft and welcoming under my fingers, and I didn't want to move.

"You can have a minute. Have as many minutes as you need, just… please, look at me." Her blue eyes were wide, and I couldn't quite read her expression.

"I am so afraid that you're going to walk in there and come up with all kinds of reasons this was a mistake."

She swallowed hard and glanced down, letting me know I was right on the money.

Shit.

"I am asking you to, please, not do that. Not that you can't decide you don't… or that this isn't… damn it you make me nervous." I laughed at myself and was relieved to see her mouth turn up into a small smile. "I am not trying to tell you how to feel. Just give this maybe 24 hours before you decide and let us talk about it." I threaded my fingers through hers and felt slightly better when she rubbed her thumb along the side of my palm.

"I will try."

"Thank you," I murmured.

Gently, I untangled our hands to rub her arms lightly, and I leaned in to kiss her on the top of the head. It was a far cry from how I wanted to kiss her, but I would be damned if I screwed this up again.

"Goodnight, Jesse," she said, finally making her way up the walk.

"Goodnight."

* * *

It wasn't too far to my apartment, around a ten-minute drive, but I might as well have teleported there for all I remembered of it. My brain was still back in her driveway. That was the best kiss of my life. It had also been impulsive—we still hadn't talked about our history, and I knew that we'd have to. But selfishly, I was so glad to have that kiss before we went there. It felt uninhibited by our past, even if that was absolutely untrue, and it was like diving off a cliff.

I grabbed a glass of water and was prepared to pass out, feeling happier than I had in a long time, but this entire night triggered the memory of our first date like a movie playing in the background of my thoughts. I cringed a little at the fact that our first date had come after we'd slept together. I should have been better than that.

Maybe something to bring up next session, I resolved.

For now, I let the movie reel take over.

I'd spent an embarrassing amount of time figuring out what to wear. Christy and I had been together since the 8th grade… the act of dating someone new had me completely out of my depth. My hair was still damp because I underestimated how long I would stare at my closet before I showered, but I showed up outside of her aunt's house in a light gray button-down open over a white t-shirt. I felt like I was dressed for a middle school dance, but Lauren had given me her seal of approval, even if it was accompanied by the threat of bodily harm if I screwed things up with Sam.

The door swung open, and all was forgotten when she smiled at me. Her hair was out of its usual ponytail and floated wildly around her. She had on a flowy skirt with some sort of top that showed her back, and I was immediately a fan.

"Milady," I said, bowing and pulling out a yellow daisy from behind my back.

"Thank you." She laughed, smoothing her skirt with one hand as she took the daisy with the other.

"There is a possibility that I picked that from your aunt's garden on the way up to the door. Just so you don't give me too much credit. You look pretty," I finished, hoping I was doing this right.

"Thank you again," she said, this time without the giggling.

My eyes darted around the room behind her before landing back on her. "Can I kiss you? Or..."

"Or is my aunt going to jump out and hex you?"

"Something like that."

"You're safe."

I immediately relaxed—being close to her was the one thing I was sure of. I pulled her hands into mine and threaded our fingers together before bending down to press my lips to hers. Goosebumps appeared on her arms as I rubbed small circles on her palms. I didn't care about the date anymore, really. I just wanted her to keep kissing me like she'd been thinking about me as much as I'd been thinking about her.

"I'm not an expert, but I think this is an excellent start to a first date," I said when I finally stepped back.

"Totally agree. Should we quit now while we're ahead?" she asked as she followed me out and locked the front door.

"Not a chance. I have spent far too long coming up with what to do tonight, and it might be boring, but now I have to see it through," I said, only half-joking. "We will have a picnic and then go to the drive-in. I brought my dad's truck and an obscene number of blankets so that we can watch the movie from the bed of it."

"That sounds like the best night ever. Definitely not quitting now."

"Definitely not." I opened the passenger door to the black Ford truck when we made it down the front walk. "Did I tell you that you're cute?"

"Not since we left the house, no."

"So, so cute." I gave her one more kiss before heading to my side of the truck, and I wondered how in the hell I was going to make it through the night without my hands on her.

We drove to one of my favorite parks that sat right on Lake Eerie, and the sun was just sinking closer to the horizon; no intention of setting yet, but that was fine with me. It made me feel like we had more time than we did.

"I did not cook. I'm sorry, but not really because I didn't want to kill you. I picked up soup and sandwiches from the cafe. For you, I got you baked potato soup and turkey on a bagel—is that right? I asked Laur."

"Thank you for not cooking. And yes, that's my order." She happily took the cup of soup and the paper-wrapped sandwich from my hand and settled in at one of the picnic tables overlooking the lake.

"So, Sam, tell me something I don't know about you."

"Ay. That's difficult. You've known me for a long time."

"Okay, we'll start with an easier one. It's also the most annoying question in the world for an almost senior, so, sorry. What are you going to do after high school?"

"Ughhhhhhhh," she groaned, laughing.

"I know, I'm the worst." I grinned before taking a giant bite out of my ham and cheese.

"Fine, fine. Probably community college. I was hoping Zin would let me live here for a while and help with the store while I take classes over in Centerville. I'm hoping to take as many online as I can. I'm thinking of graphic design? My mother is horrified that I do not wish to follow in her creative genius footsteps and be a starving artist, but well, I like not starving. I don't know. It seems very far away and like it's tomorrow. You?"

"I feel that last part in my soul," I replied, meaning it.

I'd been working for so long to get to this point that now that it was here, it didn't seem real.

"I've got offers to play at Xavier and Miami, but I haven't picked yet. No idea what I'll study. I don't think they let you pick baseball as a major. But yeah, it seems like a million years away."

"That sounds awesome. I didn't know you'd gotten offers to play college ball."

"Thanks, but I kind of killed the mood with my stupid question. No more serious topics, please. Let's just talk about our favorite cartoons or breakfast cereals or something."

"I'm down. My Little Pony, Popples, Care Bears, and Rainbow Brite.

Easy. And Honeycomb. But honestly, I like almost all cereal."

"You had those answers really quickly."

"What can I say? I know what I like." She glanced at me through her lashes while she said it, and I couldn't stop the grin that spread across my face.

A flirtatious Sam was one of my favorites. We spent the rest of our picnic discussing incredibly important topics like the best condiments, Kool-Aid flavors, cookie types, and future vacation spots.

"Well then, you can tell me other things you like as our very first date progresses," I promised, cleaning up the picnic table. "The drive-in tonight is featuring both the new Indiana Jones and the new Batman. Your pick."

"I'll go with Batman, I think."

"Solid choice. It doesn't start for a bit, so we can drive around before we head over, or I can push you on the swings if you want." I gestured toward the swing set further down the path.

"Swings, yes."

"Really?" I laughed. "I was sort of kidding."

"Do not kid about playground equipment, Jesse Garrett. I love the swings."

"Your wish is my command."

It wasn't even an exaggeration. I would have done just about anything she asked. The sun lit up her curls as it set across the lake, and I had the urge to say things I knew I shouldn't. I swallowed them instead and grabbed her hand to pull her toward the swing set. It had been here as long as I could remember, but they had replaced the actual swings recently enough. She hopped up and looked at me expectantly. Instead of pushing her, I stepped in close and bent down to kiss her, one of my hands resting above hers on the chains and the other trailing up her stomach under her shirt.

So much for keeping my hands off her, I thought, not at all sorry.

We made it to the drive-in before the movie started, but only just. I put her in charge of situating the pillows and blankets in the truck bed while I got snacks. It was also just fun to watch her crawl around in the back of the truck, but mostly the snacks thing. There was a slight chill coming from the water, and it was exactly right for holding her under a blanket. The reality of her leaving in a matter of days kept trying to claw its way to the front of my mind, *and I continued to push it back where it belonged.*

"Red Vines and orange soda and popcorn, as requested," I said when I got back, my timing perfect with the movie previews starting. She clapped a little and scooted over to make room for both me and the food. "Not a chance," I argued, going to sit behind her instead, my arms wrapping firmly around her waist.

"Ah, good call. That is better," she flirted.

I couldn't remember the last time I'd felt this relaxed with Christy—it had turned into such a production all the damn time. Sam leaned back against me while the movie started, pulling the blankets up around us. I was far too keyed up to even enjoy any of the food. Her skin was warm under my fingertips on her stomach, and her breath came in soft gasps when my lips pressed to her neck, her shoulder, her ear while the opening scenes rolled. I could not have told anyone the plot of the movie.

She sighed contentedly and snuggled into my chest even further. When that stubborn piece of reality tried for the tenth time to make itself known, I simply let it know I'd deal with it only when I absolutely had to, but otherwise, it could fuck off. I tightened my arms around the girl in front of me and gave in to the fact that I was, without a doubt, going to crash and burn.

I might as well enjoy it while I can.

Not so much had changed then. I'd still do just about anything she asked, and I would, without a doubt, crash and burn all over again if it meant I got to be near her.

Chapter 23: Sam

My lips were still tingling from the frenzy of whatever that was by the time I closed the door to my room, my back sliding down the frame until I sat on the ground.

Why did that not feel wrong at all?

I promised him I'd try not to write this off immediately, but my defense mechanisms were not on board with that plan. The ghosts of past wounds warred with the undeniable flutter in my chest in replaying the way his mouth felt on my skin.

No, no, no, no, no, no, no, you cannot do this again. Please be smarter than this.

Could I let this feeling ride for twenty-four hours?

I blew out a breath and heaved my ass up off the floor to go through the motions of getting ready for bed.

Hair up, makeup off, and fuzzy socks on, I was ready to keep my promise and just go to sleep. And yet. My deck was staring at me from my nightstand.

Six years ago, I'd refused to read about Jesse because I didn't want to know. Back then, our end was almost a foregone conclusion, and I couldn't face it. Now, the circumstances weren't the same, but the fear of knowing that I was about to have my heart broken… again… was fucking terrifying. I glared at my cards, willing them to stop taunting me, but they won. I didn't want to bury my head in the sand this time.

If there even is a 'this time.'

I huffed out a breath and shuffled my cards aggressively on the bed, putting up my standard words of protection before I cut the deck.

"Okay," I said aloud, not allowing my voice to sound anything but irritated.

Definitely not afraid.

"I am going to pull ONE card about this, and that's it. So, it better be a good one," I added, though I wasn't sure who I thought I was threatening.

I flipped over one card. Had I been reading on an actual table, I would have flipped that over, too.

"Are you KIDDING me?! You are all assholes." The Hanged Man card stared up at me, and if I didn't love this deck so much, I might have lit it on fire. A Tower, a Seven of Swords... those would have been awful, but at least they were definitive. A *Hanged Man* was a nothing. A "get out of your own way and figure out your shit" sort of platitude that gave me zero direction at all.

I should have just stuffed them back in the box and forced my eyes to stay shut until morning. But my fingers, almost of their own accord, flipped over one more card.

The Chariot. Another giant middle finger, telling me to be a big girl, make my decision, and do the damn thing.

"Thanks for absolutely fucking nothing," I declared to the room. I felt my guides retreat, more to show me that my anger meant very little than anything else.

The cards now back on the nightstand, I turned off the light, punched my pillow, and hoped I could refrain from making lists in my head about why this was a bad idea, because despite the hurricane of anger and uncertainty that was currently my atmosphere, I wanted to fall asleep thinking about Jesse's arms around me and his lips on my neck.

* * *

It was 8:00am the next morning, and I was standing at Lauren's front door having already showered, diffused my curls, done my makeup, and picked up coffee and doughnuts because my brain was *on* the moment I opened my eyes. I was trying not to spiral, but I had to call in reinforcements. During this super productive meltdown, I had texted Laur approximately sixteen times, and she had the audacity not to answer. So now, I stood knocking that cute little bee knocker to wake her ass up.

The door swung open to reveal Lauren in a still half-asleep state, red hair in a barely-there ponytail, Strawberry Shortcake robe askew. "Have you become a victim of a body snatcher? Because that is the only explanation I will accept for why you are standing here."

"Worse. I made out with Jesse last night. But I brought doughnuts. And also, coffee," I pleaded with a manic smile on my face.

"You may enter. But know that I need a minute to become a sentient being again."

I only nodded and followed her into her sunny yellow kitchen to sit and wait while she finished waking up. It was not my first choice to come and talk to Lauren about her brother. However, I had zero other friends in this town. My aunt would only look knowingly at me over her teacup and not tell me anything, and if I didn't talk to *someone*, I was going to implode.

Lauren padded back into the kitchen slowly, approaching me like I was a skittish animal that might bolt. She was correct.

"I am now awake, and you may proceed. *However*, you shall mention nothing of even a remotely sexual nature that you did with my brother. You can speak in emotions and vague explanations."

She plopped down across the table from me and grabbed the coffee and a sprinkled doughnut.

"I accept your terms."

She nodded and sipped, and I took a deep breath before I poured out a redacted version of what happened after the bar, Jesse asking me not to write it off before we could talk, and a brief explanation of how ridiculous my tarot reading had been. "So, obviously, I need to know what to do. Lay it on me."

More sipping of the coffee ensued. "Sam…"

"Laur…"

"I don't think you're going to like what I say." She bit her lip and at least had the decency to look apologetic.

"Tell me anyway." I closed my eyes and braced for impact.

"I know you, and I know Jesse. And between you both, I think you might be the more lost. It's a close race, though. Just… I know you've harbored a lot of anger toward him for what happened in high school, and I can't tell you to get over it because I still don't totally know what happened."

"Laur, I just couldn't—"

"I'm not saying you have to tell me right now. But I *do* know that he was miserable after you left. Hell, he was still miserable after he got back together with Christy. I don't think that whatever happened was intentional on his part, and I hate to say that and have it sound like I'm making excuses for him because he can be *so* dense. I'm just saying I don't think he set out to hurt you. And while he would kill me for talking about it, he's only just come back to some version of his old self recently—and I think a lot of that has to do with you, and I love that. But he was in a dark place after his injury, Sam. I don't think I can even explain the lack of life in his eyes when he was taken off the Triple-A roster… I don't know exactly what I'm trying to say, but if you're still angry and you don't think you can move past it, then maybe just let this thing with him go because I don't think he can handle the letdown."

That was the longest stretch that Lauren had been serious that I could recall, and she had my full attention. I swallowed, processing what she said and trying to take it with the knowledge that she loved me, and she was trying to be fair. "I am a little lost, huh?"

"We're all a little lost, my friend. You won't be forever, though. You're amazing, and everything will come together."

"And if I *can*… move past it." Lauren's brows raised high in surprise. I didn't blame her for her skepticism. My grudge-holding tenacity was not a secret.

"Then I think… I think you could maybe make each other happy. I knew that from the moment you two started sneaking around together that summer and thought you were so secretive. It was obvious then that there was something real there, and I don't think that's changed."

Her expression was gentle, and I really needed that. Hearing the truth about yourself, especially from people who knew and loved you, was a hard pill to swallow, but it did the trick of slowing my thoughts.

I blew out a breath, and the drop in adrenaline after the frenzy of the entire morning hit me at once, my limbs shaky and my body tired. "Thank you for saying what I needed to hear, even if I didn't want to hear it."

"You're welcome. Just try not to make me do it too often. The stress is not good for my skin." She grinned at me in a more recognizable Lauren fashion, and I knew we were going to be okay.

"I'll let you go back to sleep… but do not think you're getting out of discussing *Jer*. I just have to open the shop, and probably have an uncomfortable conversation, or else I'd force it out of you now."

"You go, Glen Coco," she responded, ignoring that I'd even mentioned Jeremy. I rolled my eyes at her *Mean Girls* reference but made a note that it should be the feature at our next movie night. I hugged her fiercely and made my way back to my car, determined to put the past behind me today. Before I could effectively do that, however, I had to relive that last conversation we'd had before I left. The one I'd let change everything. It had taken a whole two and a half minutes for me to go from being ready to plead with my mother to let me stay in Emberwood for senior year to vowing never to speak to Jesse again.

"I'm going to miss you, Sam."
He squeezed my hand tightly as we held onto the last part of the night.
"I'm going to miss you, too."
My eyes stung with the tears I wouldn't let fall. I knew it was supposed to be a summer fling, but it just didn't feel like one. It felt like there was finally

someone who knew me and liked me for who I was and didn't think I was weird for reading tarot or creepy for practicing witchcraft. It was so easy with Jesse.

"The past month has been exactly what I needed. I don't know how I would have gotten over Christy without you."

That sentence was like a bucket of ice water hitting me square in the face. The smile stayed on my face for another beat while it sank in; the reality of what all of this had meant to him as opposed to what it meant to me, adding up in my mind. I had spent so much time thinking about how much it was going to hurt when I left, and I hadn't even considered that it wouldn't feel that way for him. I stepped away from him, a look of confusion crossing his face.

"Sam… is everything okay? Did I say something wrong?"

"I am so stupid." It came out as a whisper.

"What? What are you talking about?"

"This was a rebound for you. Obviously. Why did I not see that? How did I not see that?"

I was on the verge of losing it, and I so wanted to make it inside before I did. My inner pessimist was doing a little jig in my brain and shouting, "I told you so!"

"No, Sam, that's not what I meant. I meant you were here for me, and I needed that. I wasn't using you; you know that. You have to know that, right?"

"I really, really don't."

"What can I say to make you believe me?" His eyes were searching mine.

"If this isn't a rebound. If it's not just a silly summer fling, then tell me what you picture."

"What do you mean, 'what do I picture?'"

"When you think about us. What do you picture, see, envision, imagine?"

He swallowed hard. "Like, in a perfect world? Right now? In ten years?"

"In this world. What do you want with us?"

"I don't know, Sam. What do you want with us? I would do—"

"Right. That's so interesting because I could tell you exactly what I want. I think of almost nothing else. So, if you've been able to do this for the past month, and you have given no thought to what you wish the future could look like, then we're absolutely not on the same page. So, ah, I'm going to go inside.

Have a great night, school year, whatever."

"Sam. Seriously? I wasn't even sure what you were asking. Don't leave things like that; it's not what I meant. Come on. Of course, I've thought about what I wish things could—"

"Goodnight, Jesse."

I twisted the knob to the front door of the house as he reached out for my hand, but I shook it off, harshly. I shut the door behind me and slipped into the living room, sinking into the pale blue armchair and letting the tears fall freely. Jesse knocked on the door several times before I heard his car start and back down the gravel drive.

Time had dulled the pain I felt that night, and it brought into sharp focus how insecure I'd been. It hurt that I'd let go of something that could have been great because I'd been so anxious waiting for the other shoe to drop that I'd somewhat manufactured it.

But he also ran straight back to Christy, I reminded myself, knowing I wasn't entirely wrong that night. The one thing I did know for sure was that I had to fully let it all go if I was going to be able to move forward with any chance of a happy ending.

Chapter 24: Jesse

Sleep was becoming a menace. Every time I drifted off, I thought of another thing to say to Sam that was obviously the best reason to give this thing between us a shot. I almost texted them to her in real-time, but I'd at least had the presence of mind to know that would probably come across as desperate and not endearing.

This was the reason for me having been on my third cup of coffee at 7:30am, hoping that no one would care if I took a nap under my desk at some point. I didn't know if Sam was working today, so I was trying to hold off on calling to make plans to talk. Sooner would be better than later, because I knew her, and she was going to be persuaded by our history that this was a bad idea the longer she sat with it. I at least needed the chance to get out my side of the whole thing.

Walking the aisles of the store, I jumped at any task I could to pass the time. Still, when I looked at the clock, it was only 8:30.

Fuck it.

I was just going to risk waking her up and being completely transparent. The moment I opened my texts, a new one arrived.

SAM: Hey. You in the mood to have an awkward conversation in which we discuss events that happened over half a decade ago? Or are you normal…

Oh, thank god.

JESSE: Sounds like the best time ever. I'm at the store, but I can meet you once Heather gets here at 9.

SAM: I knew there was something wrong with you. Broomsticks at 9:15?

JESSE: Done

Immediately, I began looking for things to keep my mind busy, and this consisted of refilling the nickels in the registers because they looked a little low. Our new hire wasn't on the schedule until the afternoon, but I made a mental note to check in with Heather about him when she got there.

And then follow that up with "I have to leave to dissect a sort of breakup from six years ago."

With all the business cards on the "Community Bulletin Board" now sufficiently organized, I breathed a sigh of relief at Heather's "Morning!" from the area of the break room. She gave me a full update on Bryan, and he seemed to be doing well.

No thanks to you, I admitted, having been preoccupied the past couple of weeks with getting the new logo on everything and having shirts printed. *And Sam.*

Blessedly, Heather only gave me a grin when I said I needed to meet Sam for a quick graphic design meeting and would be back shortly.

Why are all the reasons that popped up last night now gone?

What exactly was I going to say now that my brain was devoid of rational thought?

Going to have to wing it.

I parked and walked as confidently as I could with a slight limp up to the shop. The many laps around *Garrett's* probably weren't the best plan. She turned around as the bell chimed, eyes wide, and all traces of the joking tone from her texts gone.

"Hey," I started, taking in her appearance and searching for clues. She had on a long black skirt and a bright blue sweater, which made her eyes look sparkly. I started to tell her so before she spoke and interrupted the thought.

"Hey. Let's go to the back, yeah?"

She flipped the *Be Back in 10 Minutes* sign on the front door. Her voice was soft, and the worry I'd been suppressing wrapped its way around my gut and squeezed. I liked the sarcastic Sam much better. This was terrifying. My feet followed her in her swingy skirt and pulled-back curls until we were tucked into her aunt's office, though it looked less like hers and more like Sam's now—things were labeled and organized on the desk.

I stopped looking around the room and focused on her, feeling both too close and too far away, standing in the tiny room without touching her.

"I have a Cancer Venus, Jesse. Do you have any idea what that means?"

Of all the things I thought she might say, that was not one of them.

"I have *absolutely* no idea what that means."

She sighed, looking anywhere but at me. "It means that in my brain, I'm like the neediest, clingiest girl ever when I like someone. It's the *worst* because who wants that? No one. No one wants the girl who thinks about what your last name sounds like with hers on your first date. It's creepy, and I get that. And yet, I can't stop it. I also have a Capricorn Moon, and I can't begin to explain to you how much my own thoughts make me cringe."

I tilted my head, swallowing when my first thought was to put together *Samantha Garrett* in my head, and some deep recess of my mind thought that sounded spectacular.

Maybe I have this cancer of Venus, too.

"I'm so sorry, Sam, I'm just not following."

"I know. That's because I'm making no fucking sense. Ugh. I'm sorry."

She was pacing, and that was a bad sign, especially in a room where she could only take three steps in one direction. I moved toward her and caught her mid-step with my hands on her arms, silently asking her to talk to me. She looked up, and I almost abandoned the whole *talking* thing because she was so close, and it would be so much easier to lean down and kiss her.

"When we were together, before, I was… you were everything, Jesse. To an embarrassing degree, considering we only hooked up, or whatever you want to call it, for like a month."

She was keeping her voice even, and I left my hands resting on her arms, afraid that if I moved, she'd stop talking.

"And I *knew* it was doomed when it started, and I told myself not to go there, but I did anyway, and I thought you did too. And I get I wasn't fair to you that night. I ran at the first sign that you didn't feel the same as me, or at least not with the same intensity, which is fine—I'm just trying to get this out—but when it seemed like my worries were correct, it just felt so much safer to cut you out altogether."

"Sam, I *did*—"

"Nope! Not yet!" She raised her hand and put it over my mouth mid-sentence. I rolled my eyes, but I let her finish. "And now we're here, and we've been working well together, but last night was… it felt serious. And I just need to know what's different this time. Because I'm the same. Even a little more neurotic and lost now than I was then, so what's changed for you? Or maybe nothing has changed, and I'd like to know that too, because I can't do a casual thing. Not with you."

She was breathing hard, like the words had taken a physical toll on her to get out. I didn't know that I'd ever heard her say so much without an ounce of sarcasm, and that made me tread lightly. I put my finger under her chin to bring her eyes back up to mine after they'd drifted during her monologue.

"I was crazy about you then. I had *all* the feelings." I didn't look away from her because I really needed her to understand this. "Sam… I… I don't know exactly what made everything fall apart when we were eighteen, but I am happy to own my role in it. There were so many things I should have done better. I thought I knew what I was doing, and that was the furthest thing from the truth. I was just figuring myself out and trying to impress you, and I wanted you *so* badly that I cringe thinking about how I came across because you deserved better."

"I don't understand."

"What don't you understand? I'll explain anything you want."

Please just don't move.

"Why did you thank me for helping you get through your summer, get over Christy, if you wanted it to be more than the summer? You made it sound like you were okay with it being a fling—and honestly, that shouldn't have been a surprise to me, but it killed me because I was so in over my head with you."

I flinched at her words, hating that I caused her pain.

"Sam, I can promise you I suck at words. Moreso then than now because, well, therapy, right? But I was not trying to make any sort of relationship-defining statement when I said that to you." She stepped out of my grasp, and I was worried she'd start pacing again, but she stayed put, a confused expression on her face.

"But I *asked* you specifically what you pictured with us, and you had no answer. If you had 'all the feelings,' then why didn't you just say that?" Her voice was getting tighter the longer this conversation went on, and it didn't feel like a good sign.

"Sam. This is going to sound like the worst explanation, but when you asked me what I pictured, my head went to like, end game. Like did I want to get married and have a picket fence and two point five kids. At that moment, I was terrified I was losing you, and I didn't know that saying, 'Hey, it would be cool to keep talking and see if this goes anywhere because I might be falling in love with you,' was an acceptable answer. And after I left, and you wouldn't answer, saying *that* felt like such a half-assed offering when I'd clearly hurt you. I—I don't know what else to say about the fact that I just didn't communicate what I felt or what I wanted well. Or at all."

She shook her head like she was trying to clear it. Her eyes were wide.

"You were back with Christy practically before I'd crossed the state line. If you are seriously saying you thought you might be falling in love with me, then how could you go right back to her? I fully admit that I overreacted to your words that night. No question. But I couldn't have just been with someone else a week later. When I found out you were… it confirmed everything for me—that you had just been using me to pass the time." Anger swept into her voice like a wave, and I felt her slipping through my fingers.

"It was *weeks* of you not taking my calls. You wouldn't even talk to Lauren, and I didn't know how to fix it—"

"It was eight days."

My brows raised at that. "What was eight days?"

"From the time I left until you were back with Christy. I left eight days before school started, not weeks. Were you not with her when you went back for classes?"

"I—" I didn't have a crystal-clear memory of my relationship with Christy because it spanned so many years. But I remembered her making a comment about how it seemed right that we would start senior year back together and that the summer apart had been *silly.* I came back to the present, and Sam was staring at me with an expression that held both hurt and patience. It was becoming clear why she'd held onto some of this for so long.

"I'm so sorry, Sam. In my mind, it felt like forever that you'd shut me out. I am such an asshole."

"Well, I thought so too," she replied, a small grin tugging at her lips.

Maybe all is not lost, I thought.

"But I think it might at least be fair to use the past tense. Can you still tell me why?"

I let out a breath. I would do whatever I could to not still be an asshole.

"That summer," I started, trying to gather my thoughts, "I felt lost when Christy broke up with me after four years. I hadn't really experienced any of my teen life without being attached to her. But you were this girl that I *had* to be near, Sam. With you, I felt like I was my own person for the first time, probably ever. And when it all fell like a house of cards, that felt worse than when Christy dumped me because it was the *real* me that had fucked it up, you know? I couldn't blame it on anything else."

Sam just nodded like what I was saying at least resonated a little.

"When she showed up that weekend before school started and wanted to pick up like nothing had ever happened, I felt like maybe I could salvage some part of that old image of myself because the new one had failed. That's a whole other tangled web of shit that my therapist has had to untangle, okay? But please believe that you were never just a fling to me. And I can't even believe I'm going to say this because you're going to tell me it's such a cheesy rom-com line, but you've always been magic, Sam."

I swallowed, now realizing how long I'd been talking and that her eyes hadn't left mine once. I tugged at my hair on the back of my neck out of nervous habit, begging her to say something.

Chapter 25: Sam

When he said those last words, my Aunt Zin's advice came flooding back from memories I'd re-lived a hundred times. She was always the one to show me the best parts of myself, and I was starting to think that's what Jesse saw when he looked at me.

We had both been so young that continuing to hold on to this hurt felt counterproductive. The man standing in front of me now was not that guy, and I was not that girl anymore.

With the image of The Hanged Man card in the back of my mind, I made my choice, knowing that nothing would ever work out without me deciding to make it so. I wanted some of that feeling back from when I was an idealist and had let myself believe, even for a second, I could have what I wanted. I may have been dreaming then, but I was fully grounded in reality now.

"I'm planning on kissing you. So, if you don't want that…you should probably let me know."

I took two small steps to close the gap between us and pushed up on my toes before letting him steady me. He hesitated for a breath as if deciding whether this was real before pulling me into his chest, his mouth crashing into my lips. One of his hands drifted up my body to tilt my chin higher as he stood to his full height and pressed into me. His tongue traced the seam of my lips, and I opened for him, the kiss taking on more urgency as he slanted his mouth over mine and explored without hesitation.

Suddenly, I was sitting on top of the desk, my back against the calendar I'd spent two hours updating the day before. I pulled my long black skirt up to my thighs so I could secure my ankles around him and pull him closer, sighing happily as his fingers traced up my arms and brushed over my chest.

"Sam…" Jesse breathed, one thumb tracing its way down my throat.

"Jesse…" I said back, fully appreciating his muscular form leaning over me.

"Tell me what you want. Just say it, and I'll do it." He bit down, leaving a trail of marks along the side of my neck.

"I don't… mmmm, please just keep doing that." He smiled against my collarbone and did as I asked. I was in a dangerous space between knowing I was at work, that this was too fast, and not giving a shit. His hands ghosted up my sides, playing with the band of my bra, and I sucked in a breath.

"I'm sorry." He leaned back, his hands now resting safely on my hips.

"No, no. I'm just about to forget I'm at work, and I…"

"Ah. Right. Yeah, okay, maybe we got a little carried away. But Sam…"

"Right?" I let out a laugh at the state we were in—all flushed cheeks, red lips, and wild hair. I tried to force the curls that'd tumbled free back toward my ponytail while he smoothed out his shirt where I'd grabbed it.

He looked at me like he was trying to have a conversation without words. I could feel his nervous energy despite having an overabundance of my own.

"You can say whatever is screaming to get out of your head." I smiled, though I did consciously put another foot or so between us as I hopped down from the desk. I didn't feel *worried* about whatever he was about to tell me, but I wanted to protect my space, regardless.

He exhaled.

"You said earlier that last night felt serious, and I wanted to tell you I am. I'm not trying to be casual with you, and I wanted you to know that before I left. Like, I don't want you to wonder. I've been trying to figure out how to be close to you again since I saw you in this shop. Not in, like, a devious way, just, god, I want to take you out, *and* I want to keep you in my apartment and do much more of this, and I want to listen to you talk about romance books and your psychic-ness, and…okay. I have to stop before I make this worse, but point being, I have to go back to work, and I don't want you to have to figure out what this," he gestured between us, "means. I'm telling you what it means. For me, anyway."

"You're really cute when you're nervous."

He bit his lip as he smiled hesitantly. "I'm really cute all the time, so obviously that applies to now as well."

I laughed lightly.

"For the record, I'm serious too. And we can explore just how serious we are when I see you later." I was *not* the girl who did cute, flirty little lines. But this wasn't the first time he turned me into her.

"You're seeing me later?" he asked, his smile reaching his eyes now.

"Well, we have to get started on the part about you taking me out *and* to your apartment to do *'more of that.'* Is that not what you said?"

"I will pick you up at the house at 6:30."

I just nodded, unable to wipe the sunshiny smile off my face as he made his way out of the store.

* * *

After dusting, checking the tracking information for the new romance titles I'd ordered for the shop, and ensuring that all the supplies for the festival that weekend were labeled and boxed, I had run out of things to do and felt the nerves settling in. Determined not to spiral, I stopped where I was in the middle of the shop and closed my eyes, grounding myself in the space. I felt my ponytail brushing against my back, breathed in the honeysuckle candles I'd just set out and listened to the cars rolling down the street outside. My feet grew roots that sank through the floor and dug into the earth, and my crown chakra pulled in light. I sat in the little forest cottage in my mind, stirring cream into a cup of tea.

There were no knocks at the door today; I wouldn't have invited in any energy anyhow; I just needed to settle my own for the moment.

It was unclear how long I stood like that—I lost time whenever I got into a state of any sort of meditation, but I felt *right* when I came back to the room, like I could breathe in twice as deeply.

I wandered the shop with no need for something to do, trying to let it just be the comforting environment it had always been.

"It feels light in here." I jumped at the voice behind me and whipped around.

"Oh! You startled me, Aunt Zin."

"Apparently," she replied with a smirk tugging at her lips. "I just came by to chat about the festival and see if you would want to offer live three-card readings for an hour or two while we're there."

"Hmm, I could do that." My easy agreement shocked even me as it came out of my mouth. "I was also going to do a raffle for a full reading with you—people just put down their email address to sign up for our email list. I want to do a monthly newsletter with some fun things, like a Tarot Card of the Month where I break down the major arcana or something similar with different crystals? Just to keep people involved and wanting to come in for readings or to order items from the website—which Jesse says will be ready soon."

The almost-smile from before was now a big smug smirk from my aunt.

"Sounds like it's all under control, then."

"I think it is! I'm excited for this weekend. The festival is going to be good for the shop."

"I agree. Will you be home for dinner tonight? I was thinking of making something Italian and delicious."

"Ah, tonight I won't. But I can be there tomorrow night!"

"Perfect. You can tell me all about your date with Mr. Garrett then. Enjoy your evening, Samantha." Her face gave away nothing as she gathered her bag to leave.

"You're not going to give me a lecture on detours and destinations and drop some wisdom about finding my path or some other road trip metaphors?"

"On the contrary, I think you can see all of that for yourself. Do try not to be a smartass, dear. Dinner at six tomorrow!" she called as she glided through the store and out to the back parking spot.

"Unreal."

* * *

JESSE: Hey- I am finishing up at the shop, and I can either pick you up and then stop by my place to change really quick, or I can go home first then get you. I'll just be like fifteen minutes later if it's the second option.

I had been ready for over an hour, and I had run out of things to clean or pretend to read.

SAM: You can come get me first. I want to see your place anyway.
JESSE: Inviting yourself up to my apartment before the date even begins, huh? I like the way your mind works ;)

My breath hitched in my throat, realizing that's exactly what I had done. I knew he was teasing me, but after the way we'd left things at the shop, it *absolutely* sounded like—

JESSE: I can hear you overthinking from here. I was kidding. You can see my apartment, just be aware that it's boring.
SAM: I have no idea what you're talking about. I'm the psychic here. Stop trying to infringe on my territory.
JESSE: Sure thing. See you in a few.

I blew out a breath, both grateful that he stopped my spiral before it began and a little annoyed that I was predictable.

I heard the crunch of his truck's tires on the gravel. It was ridiculous that I was just going to sit here while he walked around to the guest house when I could easily go up to meet him, but I also got that this was more than just a first date.

Just let him do the gentleman thing.

He knocked twice on the door, and I walked slowly as though I wasn't just sitting here waiting for him.

"Hi," I said softly.

He was just in his Garrett's shirt and a thick flannel, but he looked delicious. Without a word, he braced his forearm on the doorframe and leaned down. His lips pressed to mine in a firm but fleeting kiss before he stepped back.

"Hi. I just wanted to remind myself that today was real," he murmured.

My gaze dropped to his lips, thinking maybe he should just come inside and stay there.

"You look amazing," he added.

I resisted the urge to roll my eyes because, again, I was letting him do this first date thing. I had on a black lace bodysuit with a soft cream-colored sweater paired with jeans and boots. The bodysuit did do nice things for my boobs, but I didn't know that *amazing* was a fair assessment.

"You look very lumberjack chic," I remarked as he held out his hand, and we finally made our way to his truck.

"Unfair. I told you I had to change. Although, I don't think that's an insult. I believe I saw a lumberjack-themed book at your shop, so maybe that's a whole fetish I don't know—"

"Stop talking immediately." I laughed anyway as he bumped me lightly with his hip.

"I know you told me to stop talking," he began once we were in his truck, "but well, speaking of books from your shop..." He grinned and shrugged, opening his glove compartment and pulling out *Pirates of Desire.* "I highlighted and annotated my favorite parts."

I held the book in my hand like it might detonate.

"You *annotated* the book?"

"I have a history degree, Sam. I know how to highlight important events."

I started flipping through the book, and he had, in fact, highlighted and made notes on a great many scenes. "I can't decide if I should be impressed or if I need to lecture you about not making fun of romance novels because it's incredibly misogynistic."

"You think I would take the time to annotate *twenty-three* scenes in a pirate romance novel to make fun of women?"

"I don't know! Men make fun of the genre because it's… well, it's…"

"Porn on paper?"

"There's a *plot!*"

"I know! Hence the highlighting."

"I don't know what to do with you right now."

"Read my notes, obviously, and then we can see if we have any of the same favorite scenes because I know you lied when you said you hadn't read it."

I shot him what I hoped was a scowl, but I had a feeling that red splotches were creeping up my neck.

It was a short drive to his apartment, but by the time we pulled in, there were *definitely* red splotches taking over my chest and neck. I never got flustered anymore reading romance novels, but something about knowing *he* also read those scenes? And reading his gods-forsaken notes about how the merchant's daughter seemed to really enjoy being blindfolded with the captain's bandana… I was going to combust.

"I really do feel like I should warn you that my apartment looks like a robot lives there," he said as he parked. His voice interrupted the little world I was in while reacquainting myself with the story, and I pulled myself back to reality to get out of the truck.

"A robot?"

"I… well, I planned for this to be temporary. Until it wasn't. But I never put much thought into decorating it or making it my own, so it kind of just looks like an IKEA catalog."

"I like IKEA. Pillows, stuffed animals, meatballs, *and* Swedish candy. It's like a theme park."

"Glad you think so."

He opened his door and turned on the lights. It was clean and open, with quite a few windows, but he wasn't wrong. It was what I would have imagined fully furnished temporary apartments to look like.

"This is the antithesis of Lauren's place," I mused.

"Don't even get me started on how she refuses to step foot in here until I agree to let her decorate it."

"That sounds like Laur."

"Do you care if I take like the world's fastest shower? I was unloading a shipment because one of my guys was out sick today, so I'm gross. Our reservation isn't until 7:30, so we're okay on time. You can watch TV, or—"

"Jesse, you're still cute when you're nervous. It's fine, you can take a shower. I'll hang out, just point me to the remote. I also have reading material," I reminded him, waving the book like a fan in my face.

His lip curved up slightly, and he looked relieved. I plopped down on the big tan couch, which was more comfortable than I'd expected, given the very utilitarian feel of the rest of the space.

I opened his recorded shows, deciding I might need to cool down from the pirate story. I felt like I could tell a lot about a person by the TV they watched. He had the newest episodes of *The Office* and *Parks and Rec*, but my heart lurched when I saw he had reruns of *Buffy the Vampire Slayer* saved. Like more than an entire season's worth. And not just saved, but *already watched*. I selected one of the most recent episodes. He was in the middle of season two, the same as me. It was a solid choice for any fan, especially because evil Angel was so much hotter than broody Angel. I wondered how Jesse felt about Angel's hotness factor, and a smile spread across my face.

I tried to concentrate on the episode, but when I heard the water shut off, my brain reminded me that one, Jesse was naked on the other side of the wall, and two, that he was still watching a show that he started watching with me six years ago. And damn it if all the fluttery things weren't happening in my chest.

"I should have known you'd be watching *Buffy*," his voice sounded from the door to his room behind me.

His hair was damp, and he was wearing a thermal that stretched across his chest, and the pushed-back sleeves revealed the fucking forearm tattoos. A girl could only be expected to take so much.

"Me, yes. But you? How long have you been watching reruns?"

He gave me a sheepish expression and walked over to fall onto the couch next to me. "I have watched all seven seasons of *Buffy* multiple times, actually. After, uh, well, after we watched some of it together, I kind of got into it. And then it became good background noise when I just needed the TV on, and then when I was laid up after knee surgery, it was an escape, I guess. But if you're wondering if I thought about you every time I turned it on…"

"No, no, I'm not saying—" My cheeks were red because that's *exactly* what I was saying.

"Then the answer is yes, Sam. I thought about you often. Not in, like, a stalker-y way. Just that I wished things went differently between us." He had picked up my hand and rubbed circles on my palm with his thumb as he spoke. The sensation was maddening in the best way possible. His ocean-blue eyes were so close, and that stupid soap smell that hadn't changed was heightened from the shower. I felt my body leaning into his with no input from my brain.

He dropped the hand he was holding and reached for me, too,

our mouths meeting as I moved to his lap. His tongue traced my bottom lip slowly as his thumb dragged down to the pulse point in my neck. He explored my mouth with just the right amount of give and take until I couldn't remember why there would ever be a time when we *weren't* kissing because this was too good.

He grazed his teeth across my tongue, then my bottom lip, before kissing his way down my neck, licking a line back up the trail he'd left. I groaned involuntarily at that. I didn't know that was a thing that I liked, but now I wanted him to do it over and over. He was hard underneath me, and I rolled my hips, earning a groan in return. His thumbs ghosted over my chest, goosebumps erupting over my entire body.

Somewhere in my brain, I heard the words "Slow down." It was hard to tell if it was my own thought or if it was a clairsentient thing, but I knew if we didn't stop now, we wouldn't stop at all.

Chapter 26: Jesse

As soon as she leaned toward me, I knew that if I didn't figure out how to stop myself, I was going to do this whole first date backwards. Again. Her skin was so soft under my fingertips, and the way she shivered when I touched her was a high I *really* didn't want to come down from. I just wanted to keep figuring out how to get her to make those sounds. But *fuck* I really wanted to do this the right way.

We both pulled back at the same time, heavy breathing in tandem.

"We should—"

"Maybe—"

We spoke simultaneously, and I couldn't help but grin up at her. She was *gorgeous* like this— her hair slightly mussed, cheeks flushed, lips pink.

"Just a breather?" she got out, slowly sliding off my lap back into the spot next to me.

I tried to be subtle in adjusting myself, but she didn't even try to contain the near-snort she let out.

"Sorry," she added.

But she didn't sound sorry at all, and I didn't want her to be. Kissing her was more than I ever thought I'd get again.

"A breather is probably good. We can still make our reservation within the time window before they give away the table." I stood, straightening my clothes and running my fingers through my now dry hair.

She hesitated for a beat before speaking. "I know you're set on this, like, first date do-over or doing everything 'correctly' and whatnot, but can we accept that we're just supposed to be ourselves and not go sit at a restaurant pretending like we don't want to be kissing?"

I was quiet for a minute. Just being with her and hanging out together had always felt comfortable, like we belonged. But I also didn't want her to think that I wouldn't put in the work to be with her.

"I can see you arguing with yourself in your head. Just say it out loud," she encouraged, pulling at my hand to get me to sit back down.

"I don't want you to think that I'm taking you for granted or not putting in the effort to, like… I don't know what word I'm looking for. Impress you?"

"You want to court me like a gentleman in a Victorian romance?" she grinned widely at that, her eyes lighting up.

"Those books set very high expectations," I complained lightly.

"Oh? And how would you know?" she questioned.

"I may have downloaded a couple of other books to my reading app." I bit my lip, starting to hate that her grin was now threatening to overtake her face. "I get bored at work sometimes! They're entertaining, Sam. Don't judge me."

"Oh, I am judging you. But the verdict is leaning in your favor." She leaned in to plant a quick kiss on my lips.

"Fine. Judge away, then. I really did sit down to start working on a slideshow about the pirate book, by the way. But I felt like I was crossing the line from funny and endearing to weird and creepy. So, I didn't do it."

She laughed in response.

"Well, A plus for effort, Garrett. But back to the point. Dinner?"

"Whatever you want to do. Just know that it was not my plan to bring you here and seduce you with a teen vampire drama to get out of taking you on a date."

"Noted. Can we order Chinese and finish watching season two? And maybe make out some more?"

"You're literally perfect." I stood and turned, looking for my phone, and I faltered, my knee not a fan of the twisting motion.

"Oh! Are you okay?" Sam asked. I hated the concern in her voice.

"Yeah, I'm good. My knee just gets angry if I move too quickly. It's fine."

"Okay. Want me to get you some ice while you order food? I like everything, so just order whatever sounds good."

I started to protest, to say that I didn't want ice because I didn't want her pitying me or feeling like she needed to take care of me. But her eyes didn't say pity. She just looked at me the same as she had been moments ago, and I relaxed. "Yeah, ice would be good. There are some fancy gel ice packs in the freezer." She nodded and flitted into the kitchen as I called the Chinese place from down the street and ordered every dish that sounded appetizing. I was going to have leftovers for a week, but then I could convince her to come back and help me eat them.

She returned with ice and two beers I'd had in the fridge, so we twisted off the tops, toasted to the slayer, and watched an episode until the food arrived. I was only slightly distracted by the feel of her nails as she traced lines from my palm up to my elbow and back down again.

"Have I told you that I like your tattoo?" she asked quietly between egg rolls and orange chicken, gesturing to my forearm.

"Oh god, this one? Really?" I laughed. I'd hated this tattoo since I got it.

"Yes! Why, you don't like it?" She ran her fingertip around the outline of the flames that spread from the skull.

"Well, I don't hate it as much with you doing that," I murmured. "But no, I was more than a little drunk when I got it. We'd just won a playoff game that we absolutely should not have won, given our ranking, and a bunch of the guys wanted to go get commemorative tattoos. I'm a little competitive, so I pitched this idea of this skull with the baseball stitching because I thought it sounded awesome. It was a lot less detailed than it is now; I added to it over time to try to make it more palatable. But anyway, now I have this very cliché skull on my arm with a symbol of a sport I can't play anymore. All in all, it's not my favorite."

I knew the words that were coming out were going to kill the vibe that we had going, but I couldn't stop them. I congratulated myself on my throat only tightening a little bit when I talked about not being able to play, though. That was progress.

"Do you want to talk about it?" she asked, her face open and caring, her fingers still tracing the tattoo.

"No. Not right now, anyway. Sorry."

"No reason to apologize. I still like the tattoo. I have a thing for forearms."

She shot me a flirtatious grin, and I breathed a sigh of relief that my bummer story was just a blip in what was otherwise turning out to be an awesome first date. I made a show of pushing my sleeves up even higher. I earned an eye roll, so I got what I wanted.

Two episodes later, Sam announced that she should head home. The thought of her curled up against me in my bed almost had me asking her to stay, but it felt like an unspoken agreement that we would go slow.

Actually, we should probably speak that agreement, I thought.

Dr. Merrill would be proud of my communication skills. We packed the leftovers into the fridge and wandered out to my truck. My knee felt better but was a little swollen, and I tried not to make it noticeable. I opened her door, got in on my side, and started the car before diving in.

"Hey, Sam?"

"What's up?" she asked, eyeing me a little suspiciously.

"I just… I thought I would ask how you're feeling. Like, tonight was awesome, but we can go slower, or whatever you want. I just don't want to assume or guess."

"Didn't it used to be me who would ask the awkward questions? Who are you?"

"I'm telling you, it's the therapy." I shrugged.

"Well, I can't argue with that, I guess. I feel… like I'm glad we stopped when we did tonight because I don't think I'm ready to jump in the deep end yet. I like you. Obviously. And I'm getting used to not holding onto the past so tight anymore, but it's new, and I—"

"You're good. You don't have to explain if you don't want to. I obviously like you, too, and I'm not going anywhere." I leaned over and pressed a chaste kiss to her lips before backing out and navigating toward her aunt's.

"Will you be at the festival this weekend? I'm going to be doing some live readings at our booth, but I could be persuaded to go on some rides and eat a giant pretzel if you asked. Does Garrett's Hardware have a booth, or do you just go for fun?"

"It would be sacrilege to miss the festival, Sam. Of course I'll be there, and I will come by the booth to formally ask you to accompany me on said rides, and we will buy all the best food." She gave a girly little clap at my words. "We do have a booth, but my dad will mostly run it. It gives him the chance to talk to literally every human being in Emberwood, and he loves it. I got extra t-shirts and stuff made to hand out. My dad insisted on *only* the ones with our logo and none of the fun ones. But I still slipped a couple of them into the pile anyway."

"Rebel."

"I can't be tamed."

I got another laugh out of her with that as I pulled into the driveway.

"Can I walk you up?"

She sighed.

"Honestly, if you do, I'm going to ask you to come in, and that kind of goes against everything I just said. So maybe not tonight."

"Whatever you want," I said, though I couldn't have wiped the smirk off my face if someone had paid me.

I got out to go around and open her door so she could hop out. I leaned down and captured her lips in a kiss, this one more serious than the last. "Goodnight, Sam."

"Goodnight," she murmured before disappearing up the walkway.

Chapter 27: Sam

After taking off my makeup and pulling on my pajamas, I sat down at the little altar table Zin had gifted to me and set out two tealights. One for Hera and one for Aphrodite. I didn't do deity work often, but after a night like this one, I needed to pay my respects to whomever was responsible for the giddy feeling I was currently experiencing, and they seemed like a good place to start.

Thank you thank you thank you. Because *what?!*

Tonight was a scene worthy of Matthew McConaughey or Sandra Bullock.

The pessimist who lived in my head was trying so hard to throw a wrench into my dizzy, bubbly emotions, but for once, I told that bitch to shut up.

* * *

I'd expected dinner with Aunt Zin to be a lot of *I told you so's,* though she would say it in the most loving way possible, but that's not what I got. She'd asked and accepted the summary I gave her of Jesse's and my date, and she didn't even roll her eyes when I asked about *her* artist "friend," who apparently was a lovely human and had painted Zin a gorgeous landscape of Lake Eerie under a full moon.

The day of the festival was chaos, and Zin and I got started at 6am. I'd made sure to tell myself in the mirror that morning that good things happen to good people and did *not* mean that they were too good to be true.

Take that, pessimist.

Neither of us were morning people. Happily, Jesse was, and he was at the park already setting up for his dad and offered to help.

"Are you going to wear the witch hat tonight?"

"Obviously. It makes me look mystical. Want me to order one for you?"

"I'm not sure I have the bone structure to pull it off. But you will look adorable. Can I come by for a reading?"

"Oh no. Absolutely not."

"Really? Why? I thought the last one went great."

"It did, but I don't want to tempt fate with the chance to fuck things up by throwing up some vaguely ominous cards. You stay far away from my table unless it's to escort me to rides and or food."

"Understood." He nodded and made his way back to his own booth across the park.

I had the raffle bowl, crystals, a few decks, some lovely, handcrafted jewelry we'd just started carrying from a local artist, and I was honestly just excited. It was Zin's shop, but the booth set-up, the new business cards, the new products— those were from me, and it felt right to have something that was mine again. The official start of the Golden Harvest Festival was soon, so I started shuffling my cards, got my hat on, and double-checked everything once more.

Once the crowd started to thicken, I lost track of time. I did more readings than I'd anticipated, and we were on the third page of our email list sign-up when we finally hit a lull in traffic. I took a minute to ground myself. My own energy tended to seep out the more readings I did, and I hadn't been in the zone that long in years. Or ever. I knew I needed to be done soon and just focus on being a salesperson again. I rolled my shoulders when a familiar energy rolled over me. It was the feeling of sand on the beach that was just slightly too hot when it hit your skin.

"Mom?" I asked aloud, whipping my head around to find my mother, the critically acclaimed Nora Marsh, standing in my booth, looking at the crystal display. Her cinnamon and sugar hair was pulled back into a loose braid, and she was dressed in her signature all-black. *"People should focus on my art, not my clothes,"* was her explanation when I asked her why she always looked like she was attending a funeral.

"In the flesh."

"What are you… I mean hi!" I moved in to give her a hug, and she squeezed me tight like I was a child. I tried desperately to visualize my shields before I engaged with her. I needed to be able to remain detached from whatever she was going to say during this visit. It was weak though; I could feel it barely coming together.

"Well, when you either ignore my texts or send two-word responses, this is the outcome. Plus, I haven't been to the Harvest Festival in a long time, so I thought it was the perfect time for a quick visit."

"I'm sorry. I've been preoccupied with getting the new systems at the shop in place and preparing for this… but I should have texted."

My mother just hummed at me, and that usually meant that she wasn't pleased but wasn't going to argue about it.

"Do you want to do a reading for me?"

"Oh, I was just cleaning up. I'm spent after reading for strangers all day. But another time, sure. How long are you here for?"

"Just through tomorrow. I leave for a show in Colorado on Wednesday, so I need to pack and get ready for that."

My mother was a former starving artist turned quite successful artist in the last ten years or so. Her eyes assessed me, and I pushed everything I had left into that shield, only for it to wobble. I saw Zin making her way back to our booth after having gone to visit some other local businesses, and she looked wary upon her approach.

"Nora, this is a surprise," she said in greeting, opening her arms to hug my mother.

She got the same spiel about my failure to answer texts and a repeat of the rest of the information.

"Well, you'll have to come over for brunch tomorrow before

you head home." My mother agreed pleasantly before turning back to me.

"Let's walk down by the lake before you have to get back to work." The way she said *work* was the way I'd imagine a chef with a Michelin star would refer to fast food chicken.

I joined her in sauntering through the maze of booths and food trucks toward the lake until she came to a stop at a bench.

"So, Samantha, what is your plan?"

She tried to sound interested and encouraging, but I knew it was killing her not to just tell me exactly what I was doing wrong. My mother loved me, but I triggered things in her that made our relationship difficult at times.

"For tonight? I'm going to ride some rides and have a big pretzel." Her eyes narrowed slightly, knowing exactly what I was doing.

"And after tonight?"

I sighed, resigned to this conversation. "I don't know, Mother. I'm in an okay place right now, and that's enough for me."

"The idea was for this to be a temporary landing place, no? That's what you told me, anyway, but maybe I'm not privy to changes in that plan. And can you take off that hat? It's very hard to take you seriously."

Here we go.

I slid the hat off my head and smoothed my hair. "That was the plan. I don't know if it is anymore. I'm *happy* for the first time in a long time, and—"

"It makes you happy to work retail and live in my aunt's guest house?"

I winced at her words. Because she had a way of twisting whatever I said to help prove whatever point she was trying to make.

"Mom. Just tell me what you want from me. I don't want to do this. I'm tired."

"Hey!" a voice came from behind me.

No. Please, just not right now.

I mustered the brightest smile I could before I turned around.

"Hey, Jesse. You remember my mother?"

"Oh, wow, yeah, it's been a while. Good to see you again Ms. Marsh."

"Please, call me Nora."

"Well, I was coming to see if you had a break and wanted to go ride some rides, but I didn't realize your mom was in town. Just let me know if you want to do any of them later, yeah?"

His open expression and genuine smile melted me a little inside because that was the *only* thing I wanted to be doing right now.

"I'll text you," I answered softly.

He just nodded and walked away. She barely even waited until he was out of earshot.

"*Really*, Samantha? You're sticking around this town with *no* plan because of the Garrett kid? *Again?* You are smarter than that."

"Mom, it's not like that. I'm not staying here *for him*. There wasn't even a '*him*' until a couple of days ago—"

"I realize that you're twenty-four, and there is very little that I can do to keep you from making a colossal mistake. But know that you were not made for a small life, and that's what this town is. You are a lovely writer, a painter— you have so many talents that could feed your soul if you were dedicated to them. This? Here? This is not for you. And Zinnia is an enabler. She's wonderful, but you are not her, Sam. She had her years of being wild and free before she settled down with my Uncle Linden. You haven't done that. You can't just come here and think you'll be satisfied working in that shop, throwing away your chance at making something of yourself on a pretty boy like Jesse Garrett, who is going nowhere now that his baseball career is over."

It was like she had physically slapped me. The tears were already overflowing, and I tried to wipe them away with the palm of my hand to no avail.

"Why is me being happy not enough, Mom?" I whispered.

Her eyes half-rolled at me in response, cutting even deeper.

"You're being dramatic. If I thought this could make you happy, I'd throw you a party. I'm only trying to save you from yourself. My offer stands… if you want to come home and figure things out there, without the influence of your aunt, I'd love to help you find something that's worth your time and energy."

"Right."

I couldn't argue anymore. She might as well have stuck me with a pin and deflated me.

"Just think about it. I'll see you at brunch tomorrow." She reached over and tucked a piece of hair behind my ear that had fallen from my braid, and it took everything I had not to flinch.

"I'll see you tomorrow."

She walked away, apparently satisfied that she'd really shown me the error of my ways. In reality, all she'd accomplished was making me want to crawl in a hole. What I wanted at that moment was for Jesse to come back, wrap his arms around me, and let me complain about how awful my mother was to me.

And to him… she had no fucking right to talk about him like that.

But running to him felt like exactly what she'd said. That I was throwing myself into this thing with him to avoid making plans, figuring out my shit. And I *hated* that.

SAM: Hey. Could you drop me at my house? I came with Zin, and I need to go home.

LAUR: Of course. I'm on the carousel, but I'll meet you at the entrance when I'm done. Everything okay?

SAM: I'm okay. Just need to get out of here.

LAUR: See you in 5

I shot off another text to Zin to tell her I had to go home. She just wrote back that we would talk later and not to worry about the booth and that the neighbor boys were going to help break down everything.

Great. Now I'm not even capable of following through with the one *thing that was mine. My vision, my plan.*

The sting of failure and disappointment lingered and showed no signs of retreating anytime soon.

No matter what, it's never quite enough.

I heaved myself off the bench and tried to be invisible as I wove my way back through the festival to get to the parking lot. I just needed to get to someplace quiet to re-ground myself and cry for a good solid hour.

JESSE: Hey. Laur told me you needed to go home. I hope everything is okay. You know you could have asked me to drive you, right? Text me later if you want to hang out.

Another tear forced its way out and slipped down my cheek because this was what I'd always wanted. To be in Emberwood doing fun witchy shit with my aunt, hanging out with Lauren, and being with Jesse. Just because I'd been a teenager when I wanted it didn't make it less real, did it?

Is a "small life" even a bad thing?

It sounded like a bad thing. Between the energy suck of reading all day plus the energy suck that was my mother, I knew I couldn't think big, heavy thoughts right now. I saw Lauren up ahead talking to someone, and I slowed my pace, hoping she'd be done before I reached them and had to fake cheerfulness in front of a stranger.

They both seemed to register my presence at the same time because they cut their conversation short.

"It was wonderful to see you, Laur. I'm serious about doing that piece about you and the salon, so email me."

"Will do, thanks Christy." The woman turned to walk away, only giving me a cursory glance.

My eyes snapped to Lauren, who just shook her head slightly and mouthed, *"car."* My tears were almost forgotten, and a whole new feeling crept up because that was, without a doubt, Christy

Covington, and I was in no state to filter out the pessimist in my brain at this moment.

She is still stupidly gorgeous, like a Midwest Barbie. Does she still live here… like does Jesse see her on a regular basis. Are they friends?

I wanted to vomit.

Breathe. Breathe. Breathe.

I practically flung myself into the passenger seat of Lauren's car and put my head on the dash, willing myself to return to the fluttery happy me that I was two hours ago.

"What happened?" Lauren asked.

"No, no. Christy first," I insisted.

"Christy is inconsequential. She and Jesse broke up years ago when he was a freshman in college, and to my knowledge, that was that. She lives in Toledo and is here for the festival. She's writing about it in her *lifestyle blog*. Now, what happened?"

"She has a lifestyle blog?" I briefly wondered if it was called *Musings of a Midwest Barbie*.

"She does. We can search through it later. What the hell is going on, Sam?"

"My mother showed up unannounced."

"Ughhhhhhhh, fucking Nora." There was no love lost between Lauren and my mom. "What did she do?"

I gave her a summary and almost managed to do it without crying, but I left out the insult about Jesse because I thought that might lead to murder.

"And now I have to have brunch with her tomorrow."

"Zin will be there, though, right?"

"Yeah. But Zin has always been weird when it comes to my mom. I think she doesn't want to step on her toes or something, but I really wish she would. Her whole foot even."

Lauren was quiet for a minute as we neared the house.

"Do you want to hear my opinion?"

"I do, Laur, but I don't think I can handle any more opinions today. I just need to think."

She nodded her understanding and pulled into Zin's driveway. When I finally made it to my room, my back hit the door, and I slid to the floor before a sob worked its way out from my chest.

Chapter 28: Jesse

I should have rescued her when I saw the look on her face.

I'd called Lauren after she drove Sam home and at least made her give me the bullet points on what the hell changed since last night. I *hated* that Sam felt like she couldn't text me for a ride. I understood not wanting to be vulnerable in front of other people—I'd become quite good at deflecting in the past year or so, but I wanted her to know that I wouldn't feel sorry for her or make her feel small.

"Hey, Jesse," a once-familiar voice sounded from behind me on my walk back to the booth.

I turned and tried to wipe the panic off my face.

"Christy, hey. How're things?" I stood still so she could catch up. She looked the same since the last time I'd seen her in passing a few years prior, and really hadn't changed much since we graduated.

"Good! How's the knee? I heard—"

"Well, it was great to see you. Have fun at the festival."

I nodded politely at her and walked away, not caring about what I was sure was an offended look on her face. I held no leftover anger toward Christy. Well, I really didn't hold leftover feelings for her at all; we had let things run far past their course, and I didn't feel obligated to put energy into a conversation for the sake of social niceties.

Fuck.

I just wanted to drive over there and knock on Sam's door until she answered, but Lauren told me to give her until her mom left the following day before I demanded anything else from her. It was a fair request and probably the right thing to do, but I didn't have to like it. I walked the rest of the way back to the Garrett's Hardware booth and offered to take over for my dad so he could go home.

"Nah, you can go enjoy the festival or go home if you need to rest your knee."

My father was almost a copy of me, just a few decades older. He'd aged significantly since his heart attack though, gray overtaking his blond hair, deeper wrinkles around his eyes.

"Okay, if you're sure. Need me to do anything while I'm here?"

"I said I've got it, son." His voice was soft but firm, and it made me feel like a child being chastised.

I just shot him a thumbs up and walked away, shoving my hands in my pockets. What a spectacularly shitty day it turned out to be. His refusal to admit that I had taken over at the store and done a *damn* good job was more than irritating. Maybe even moreso because I didn't *want* to be damn good at this job, but *that* line of thinking led to a dangerous place called *What the Fuck am I Going to Do with My Life.*

Not a problem you're going to solve today. Just go home, ice your knee, and call Sam tomorrow.

Dr. Merrill taught me that small actionable steps helped calm the panic. It worked. I just didn't know how long I could avoid the big, abstract, life-determining questions.

Chapter 29: Sam

While I eventually made it to the shower and then to bed, I couldn't say that sleeping on things made them any clearer the next morning. If anything, the strongest feeling I had was dread at seeing my mother at brunch.

Zinnia had come by my room and knocked, but I was already committed to sleep at that point and ignored her. I felt guilty, but guilt was just a drop in the bucket.

Jesse hadn't texted again. Lauren told me she was going to instruct him to give me a day, but I didn't know if he'd listen. I couldn't decide if it was a good sign that he was respecting my boundaries or a bad sign that he just didn't care all that much.

It's too early, pessimist.

The affirmations had to wait until tomorrow, but I did decide to pull an oracle card just for some guidance on how to go about my morning.

It said, *I trust my intuition to guide me.*

I wanted to roll my eyes, but if I *was* capable of picking up my own intuition right now, it would be decent advice. I pulled my hair back into a tight ponytail and slipped into a pair of leggings and a sweatshirt. If I had to be emotionally uncomfortable, I was going to be physically comfortable. A light knock sounded on my door as I was pulling on my socks.

"Come in."

Zin entered with a large mug of coffee, and I breathed a sigh of relief. She sat across from me at my little bistro table.

"I'm so sorry I couldn't protect you yesterday."

Wow. Right to it.

"It's not your job to protect me, Auntie. I'm a big girl, and she is my mother."

"I sat up for a long while last night. With my cards, with my own guides… and it is so hard for me where Nora is concerned because I have to honor her role as your mother. Even if I disagree, your relationship is part of who you are, and it's something I've never experienced."

Her voice got quiet as she spoke, and I realized I didn't know much about why Zinnia never had kids. I'd always assumed it was by choice, but I'd never thought to ask.

"I want to be here for you, and I want you to be *here*, in Emberwood, period. But I realize that I may have pushed too hard. I thought it was the right thing to do, but if you don't think it's best, then I won't press the issue. I support you always."

Her eyes were misty, and I hated it. She was my Yoda, and she was supposed to be calm and have all the answers.

"You know that I wouldn't have come if I really didn't want to. I'm a little bit stubborn that way."

"Thank the universe for that," she said, laughing. "What can I do?"

I'd been thinking about that for a while. I knew that she wouldn't try to take on my mother, and now I kind of understood why. I just needed to know she was in my corner.

"Can you tell me if *this*," I gestured at my surroundings and then again at myself, "is a detour or a destination?"

I wanted that direction *so* badly. I'd finally felt like I was picking up the pieces after losing my job and essentially my independence, and I thought maybe this was where I was supposed to be all along, and getting fired was the course correction I'd needed. But now, replaying my mother's words over and over in my mind, I wondered if I was here because it was safe, and there was very little risk of failing again when I had Aunt Zin to hold me up.

And Jesse to distract me.

"I… I think I should let you decide that for yourself. I will say that you should hold on to that stubbornness you mentioned. It serves you well, Samantha, and it's tied to your intuition. When you feel like you need to dig in your heels, it's because you probably do."

"What do I do? Do I make a big pro/con list for my life? Look for graphic design jobs on Craigslist and see if a good one pops up? Start over *again* somewhere else?"

My voice was getting higher the more questions I asked because I truly had no idea.

"Or do I stay here and live in your guest house and eat tacos and drink margaritas and read tarot cards for people?"

I didn't list the option of going to stay with my mother because that was the worst option. The nuclear option.

"I think all of these are questions you need to sit with and sift through your feelings about. When you're clear-headed and grounded, not right now. I am confident that you will come up with the answers you need, and that this, too, shall pass. And so will brunch."

We both grimaced at the thought of brunch, but the time was drawing near.

"Let's just get it over with. I will try to stay shielded now that I've slept, and you can turn all the brooms in the house upside down."

"I did that at six this morning."

Zinnia just smirked slightly at that before she made her way back to the main house. I finished my coffee, tried to meditate through my nerves, and built the most complex, mirrored shield I could envision before I followed.

* * *

She brought a fruit plate from the grocery store that paled in comparison to the one Zin had prepared, but okay, it was an effort. I sipped my orange juice, cut my pancakes, and seasoned my eggs. I answered when asked a direct question and nothing more. My mom played along for a while until she was done.

"Are you going to drop the childish act anytime soon,

Samantha? Or are you committed to this bit?"

"Not a bit, Mother. Just trying to make it through brunch without you telling me how mediocre I am."

"Dear god, this again. I have never once in my life said that you are anything less than amazing. I just want *you* to know that and to create something for yourself that is *also* amazing. I'm sure even Aunt Zin agrees with me here." She shot a look at my aunt.

"We do agree on the semantics, Nora. I just think we may differ on what constitutes amazing. It's really neither here nor there, though. I've told Samantha I will support whatever she chooses to do without attempting to persuade her." My mother's eyes narrowed.

"So, does this mean—"

"I'm not coming home with you, Mom." She was quiet. "I'm not saying I'm going to stay in Emberwood long term. You're right. That wasn't my plan, and it was easier to stay busy and put off making a plan. But I'm going to do it here because I'm doing well. I'm not going to move my life again in the name of figuring out said life. So, I love you, but I'm staying here for now."

"Okay. Well, I had better be getting back so I can prepare for Colorado. Thank you for brunch, Zin. Samantha, try to text me back sometimes."

She tossed her folded-up napkin on the table, walked by my chair, kissed the top of my head, and then she was out the door.

My posture deflated, and I dissolved the shield I'd been holding, sucking in a deep breath.

"Mimosa? I have pomegranate juice and lavender for garnish."

"Best idea ever."

Chapter 30: Jesse

I waited until 12:31pm. This technically counted as afternoon. I typed out six different versions of my text before I gave up and just hit send.

JESSE: Hey. I'm sorry things with your mom were difficult. Can I take you to dinner?

I now had the displeasure of checking my phone every thirty seconds to make sure I didn't miss a response. My alternative was returning calls to new contractors and trades who wanted to set up delivery accounts with us. This was positive, but it was not what my brain wanted to focus on. Three phone calls were done before I saw her name on the screen.

SAM: Hey- that's okay, it's… complicated. Anyway, I think I just need a little bit of time to recover? For lack of a better word. It's nothing to do with you, I just have to figure some shit out on my own. I'm sorry :(

I hated that response. It felt like I'd been racing full speed toward a dead end.
No. Not a dead end. Just a stop sign.
I could give her some space to figure shit out. My worry was that then I'd have to also use that time and space to figure *my* shit out.

JESSE: Of course. Don't apologize. I'm here when you want to talk.

I forced myself to move and get the afternoon deliveries

together. My dad kept hounding me to hire a delivery driver so that I wasn't out of the store as often and wasn't hauling tools up flights of stairs at times, but honestly, I just didn't want to. I had to get out of that office sometimes, and this gave me a reason that didn't look like I was running away. I was pulling some pieces of trim when I felt someone behind me.

"Jesse Garrett," a warm voice said.

I turned, half expecting to have to disappoint someone by telling them I wasn't going back to the Mud Hens, but the thought fell away when I saw who it was.

"Coach Brown? It's been a minute, how are you?"

A genuine smile took up residence on my face. This man was my coach from the time I was playing tee-ball all the way through eighth grade. He'd ended up coaching community college ball and then at one of the smaller university teams, but I'd not kept up over the years.

"It sure has. I can't complain—just officially retired, for the second time, and Claire said it was time to come back to Emberwood. We just moved in a couple weeks back, and now I'm to start on her honey-do list of projects at the house, which brings us to my visit here." He gestured around to the store.

"That is awesome; Emberwood is glad to have you back. It was never quite the same without you."

I meant that. He had been my coach when I fell in love with the game and the game had loved me back. The stakes were low, but the payoffs were sky-high when you were a kid who'd just won a championship.

"Well, I'll let you get back to it; you looked like you were on a mission. But Claire would be madder'n a hornet if I didn't invite you to dinner soon, so just be ready to come and eat more food than you've seen in a month. Don't think you can get out of it either, because she's persistent."

"I wouldn't dare turn down Claire. I'm running the store now, so you can pretty much always find me here. It was good to see you, Coach."

"You too, son."

He shuffled down the aisle with his list, and I finished gathering everything for my deliveries and loading the truck. I wasn't sure how to turn the day around, but it felt like Coach Brown came across me for a reason. I felt myself come out of a spiral and back to baseline while we were chatting, and now I felt more rational about the whole Sam situation. I had to respect that she needed some time, and I had no choice but to believe her that it wasn't about me.

* * *

Same essential oils. Same white noise machine. The last time I was here, I felt like I had made so much progress, but it had now been five days since I'd heard from Sam, and it was too much time with my thoughts. I could only go out with Jer so many times in a week, plus him asking about Lauren was starting to make me cringe.

"Come on in."

I stood and took my familiar spot on the chair opposite her and leaned back, trying to appear relaxed. Rational.

"It's been a while since you called for an extra session. What's happened?"

I launched into a veritable avalanche of everything that'd gone on with Sam since my last session. There was no point in holding anything back; this woman had seen me at my worst, so I figured she could handle me pining over a girl.

"And now my mind is so loud because everything else is so quiet, and I feel like the time I'm going to be able to coast and ignore the 'life plan' questions is rapidly coming to an end."

"I know that feels overwhelming because when you think about planning for an entire lifetime, it's too much. Too many decisions, too many possibilities and variables. Instead, let's start

171

with what you can and cannot reasonably do right now or in the very near future."

"Okay. Let's do that."

We went through what felt like a million questions, but in the end, I had concluded that I *could* eventually leave the hardware store if I wanted, but not tomorrow. I *could* also continue to work there and just treat it as exactly what it was: a job, and I could find fulfilling things in other parts of my life. This meant finding a hobby that wasn't playing baseball. So, my new, actionable plan was to do some interest surveys that she gave me like I was a high school junior to help me "open my eyes" to new possibilities. From there, I was supposed to come up with a list of hobbies or activities to try, as well as a list of jobs or careers that sounded interesting, and we'd make more plans at the next session.

"Before we finish, do you want to talk more about Sam?"

"I... Should I leave her alone? It feels like when I did that before, when I just accepted her shutting me out, it was the wrong move. But now, it is different, and I don't want to make the wrong move again."

"Relationships are hard. I wish there was some way you could read her mind and know exactly what to do, but the reality is that you have to balance respecting her boundaries and respecting your own. If you want a relationship, meaning you want to be with someone seriously, and she's not in that same place? It is okay for you to walk away. Not in anger or resentment, just because that's your boundary. You're looking for something stable in your life, and you'd like to build that something with her, it sounds like. You can respect her need for time and space, but at some point, it is okay to ask if she is interested in building that something with you. Then, you accept what she tells you."

"You make it sound so simple."

"It is rather simple in theory. But that doesn't mean it's easy."

"Understood. Thanks, Doc."

I walked out of there feeling fifty pounds lighter.

Chapter 31: Sam

"Show me the blog, or so help me, Lauren, I will come in and redecorate this townhouse in all neutrals. Beige and gray and chocolate brown."

The lack of sleep had caught up to me, and I was nearing a level of unhinged that I hadn't seen in a while.

"You're cruel. I just don't think it's going to do anything positive."

"Mhm. Show me."

I pushed my laptop across her counter. I'd been trying to just focus on myself and push Jesse out of my mind, which also meant ignoring the Christy Covington sighting from the festival. But now I had to know. Lauren flipped her hair haughtily and typed in the website: *HeartlandHypeAndHappiness.com*

Okay, not Barbie, but bleh.

I greedily took back the laptop and started scrolling. Most of her posts seemed to center around event planning, dinner parties, some recipes, and reviews of local places. It wasn't terrible, honestly.

She could use a better logo, though, I thought.

I clicked to open her most recent post, which was about hosting a Halloween party. Halloween was kind of my jam, so I figured it was a good place to start.

"Before you decide to host any type of Halloween event, you must decide what kind of Halloween you want to achieve. Is it slasher style blood and gore, old-school bats and ghosts, magical witches and potions, or more whimsical painted pumpkins and fairy costumes."

My jaw dropped in shock.

"She stole my fucking idea!"

"What?" Lauren asked, eyeing me warily.

"This… Christy, about Halloween. The explanation is mine!"

"You're going to have to explain."

I re-read the selection for Lauren before I launched back in time to re-live for her in painstaking detail the day that Christy Covington and I had our only real conversation.

I popped my headphones in while I dusted, pulling books off shelves and trying not to add to the stack of "books for Sam" any more than I had to. I saw a copy of Practical Magic *placed in the wrong section, and I determined it was clearly waiting for me, adding another to the stack.*

The bell above the door jingled me out of my very pleasant daydream about Jesse, and I pulled off my headphones to go help a customer. My salesperson-perma-smile stayed on my face until the customer turned around and I saw who it was. Christy Covington, Jesse's very recent ex. Plus her sidekick of the week, I thought I remembered her name being Paige. I swallowed painfully, really hoping this was a quick encounter.

"Hi, what can I help you find?"

Christy's eyes roamed over me, not unlike an appraiser would look at a counterfeit piece of art.

"I'm having a Halloween in July party, and it's completely impossible to find decorations. So, I thought I'd try here." Her words were innocuous, but her tone sounded like the store had already disappointed her.

"Gotcha. Do you know what kind of Halloween vibe you're going for?"

"Yes. Hal-lo-ween."

This girl was so pleasant.

"Right. Just, like, witches and potions, fairies and princesses, fake blood and axes, or skulls and spiders?"

Christy rolled her blue eyes and flipped her blond hair in a way every teen-movie heroine would have envied. "At this point, anything."

"Okay. We don't have much stuff out here on the floor, but I've seen some old Halloween inventory boxed up in the back. I'll pull it out and be right back." I quickly made my way to the storage area.

"Who even is she?" Girl-Maybe-Named-Paige muttered as I walked

away.

"I don't know. The owner lady's chubby granddaughter or something."

I winced at that, though I hated that I did. I didn't really have an issue with my weight or my body— I was comfortable in my skin. Being that my mother was an artist, I learned to appreciate all kinds of bodies from the time I could toddle around a museum, but it still flustered me to hear people make comments or judgments about it, especially someone who had been with Jesse up until a month ago. I was resisting comparing my short, curvy figure to her tall, lean one so hard that I could physically feel it in my muscles.

I tried to physically shake off the reaction and pull down the boxes I'd seen earlier. There were quite a few packages of fake webbing and pumpkin and spider decorations. Aunt Zin hated the cheap crap all the stores put out at Halloween, but she also needed to stay in business and had to try to compete with their stock and prices. October was good for a business with broomsticks in the name. I dragged the boxes up front, by which time Aunt Zin was behind the counter, making the two girls uncomfortable with her patented brand of silent judgment. I bit my lip to keep from smiling at her.

"Here you go. Feel free to sort through what we have and see if any of it will work for your party."

Please just leave. As quickly as humanly possible.

Reading my mind, Aunt Zinnia went to the door of the shop to the hand-made broom she kept there, the handle wrapped with crystals, and flipped it upside down. A small, but usually effective, energy shift to get your guests to leave.

"Yeah, sure. I'll take all the webs and the pumpkins and five strands of the skull lights. Oh, and the inflatable cauldron," Christy added, looking up.

Flipped broom for the win.

I rang up the items, and I may have added an "inventory fee" for the fatphobic comments. They paid and left in a hurry, and my aunt flipped the broom back to its original state. She lit some juniper by the door for good measure.

"Hmph," was all she said before going back to the office to work on ordering stock for the following season.

I agreed with the sentiment. I took some deep breaths to rid my brain of

"So you see… mine."

"Well, it does certainly seem like you made an impression."

"She's a plagiarizer."

Lauren practically scoffed at me. "I know that you know that's not what that word means. And you're projecting your frustration with your mom, your job, *Jesse*, onto a girl you've spoken to once. Granted, she was a bitch then, and she was probably jealous that you had boobs and an ass, and she didn't, but I digress. I'm just saying that if we're going to sit here and do a deep dive into your emotional baggage, can we at least make it about the real shit and not the made-up stuff?" Her gaze nailed me to my spot.

"Only if you tell me what's going on with Jeremy." I thought this might at least buy me some time to think of reasons why she was wrong.

"Sure. He's hot as fuck, has a wicked sense of humor, *and* he's my brother's best friend, *and* he has kind of a reputation from when he was younger, which is why I'm sure Jesse is such a buzzkill anytime Jer flirts with me. He's never said anything serious, asked me out, or made me think that he's interested in anything more than being friends, and even if he were, I don't think he'd be willing to cross Jesse. So that's that. Go."

"Why must you be the way that you are?"

"Just lucky, I guess."

"Well, I still want to read for you about Jeremy. But fine." Lauren just looked at me expectantly and ate a cookie. "I've been working through this 'shadow work' book that Zin gave me, which is just like, questions to make you examine all the shit that's wrong with you and why… so therapy without the trained professional."

"That sounds promising."

"Oh, for sure, it's an excellent idea to sit in all my feelings every night and write down how messed up my brain is. I love it."

Lauren snorted lightly. "Tell me some of the questions."

"Hmmmm, one was about figuring out what my childhood-self wanted more than anything in the world, another was the same but for my inner teenager. The teenager one was a little rough because all I wanted then was…"

"Jesse. Same rules apply to this conversation. Vague generalities, nothing specific."

"Understood. I guess it was a hard one because it made me wonder if I'm trying to satisfy my teenage self or if there's still something real there as an adult Sam and Jesse."

"This sounds like a truly horrible book."

"You're telling me. My most favorite so far is that I had to write a journal entry from the perspective of my mother on the topic of how she feels about me, or what she thinks when she looks at me. That one took a full business day to recover from."

Lauren sighed. Loudly.

"I know that things with you and your mom are complicated on a good day, but Sam, you know she is just pushing her own bullshit onto you, right? Like she's always wanted to be this big-time artist, and so yeah, living a 'normal' life might feel suffocating… *for her*. But that doesn't mean it is for you."

"I… I do know that she's trying to fit me into a vision that has very little to do with me. But Laur, it's so hard to try to let it roll off my back. She is my *mother*, and she thinks I'm failing at life. It's… it's a lot. I wish I could say I don't care and that she's just a bitch, but she's in my head."

"I get it, I really do. I just want you to know that for every negative thing she says, I could say ten positive things about you, your talent, your *life*. So just try not to let her thoughts drown out all the others. Okay?"

"I'll try. Yeah."

"So has any of this soul-crushing 'shadow work' done anything to help you figure out what you want to do?"

She pushed the box of cookies across the counter to me, and I happily partook.

"It's made me at least take my head out of the sand. I've been looking at job listings for full-time graphic design work anywhere from Chicago to Toledo to Lansing. I don't know if I want to move further than that. I'd like to be able to drive back to Emberwood if I leave. But the listings are so depressing. I'll have to completely start over as an assistant, and I won't get to do any real designing for possibly years. I guess it's just hard to remember anything I liked about my old job. I always just liked the idea of where I'd eventually be, not where I was."

"Barf."

I laughed, surprised. "Barf?"

"Yeah. Honestly, just cross that off your list."

"You're completely serious. Just don't even consider the job I went to school for."

"So so SO serious. I mean, you can design, obviously. You've been creating designs since you got here. But can I tell you that when I go to work? I'm generally happy to be there. Like, yeah, I have some clients that annoy me. But making people feel great about themselves is just fun. I like the conventions, I like the people I work with, well, mostly just Christian because he's snarky and fabulous, but that's working anywhere, right? I just can't imagine getting up every day and *not* liking where I was going or just waiting for it to get better for *years*. I'm not a psychic, and I don't read tarot, but I'm telling you that I'm right about this."

"Am I just completely obtuse that I've never even thought about it like that?"

"Yes."

"Shut up." I tried to sound mad, but I laughed anyway.

Can I just take it off the list?

"Do you hate going to *Broomsticks* every day?"

"Of course not. It's just not a *real* job."

"Does it pay real money?"

"Yes, but—"

"Has your aunt lived off of the profits from said business for decades?"

"I mean, sure, but there was also my uncle and—"

"It's a real job. You're a weirdo."

I frowned, contemplating her questions.

"I do like ordering books. And I liked organizing the event and doing readings and stuff. Though it literally has nothing to do with what I've been working toward for the past five years."

"And? Design your own deck of tarot cards and sell them at the shop. Create less-conspicuous book cover jackets for all the shirtless man books so women can read them in public without feeling weird. Design t-shirts. Jesse runs a hardware store, and the t-shirts might be the best-selling item there.

"I'm just saying maybe it doesn't all have to fit into one box. You can have multiple boxes and just pull from each of them when you want. And for the record, because I can't let this one go— there *is* something there for grown-up Sam and Jesse. I won't be taking questions on that at this time; there just is."

We each stared at the other for a good ten seconds, Lauren daring me to contradict her. In the end, I didn't.

"I will take your suggestions under advisement. Now give me another cookie."

Chapter 32: Jesse

It was day ten, and I was losing my ever-loving mind. I snapped at Bryan that morning when he was asking for clarification on something, and I'd already apologized twice, but I needed to get it together. It felt awful to be this anxious all the time. Lauren was ready to block my number if I called or texted her anymore for her opinion on where Sam was on the whole "needing space" thing. I just couldn't deal. I wanted to be making progress and planning a stupid couple's Halloween costume that would make Sam blush and roll her eyes at me. I had been thinking about what Dr. Merrill said over and over again, and I knew it made sense, but I was terrified to push Sam and risk her walking away for good.

I'd struggled to finish the lists I was supposed to make. The hobby one was easy. I worked in a hardware store, so I figured I could try building something. My apartment needed character anyway, so I was going to attempt to make a coffee table. I'd already found plans and procured all the tools I needed, mostly from my parents' garage, and I was set to give it a shot that weekend. However, I was concerned I might slice my thumb off or something, given my level of preoccupation.

So, I was going to talk to her. I didn't think I was ready to make any proclamations or lay everything on the line, but I needed her to know that I was still here, and I wasn't going to let her disappear again.

* * *

My heart thudded in my chest as I put my truck in park in Zinnia's driveway. I'd driven around the block twice considering if this was too invasive and maybe I should just text. But it was too easy for her to play off like she was just *working things out* and that she was *fine*, and I needed to see her. The fact that she was straddling me on my couch two weeks ago was starting not to feel real.

I knocked twice, again feeling like I should have texted first. I still had on my Garrett's t-shirt because I knew if I went home first, I'd chicken out.

"Jesse," she said as she opened the door wide.

She looked gorgeous even though she was clearly already in for the night in a pair of sweats and a hoodie.

Holy shit, that's my *hoodie.*

I'd forgotten I never got it back the night I brought her home from The Bar. Blood rushed in my ears seeing her wearing my clothes, and I effectively forgot everything I'd come there to say.

"Hey… I'm sorry to just drop by…"

I'm not really, though.

"It's okay, here, come in."

She stepped aside to let me into the guest cottage and gestured to a small table in a makeshift kitchen. The whole space was warm and inviting, and it made me wonder how to get that feeling in my own apartment. "Can I get you something to drink? I could make tea, or I have water or beer or —"

"Water would be great, thanks. This place is homey. I like it."

"I wish I could take credit, but most of this was Zin. You're right, though. I felt at home as soon as I walked in."

She seemed to falter over her last sentence and her brows drew together like that statement confused her, but she recovered quickly and set down a glass of water in front of me.

"How've you been?"

That's good. Start small. Work up to telling her you're pining away for her and want her to stay in Emberwood for you.

"So rude to start off with such a loaded question." She grinned at me, but it didn't quite reach her eyes.

"Sorry, should we start with politics or religion?"

"Gladly," she laughed. "But no, I've been… managing since

the hurricane that is my mother destroyed my carefully built walls that kept out reality. I'm trying."

"Do you want to talk about it?"

"About my mother? God, no, that sounds terrible. How are things with you?"

She sipped her own water, and I wanted to break through this awkward polite thing we were doing.

"Ummm, well, I wish I could say I was managing, but I'm kind of losing my mind, to be perfectly honest. I, um, well, I miss you. I know we'd just sort of started hanging out again, but that's the only way I can describe it. I want to text you about new shirt ideas and have you explain to me what moon water is because Lauren mentioned that the other day, and I hate not knowing if I can. I'm not trying to pressure you into anything you're not ready for, and I'm fine giving you space or time or whatever it is that you need… I just wanted to tell you that I'm here."

"See? Totally loaded question." She smiled apologetically.

"Yeah. I didn't really ease into that, did I?" I ran my hand through my hair, wishing I could go back and try that whole explanation again.

"I miss you, too," she said quietly, but her eyes looked serious, not like she was saying it to make me feel better.

"Yeah?"

"Yeah. I really did mean it the other day when I said this wasn't about you… I sort of got here and jumped right into my denial phase and never looked back because it was hard. But the more I think about it, it was about you a little bit." She shrugged. "I wasn't dealing with losing my job or even thinking about what comes next because being with you made it easy to ignore."

"I don't know if that's a compliment or not."

"It is. I was a wreck when I left Rockford. I felt like I didn't even know who I was, but with you, I remembered. It's a compliment."

Her hand started to reach across the table, and my heart froze for a second, but she seemed to realize what she was doing and pulled back.

"I feel like there's a 'but' coming. And I really don't want there to be." It felt like she was saying goodbye, and that was exactly what I was afraid of if I pushed.

"It's not a 'but,' it's just an 'and'."

"Okay, shoot."

"I like being with you. *And* I think there's something more here than just leftover feelings from six years ago. *And* that is terrifying because I may have come to a decision about staying here in Emberwood— don't tell Laur I told you first, though, or I'll call you a liar." I chuckled at that. "Because if it is something real, and it doesn't work out, which if I look at my track record, it's statistically likely that it won't, I will have committed to being in this town for the long haul. The thought of seeing you all the time after everything falls apart… it makes me wonder if we should just not go there."

My heart sank into my stomach. I didn't know how to convince a psychic that her version of the future was wrong.

"I understand what you're saying because I think you have the power to absolutely break my heart. It *is* terrifying. And if you tell me you don't want to see me anymore, I'll respect it, Sam, and I'll try to move on, too. But I made the mistake of letting you shut me out six years ago and not fighting to give us a chance, and I won't do it again. So, I guess I'm asking you not to decide tonight. I know you still have things to solidify, and I've got my own stuff I'm still working through. We both have a lot of crap to do to build our new lives. But I'm telling you that I'm in if you'd like to try to build something together."

She just swallowed hard, and I pushed back my chair to stand. She scrambled to walk me to the door. I paused before I walked out and let my hand rest lightly on her hip.

"Goodnight, Sam." I bent down and pressed a kiss to the top of her head, hoping that it was platonic enough that it wasn't

inappropriate, and I made my way back to my truck. It wasn't what
I had hoped for when I knocked on her door tonight, but at least
it focused my intentions. I knew *exactly* what I wanted now, and I
wasn't going to take the easy way out.

Chapter 33: Sam

The world of my room slowly fell away as I envisioned my body sending roots through the floor and into the earth, branches into the sky to soak up all the light. I had been on a pretty good stretch there for a while of meditating in the mornings when I got to the shop. Then I got busy with preparing for the festival and thinking about Jesse and then obsessing about everything my mother said. Since Zin had given me the shadow-work book, I'd been trying to get back in the habit.

I sat at the raw wood table in the woodland cottage in my mind and poured a cup of tea. The knock came on the cottage door, and I invited the energy in. I'd set the intention for this session to try to sort out how to separate my feelings about Jesse from my feelings about staying in Emberwood and carving out a real life here. No matter how many times I went round and round in my brain, I couldn't imagine staying and just ignoring him or the way I felt when I was with him. But I also couldn't imagine staying and things falling apart with him and being forced to see him settle down with someone else. I *had* to want this enough that I would feel confident about the decision independent of whatever happened with Jesse.

My guides entered the cottage, and their presence felt warm and familiar, like the scent that hung around hours after baking cookies. Today, I waited calmly. I'd already apologized for yelling at them multiple times for their lack of guidance, and I was trying to do better with the whole patience thing. Something akin to a scrapbook was placed in front of me, and it flipped through pages on its own. I watched still images of myself in the shop—organizing, doing readings, changing displays, and in all of them I looked genuinely happy. My body relaxed even further into the meditative space as uncertainty fell off my shoulders little by little.

This will be the right thing for me whether Jesse is there or not.

Then, the book flipped back to the beginning, and my guides showed me the same series of photos but zoomed out. In them, Jesse was either dropping off coffee, leaving me notes on the checkout counter, or sitting across from me during readings. And he looked stupidly happy too.

Wait, I thought. *So, I can't separate the two?*

The answer I heard back was, "You can if it's what you decide. You just don't need to."

Those words settled over my skin like a blanket, and I let the weight of it sink in. The energy of my guides retreated out the door, having done and said all they needed to for the moment. I began to wiggle my fingers and toes in my meditation until I could feel them in my physical body, and I slowly came back to my room.

I had not considered the idea of just *not* separating my feelings about staying and my feelings about Jesse, but yeah, what if I just... didn't? What if I just got to be happy about both things, and I didn't actively prepare for the worst? What if I got to be the exception this time? The girl who gets what she wants and isn't someone's second choice. What would it feel like to just accept that I got to be first?

Zin *wanted* me to be more active with the shop. She wanted to have more of a retirement, and she trusted me to take care of the store. Jesse said point blank that he wasn't giving up on us... that he *wanted* this. *It can't really be that simple, can it?*

* * *

"I think very seriously that this might be the best Halloween set-up the shop has ever had, Samantha." Zin looked around, pride radiating out from her.

"I've got all of the crystals organized into different Halloween vibes- I've got the amethyst and rose quartz our for the fairy princess crowd, tiger's eye and obsidian for the horror fans, and even crystals set out for all of the Hogwarts houses for the witch and wizard clients."

I had decided to take back the ownership of my Halloween descriptions from Christy. Lauren made me understand that I was being a little petty with my initial reaction, so I thought this was a nice compromise. Plus, I could live with a little petty.

"I also sent out the new flyer with a coupon for fifteen percent off a 'Samhain "Thinning of the Veil" Reading.' It sounds *very* magical. Plus reading on Samhain *is* magical so it's not just a marketing scheme," I said, grinning.

"Sometimes I think I've been doing this so long that I forget how much fun it can be," she replied. "Your energy is good to have here."

"I'm glad I'm here too, Auntie." Her gaze focused on me a little harder, and one of her brows raised up impossibly high. "Anyway, do you want to grab lunch or—"

"You know better than to think you're going to beat around the bush with me."

I grinned. "I know, I know. I just had to make you work for it. I've decided I'm staying. Like, really staying. I do have some specifics to work out with you because I'm not just going to keep living at your house for free. But I feel really excited about what I can bring to the shop, and it's already amazing how much more focused I am on my craft since I've been here. I want to keep learning from you, and— where are you going?"

I was in the middle of a well-practiced explanation when Zin darted toward her office on a mission.

"Keep talking. I'm listening!" she called from the back room.

"Well, now it just feels silly!" I waited a few moments for her to return to see her holding a thick folder.

"Nothing you say is silly. Go on."

"I just... I'm excited. To come to work every day. It makes me happy to be here, and I think I can add some of my own flair to the shop, maybe do some designing, if that's okay with you. I mean,

I know it's not *my* shop. You know what I'm saying."

"I do know what you're saying, and I'm prepared to remedy that immediately."

"Remedy what?"

"It being only my shop."

"What are you talking about?"

Zin flopped the folder open on the checkout counter and turned it around so I could read the first page. I skimmed through the words, and then read it all again more slowly.

"You're… making me your business partner?" My heart thudded in my chest.

"Of course, dear. I can't fathom you thinking I begged you to come here just to work as what, a clerk? A manager? You're a part of this shop, and you are its future. I had your father work with my lawyer and draw up all the necessary paperwork to make sure we're both getting everything we need, legally speaking. Your dad also said he's going to come down and make sure you get your old 401k rolled over into a new retirement account and that you're set up for financial success for your future."

"When… what? I've talked to my dad like five times since I've been here, and he never…"

"Ah, he's been an excellent co-conspirator. Very impressive."

"I don't know what to say. Why wait until now to tell me this?"

I felt heat rising toward my ears and tears pooling in the corners of my eyes. This was more than I'd ever anticipated.

"Because you had to decide for yourself what you wanted. I could tell you all day about how obvious it was to me that you belonged here, and how you would make not only the shop but people's *lives* better here, but it had to come from you. For the record, I'm ecstatic that you decided this way because it has killed me not to tell you."

I walked around to the other side of the counter, threw my arms around my aunt, and let the happy tears spill over. I had never felt so seen before in my entire life.

Chapter 34: Jesse

I'd gotten one of the *Books and Broomsticks* coupons as part of Sam's mailer campaign. She'd even set up a way for people to book their "Thinning of the Veil" readings online using their coupon.

She is killing it.

I wanted to feel like I'd helped, but she was unstoppable when she wanted something. Impulsively, I scheduled a tarot reading for Halloween, or Samhain, as it said on the flyer. It was also smart of her to include a pronunciation key because I absolutely would have said "Sam-Hane" instead of "Sow-in." Anyhow, I booked the appointment under Captain Cerulean SeaWolf, the not-at-all-over-the-top name of the pirate in our now-shared book, and I had a whole idea forming for my Halloween costume.

I left the office to check on the floor when I saw Coach Brown chatting with Bryan at the checkout.

"Hey! Just the man I was looking for," Coach Brown called when he saw me approaching.

"Hey, Coach, good to see you again. How's that list coming?"

"Well, every time I check something off, something else gets put on, so I don't know if that's good or bad. Either way, Claire told me to invite you to dinner tonight. I told her it was short notice and you're a young man who probably has a social calendar to keep, so don't you go feeling obligated, but she is making pot pie. Just in case that sways your opinion."

The dark skin around his eyes crinkled in pride for his wife's cooking.

"I would be crazy to turn it down. What time do you want me there, and what can I bring?"

He assured me to just bring myself, but I'd already decided to at least pick up some flowers, if nothing else. The idea of sitting down and reminiscing about baseball actually filled me with warmth instead of dread for the first time since my injury.

I left Heather to close that evening so I could go home to shower and put on a button-down shirt of some kind. Claire was a stickler about dinner etiquette, at least she was when they used to host team meals, anyway.

I stopped in at our local flower shop and picked a bouquet that the florist assured me was a beautiful fall arrangement for Claire. Before I paid, I stopped in front of a Halloween display and knew that I had to get something for Sam and drop it off, even if I didn't get to talk to her. I had no idea what any of the flowers were, but they were labeled as *Full Moon Magic, Witch's Potion Petals,* and *Wednesday Addams.* The *Witch's Potion Petals* had a mixture of black and purple flowers with a couple of shockingly bright pink blooms. That one looked like it would fit right in at *Broomsticks.*

"Would you like these delivered? Or did you want to take them as well?"

"Oh, I guess I didn't even think of that. Yeah, actually, if they could be delivered just across the street to *Books and Broomsticks?* That would be perfect."

"Absolutely! I was headed there after work anyway because I got their new flyer! I won't even charge you for the delivery since I won't need to add them to the truck tomorrow."

I just grinned at how perfectly that fell into place, and I figured I should thank my "people," as Sam would say. I left for Coach's house feeling optimistic that Sam would at least have a difficult time ignoring me after the flowers and the tarot reading I was scheduled for the following night.

* * *

"Mrs. Brown, thank you so much for the dinner invite. You've saved me from a frozen lasagna."

I handed her the flowers and accepted her hug when she opened the door.

"Jesse Garrett, you know better than to call me Mrs. Brown. That was my mother-in-law, and God rest her soul, that's not me."

"My apologies. Claire."

"Better. And, if I hear about you eating frozen lasagna again, I'm liable to set up a dinner rotation with the ladies in my bridge club. So, you best learn how to cook, or you're going to have a whole host of elderly women knocking at your door."

"While that doesn't sound terrible, I promise I will try."

"Good. Now, come in and sit down and tell me what you'd like to drink."

She ushered me into their home, and while it was smaller than the one they'd had when they'd previously lived in Emberwood, it felt the same. It smelled like freshly baked bread and cinnamon. Claire was always dressed in her Sunday best no matter where she went, and tonight was no exception. She reminded me of Claire Huxtable more than a little bit.

Coach Brown regaled me with tales from the last decade of coaching, and it made me miss the game so much my chest ached. He was always the coach that cared about your mental state first and your stats second. The pot pie was also maybe the best thing I'd ever eaten, though I would never tell my mother that.

"So, Jesse. I know you probably expected me to ask about your knee, and I just want to let you know that I'm not going to. I know that if you could be playing, you would be playing, and I don't need you to explain it beyond that—actually, no one does, so you can tell all the busybodies in this town to stuff a sock in—"

"Gerald…" Claire said with a warning tone.

"Well, they can," he mumbled, and that made me smile a little.

"I'll try to refrain from using those exact words, but thank you for the sentiment. It has been, well, a rough year and a half."

"I believe that, son. I did want to know… are you planning to stay at the hardware store for your daddy long term?"

Isn't that the million-dollar question.

"For the foreseeable future, I think I'll be there at least in some capacity. I'm trying to work out what I'd like to do now that baseball is off the table." I was getting a lot better at admitting that out loud, and I kind of thought I deserved a therapy-gold-star.

"Would you consider putting it back on the table if it wasn't as a player?"

My eyebrows drew together of their own accord. "I'm not sure what you mean, sir."

He just held up a finger and shuffled through the doorway to their kitchen. He came back holding a thin packet. Once he sat back down, he shot the packet across the table toward me with an unexpected speed, and it fell into my lap.

"Sorry about that; aim's not what it used to be." Coach chuckled as I recovered it and started scanning the text.

It looked to be an informational packet for a new baseball rec league one town over.

"Cloverdale is starting a new rec league? Didn't Emberwood usually just encompass Cloverdale and Milton?"

"They did, but Cloverdale has had a mess of new construction homes and a population boom over the past several years, and they have enough kids to have their own youth leagues now for at least five sports. This will also open the chance for inter-league games."

"That sounds great, kids can always use more rec sports experience. Those were some of the best times of my life playing ball. But I don't understand how I would fit into that. Are you looking for volunteer coaches?"

"As it happens, the Parks and Rec department over there has asked me if I'd like to be the director of this here program. Not just for baseball, but for all their recreational sports. Now, I'm supposed to be retired, but it seems as if that's not in the cards. They'd like me to hire my own team to round out the department. I want you to be the assistant director of the youth sports division."

I was quiet for what felt like the longest minute ever. The first feeling that crept up when I thought about being around the baseball world again, even at the rec level, was fear. Fear that I'd see kids whose sights were set on the big leagues and see myself, and I worried that it would hold me back from moving on. But as quickly as that feeling came up, it passed. And I thought about the friends I made then, friends like Jer whom I still considered my family, and the feeling of Saturday games and cookouts afterward, and the feeling of spring evenings out on the diamond, practicing because I loved it. Those were the highlights of my childhood.

"Am I even qualified to do that? I have a degree in history…"

"Do you think there are many athletes who played at your level who would be willing to coach the next generation? Especially in a rec league where the goal is for all kids to be able to get the benefit of playing sports and not a fancy, expensive club league? I don't think anyone could give a fig what your degree says."

"I… I don't know what to say. I hadn't really thought about coaching because, up until very recently, even talking casually about baseball was too much. But I've been doing the work, and I feel like I'm in a much better place now than I was. So… maybe, yeah. Can you tell me more about what it would entail, and I can think about it for a day? Depending on the time commitment, I may need to talk to my dad and the store managers, but… the more this kind of sinks in, I think I'd like to give it a shot if I can."

"Wooo Pig Sooie!" Coach Brown hollered. A genuine laugh escaped my throat at that. I'd forgotten about his hog calls.

"Let the boy think about it, Gerald, before you go gettin' all over-excited," Claire admonished.

But honestly, it felt good to have someone that excited when it came to talking about me and baseball in the same conversation. The rest of dinner was a blur of nostalgia and anticipation for a future that might include me getting my passion back in one way or another. I couldn't wipe the smile off my face, and I didn't try. I wore it all the way back to my truck.

I thought my face might split in half when my phone buzzed on my way home, and I saw a message from Sam.

SAM: These might be the witchiest flowers I've ever seen. The only question becomes whether I take them home or keep them at the store to add even more magical ambience to our Halloween displays. I voted for taking them home, but Zin says that would be selfish. She'll probably win. Seriously, though, thank you. They're perfect ♥

JESSE: Glad you like them. Happy Almost Halloween ♥

That single heart at the end of her message did more for my emotional state than I cared to admit. It also made me decide that I'd pick up one of the other bouquets when the flower shop opened and drop it off at her house in the morning. I kind of figured that for Sam, Halloween was a bigger deal than Valentine's Day anyway, and I wanted to make sure I knocked this one out of the park. Baseball pun intended.

Chapter 35: Sam

The energy on Samhain was electric. Even as a kid, I always felt like there was an excitement on Halloween that was completely different from the excitement I felt around the winter holidays. I think it had something to do with the mounds of candy back then, but as a witch, I got that my intuition was just sharper on this day.

I'd been up early, even without my alarm. Originally, I'd planned to wear my fancy witch hat and call it a day as far as a costume went, but there was a vintage shop two doors down from *Broomsticks* that had a Victorian-esque gown in their window in the prettiest shade of lilac. It was so stupid, but it made me think of the merchant's daughter-turned-damsel in the pirate romance novel Jesse had apparently decided was his favorite book of all time.

I definitely hadn't read over all his notes multiple times.

I walked by the window for days, but after I'd gotten Jesse's flowers, I'd marched in the shop to look at it up close. I assumed it would be the wrong size, and I could stop thinking about it, but the tag read *almost* my size, and with it being a corset back, I knew I could make it work. As I twisted my hair into a braided crown that morning and took in my overall appearance, I felt pleased with my decision. Even more pleased when I opened the door of the guest house and found another, maybe even more beautiful, bouquet waiting for me. This one was all shades of purple with deep emerald greenery and baby's breath dipped in silver glitter. The card read: *I didn't want you to have to choose. Now you have one for home and work. Happy Samhain.*

The fact that he'd called it Samhain made my heart do a tap-dance. It was one thing to think what I could do was "cool," but he was actually trying to learn. I pulled out several of the stems and dried them off before weaving them into my braid.

Perfect.

The store was dead during the day except for some last-minute people in need of costume accessories, but that was to be expected. I didn't sit down once anyway, determined to re-familiarize myself with every square inch of the shop now that it was going to be partly *mine*. All the little ideas that had popped up over the last several months that I'd pushed aside because it wasn't my store, my business, I was now trying to recall.

"You can take a break, you know," Zin said as she entered the shop from the back.

"Is it already three?" I asked.

The day had flown by. I found myself moving the flower arrangement from Jesse to another table, again, convinced it looked better near the checkout than the front.

"It is. You should get something to eat before the sun goes down and we are swamped. How did your fancy new website work for booking readings?"

"Oh! I haven't looked since this morning, but even then, we only had four or five open spots." I pulled up the admin side of the site and felt triumph spread across my body. "Completely booked."

"Excellent work, Samantha. I also love this dress. It's worthy of its own romance cover."

"Thank you. I kind of want to wear it every day." I did a dramatic twirl and let the fabric float around me.

"Absolutely perfect. Now eat."

She shooed me out the door, and I didn't even feel out of place in my costume at the cafe because all the workers were completely decked out. I ordered my favorite bagel sandwich from a Beatnik poet and was handed my iced tea by Lydia from Beetlejuice. *I love this town.*

I decided to sit and eat in the café instead of hurrying back. I looked out at the shop-lined street and sighed. The way I looked at everything had shifted just slightly since I'd decided to stay. The trees along the sidewalk made their own version of a sunset with the array of reds and yellows and oranges, and all the street signs had Halloween-themed banners. I hadn't felt this way often, but I was pretty sure the emotion was *content*, and it was so peaceful.

The only remaining worry was that I needed to talk to Jesse, like, *really* talk to him, and hope that he'd meant what he said. I just wanted to get through this event tonight, and then I would happily tell him I was all in, too. That thought no longer struck fear deep into my core. Instead, it sent little lightning bolts down to my fingertips, remembering how they felt on his skin. I gave an involuntary shiver and decided it was probably time to go and get my Halloween on.

Chapter 36: Jesse

I decided to swing by my parents' house and have the face-to-face I'd been dreading. I thought it would be best to do it *before* I got dressed in my pirate costume, just because I wasn't sure if I could even take myself seriously in that. I wiped my palms on my jeans again so I could pretend like they weren't sweating. I thought about putting it off, but I wanted my brain to be clear of anxiety when I saw Sam tonight. *Needs to be now.*

I let myself in through the garage and entered to find my mom filling massive bowls with candy.

"Are you planning on getting an entire Spartan army as trick-or-treaters?"

"You know? You're not far off. I think we got every child in this town at our door last year. Apparently, several of our neighbors do full sized candy bars and the neighborhood has gotten a reputation."

"Well, feel free to send any leftovers to my apartment."

"If your dad doesn't get to them first, you can count on it." She finished with her last bag and walked over to give me a delayed hug. "Not that I'm not glad to see you, but what are you doing here? Do you want to stay and hand out candy? Your dad is going to grill, or—"

"No, but thank you. I just need to talk to Dad before I head home. Is he around?"

"Yep, he's in the back prepping his burgers. Everything okay?"

"Yeah. Things are good, actually. I just need to talk to him."

I kissed her on the head and made my way out to my parents' back deck to find my dad cleaning his grill with a *Kiss The Grill Master* apron on.

"Hey, Dad," I said, hoping I could do this quickly.

"Hey, son. What are you doing here? You want me to make

you a burger?"

"Nah, I gotta head out here in a minute. I just wanted to talk to you about something."

He looked over at me and stopped his cleaning. I cleared my throat, which was apparently my accepted nervous tick now.

"I'll start by saying that this doesn't have to change very much about my involvement at *Garrett's* right now. But, uh, I got an offer to be the assistant director of youth sports for the new rec program over in Cloverdale. Coach Brown, he moved back, I don't know if you knew that?"

Now you're rambling. Wrap it up.

"Anyway, he's going to be the director. I can do a lot of it on my off days or late afternoons and evenings for now, so I don't want it to seem like I'm just abandoning my responsibilities at the store; it's just that this is the first time I've been excited about something since, well—"

My dad just held up his hand to stop me, and my heart slowly lowered into my stomach. I bit the inside of my cheek to try to direct my attention to that instead of the feeling of being a disappointment. Again. But this time at least it was a choice I made and not something that happened to me, and I could live with that.

"It's about time, son." My dad's hand ran over his face, and he took a ragged breath.

"Wait, what?"

I was so confused. Did he *not* want me at the store? I thought I'd been doing well.

"You have exceeded all my expectations taking over at *Garrett's*, but Jesse, that's not your life. It was my life, and I hate that I can't live it the way I wanted."

His words hit me somewhere deep, and I'd never considered that my dad was dealing with a lot of the same things I was after his heart attack took him out of commission from his normal life.

"I… I'm not sure what to say to that."

"That's all right. Just… this new job. It'll make you happy?"

"I think it will. Or it's at least a step in the right direction."

He just nodded for a moment.

"That's all I wanted. And for what it's worth, I'm sorry I've been pretty worthless when it comes to fathers this last year. It about killed me to see you in so much pain, and then my own heart actually did about kill me. But I'm going to do better."

Someone could have scraped my jaw off the deck at that point. In my wildest daydreams I could not have imagined this as the outcome to me getting a job offer.

"I... okay. Thanks for saying that, Dad."

"You know I'm not much of a hugger, but I'm gonna hug you anyway."

He shuffled over to me and pulled me into a tight hug. The last time I remembered him doing that was when I got signed to the Mud Hens.

"I'll get you more information about what hours I can work once I sit down with Coach Brown next week; I just wanted you to know now."

"Heather will be more than happy to take on whatever you need, and my doctor has cleared me to work in a 'low-stress capacity,' so I'll probably be putting up sale signs, but at least I'll be back to some kind of normal. All that to say, whatever you need to do, we'll make it work."

I just nodded at him and made my way back inside, wondering if this had all been a dream and I'd wake up still needing to have this conversation.

"Oh, and Jesse?"

I turned back, my hand already on the sliding glass door. My dad took off his apron and held out his arms as if displaying a car I'd won on a game show. The confusion died in my throat when I realized he was wearing one of the long-sleeved **ALL MY TOOL NEEDS ARE MET AT GARRETT'S** shirts. I laughed as warmth spread through my chest.

"It looks good on you, Dad." He just nodded, happily putting his apron back on. I caught my mom up on my job offer before I left, and her reaction was much less surprising because she cried, but she's a crier.

On my way home, I decided that if that exchange was any kind of indication of how tonight was going to go, I was *really* looking forward to my tarot reading later. Also, I was really digging whatever these pirate pants were doing for me.

* * *

Broomsticks was as busy as I'd ever seen it. The place was filled with witches, fairies, definitely a Wednesday Addams, and Sam, who could not have looked more like the matching counterpart to my costume if we'd tried to plan the most obnoxious couple outfit ever.

I adjusted the dark red fabric tied around my head and hung back a minute, watching her in her element. She was reading for a girl who looked about sixteen or so, and Sam's whole face was lit up and animated as she delivered information that she seemed *very* excited about. The girl kept nodding and smiling, practically bouncing in her chair. I was mostly ignorant of everything Sam did in terms of witchcraft and her fucking insane 'intuitive' abilities or whatever she wanted to call them, but I knew that I was in awe of her.

When the girl stood up, finished with her reading, I was next. I saw Sam check a printout of what I assumed was her client list, and I watched as she started laughing. Her eyes started roaming the shop until they came to rest on me. I started toward her, not hating how she tugged her lip between her teeth and let her eyes roam over my costume.

"If you're done checking me out, I do actually have an appointment."

I liked that pink crept into her cheeks at my comment, but I was a complete hypocrite because I'd been memorizing how she

201

looked in that dress for ten whole minutes before she saw me.

"*So* conceited," she muttered, but she didn't try to hide her smile.

I sat across from her and rested my chin in my hand.

"You look incredible, by the way. I should have led with that; I'm sorry. You *were* totally checking me out, but I liked it, so it's fine."

"Well, you don't look hideous, I guess. *Captain.*"

My smile grew wide at the flirty tone in her last word. I leaned in closer across her table. "You mean you'd let me carry you back to my ship to do unspeakable—"

"Do you have an off switch somewhere?" I laughed and sat back, letting her have more room to finish shuffling.

"Question?"

"How does my new job turn out?"

Chapter 37: Sam

I felt my eyes get big as I stared at him.

"You have a new job?"

The level of the playful energy I felt from him tonight started to make sense. I started to let my eyes unfocus a little bit until I could tune in to his people.

"You're the psychic, Sam. I feel like you should know."

I ignored him as I took in information and laid down some cards. My smile grew until I feared it might take over my face, and I bit my lip to try to keep it from getting out of control.

"This is the one that fell into your lap?"

His playful expression froze on his face, and I worried for a split second that I'd said something wrong, but then I recognized *the look*. The one that people had when they realized I had predicted something so accurately that they were a little freaked out.

"Yeah. That would be the one," he choked out.

"Not to sound dramatic, but it's going to change your life. In some small ways, and some larger ways, eventually. But just yes to everything about it. The people, the work, the… kids? All of it is going to click."

He nodded at the *kids* part. He was looking at me like I was a little bit scary, but when I met his eyes, his expression turned into something else entirely. I felt heat creep up my neck.

I should have bought the fancy fan to go with this dress. "My only other real question is… do I get the girl?"

The breath caught in my throat, and the din of the shop fell away. I didn't even touch my cards because I knew that's not what he was asking anyway.

"Yes. Without a doubt, Captain Cerulean SeaWolf."

A low chuckle left his chest before he stood and leaned across my table. His fingers traced up my jaw and angled my face up toward him. Our lips hovered a whisper apart for an impossible moment where every inch of my skin could feel his energy, my shields non-existent. Finally, his lips pressed to mine, and I remembered to breathe again. He ended it far too soon, but the loss of contact brought the noise of the store rushing back in. My lips were still tingling, and I pressed my fingertips to my mouth.

"That was an excellent tarot reading. I am leaving you a five-star review on Yelp," he murmured in my ear.

Goosebumps broke out down my arms as I laughed in response, wondering how he made internet reviews sound hot. I stood with him to… *walk him out?*

Did you walk any of your other clients out?

But I didn't want him to leave. I *wanted* to pull him into the back room and unlace his stupid puffy pirate shirt that I was hoping he bought rather than rented.

"Can I go grab some food and pick you up once you've closed?"

His eyes kept dropping to my lips as he talked, and it was not helping my runaway imagination. Not trusting myself with words at the moment, I just nodded and watched him walk out of the store, striped pirate pantaloons and all.

* * *

"That was the busiest Samhain I can remember. You did a wonderful job, dear," Zin said as she gracefully retired to one of the armchairs.

We'd finally made the last crystal sale and locked the door. I made a much less graceful plop into the other chair and kicked my feet up over the arm.

"It was kind of awesome, wasn't it?"

My readings had brought tears to no fewer than three clients, and I felt like I was floating, finding a cloud of *happy* in my exhaustion.

"Are you ready to head home?" Aunt Zin asked.

"Oh, um, I think I'm going to go to Jesse's and get takeout or something."

"Mhm. He looked quite dashing as a pirate."

"He really, *really* did." I grinned.

"At least you're over your denial. It was exhausting, to be frank. Have fun, Samantha. You deserve it."

She turned off her office lights and made her way out to the parking lot just before I heard a light knock on the glass.

He was holding a 6-pack of Corona in one hand and a paper bag in the other, grease already soaking through the sides, from the taco place.

This man…

I wanted to hear all about his new job and tell him everything that had happened with the store, but above all of that, I needed to breathe him in and know that we were *doing* this.

I unlocked the door and pulled him in by the front of his pirate tunic. As soon as his boots were in the building, I wrapped my arms around his neck and tip-toed to meet his mouth. If he was surprised, it lasted for only a split second before he dropped the bag of tacos on the ground and pulled me in tighter.

He teased my lips open, and his kiss was even better than the one I'd been replaying for weeks in my head. The beer found its way to a display table without him ever leaving my mouth, and with his now-free hand, he tugged gently at my braid to deepen the kiss. My nails traced their way from his belt up his sides where he tensed, apparently ticklish there.

I tucked that information away for later and pressed my palm to his warm chest, where I could feel his heart beating as rapidly as mine.

He had somehow walked me backward until my back hit the check-out counter, and both his energy and his body crowded me in the most delicious way. That flutter of *new crush* and *first kisses* that his aura always brought was heightened exponentially by his mouth tracing open kisses down my neck. I sucked in a breath as he pulled me impossibly closer, his hands no longer pretending to be on my lower back, and I let out a groan when his teeth grazed my pulse point in response.

"Sam," he ground out, sounding almost pained.

"Mmmmm," I answered, still not feeling the whole *words* situation.

"I need to bring you home with me before I drag you into Zin's office and get rid of this dress."

"It wouldn't be the first time…" I whispered, thinking that sounded like a much better solution than driving to his apartment, where I'd have to sit all the way on the other side of the truck.

"You're going to be the death of me," he groaned, his body not at all committed to the idea of leaving. "I was a prick then; please, let me do it right this time."

He rested his forehead on mine, and I knew he needed this.

"Okay, we can go. But only if you promise to drive slightly over the speed limit and tell me about your new job to distract me on the way there."

"Deal."

He was pulling me out the door before the word was even out of his mouth, and I had to force him to let me get my purse so I could lock up.

"You look impossibly beautiful in this dress," he said when he finally pulled away from the next round of toe-curling kisses with me pressed against the door of his truck.

"I thought there was something you said about getting rid of it, so I wasn't sure how you felt—"

He stopped me with another searing kiss, his tongue now well-versed in the pressure that made me tighten my fists in his hair.

"In," he commanded, finally opening the passenger door and helping me inside.

"Mmmm, I kind of like bossy pirate captain."

I grinned broadly as he let out a strangled sound and slammed the door, mumbling something that sounded like *the death of me.*

He did as promised, driving only just over the limit, and he shared everything he knew about the new job. My eyes welled up when he recounted the conversation with his dad, and I pretended not to notice that his did too.

"I am… that's the most perfect first chapter of your new story."

As soon as the words were out, I recognized that they weren't mine, but his guides'. Every once in a while, I tuned in without meaning to and found unfamiliar words in my mouth. My heart warmed as they clearly resonated with Jesse, though, his hand sliding over and his fingers weaving together with mine and squeezing.

"Also… Zin is making me part owner of the shop," I said casually as we neared his apartment.

If we didn't keep talking, I was going to make this a very unsafe driving situation.

His foot pressed on the brake just as he pulled into his complex.

"She *what?* Sam! How did you let me go on for ten minutes about the rec league and not tell me that?"

"It was only seven minutes. And I like listening to you talk when you're excited about something." I shrugged, meaning it.

He reached across and gripped my chin gently, pulling me toward him. This kiss was short, but it made me feel seen. He got what it meant to me to have a piece of the shop officially.

"You're going to make that place even more magical. But don't tell Zin I said so because I've heard stories about her."

I laughed and agreed to keep his secret.

The frenzied electricity from the shop had subsided a little, but I could feel it buzzing just beneath the surface when he helped me out of the truck and tugged me forward toward his door. I walked in and looked around, confused. Because this wasn't the same apartment I had been in a month ago. The living room was painted a muted green, and there was a beautiful warm wood coffee table in front of the couch. There was framed art on the walls.

"What happened in here?"

"I decided that Emberwood was home, and it should feel like it."

This time *he* shrugged, and I smacked his shoulder. "Lauren is responsible for the art though. I think it's by some guy your aunt knows… she said it was a friend and that he gave her the prints." I then realized why the style looked familiar since Zin also had an original hanging in her house.

Okay, we officially like Jack.

"Oh, and I made the coffee table." I whirled around and marched over to the beautiful table.

"You *made* this. Like, not that you built it according to the IKEA directions, but you cut the wood and used power tools?"

"I do run a hardware store."

"Yeah. I guess. Just…"

"Just what?"

"I thought a pirate romance was my thing, but now I'm having some kind of feelings about a sexy carpenter who sweeps the merchant's daughter off of her feet with his beautiful furniture, and then he makes some sort of magical bed, and they—"

I let out a little shriek as he whirled me around and attacked my mouth. I held onto him and let him devour me.

"No more talking. Please," he pleaded when he came up for air.

The heat from earlier bubbled up with a vengeance.

"Aye aye, captain," I agreed breathlessly, amused and absolutely drunk on the power that came with working him up like this.

He let out a low laugh, and his fingers pulled lightly at the bow of my dress's corset top. He tugged me toward his bedroom without breaking contact. We moved until he hit the bed, and he pulled me to stand in between his legs.

My lungs expanded as the corset finally came loose, and the soft purple fabric pooled at my feet. Jesse pressed open-mouthed kisses up my rib cage, and I shivered when he grazed his fingers over my chest before unhooking my bra and sending it to join my dress on the floor.

He looked up at me with something akin to reverence in his eyes, and he gently pulled at the back of one thigh and then the other until I was sitting in his lap, pulling his pirate shirt up over his head and going to work on the ridiculously large belt buckle. Sparks radiated from my shoulder where he was dragging his teeth along my skin.

"You are so gorgeous," he murmured against my neck as I finally worked his belt out of those stupid pantaloons.

My thighs tightened around his hips, and we refocused on each other. Being with him now was not the same as being with him then. I closed my eyes and let his energy surround me in addition to his arms, which were now covered in goosebumps, as I let my nails roam freely down them. The normal images I got when I dropped my shields had intensified from the sweet offering of a jacket on a cool night to a fierce need to protect me. That intensity made sparks flicker in my belly as I recognized the same want *from* him that I felt *for* him.

"Jesse… I need…" I got out between breaths.

"Tell me what you need, Sam, and it's yours."

"Just… touch me," I managed.

The calm ocean of his blue eyes was just a ring now, his pupils wide with the same feeling of must-have-right-now that was coursing through my veins.

Do you want this?"

He squeezed my leg where it met the curve of my ass before he left it, trailing his fingers around to the crease of my hip, and finally making it to his destination between my thighs.

"Y-yes." He captured my mouth again and brushed my underwear to the side to slowly press his fingers to my center. My body lit up like the 4th of July when he guided me against him. The pressure made me dizzy, and I was almost certain my brain was going to leave my body. The band of tension that had been building all night, maybe for weeks, or hell, even years, came to its breaking point.

"Let go for me, Sam. I've got you."

It would have been embarrassing how quickly I followed his directions, but the stars bursting behind my eyes couldn't have given less of a fuck. He held me as I came down, my heart threatening to burst out of my chest. I needed more of him.

Shakily, I planted my feet back on the ground and then sank to the floor. He took in a stuttered breath. "You don't have to—"

I stopped him with a pointed glare, and he shut up. I argued with his pantaloons until I won, and I lowered my mouth onto him. His fingers lightly found their way to my hair, my braid already coming loose. His hips move in time with me, and his breaths come out in small bursts.

"Jesus *Christ*, Sam," he groaned, and I soaked in the high of making his muscles twitch the way they were.

Chapter 38: Jesse

The sight of Sam on her knees was too much. I was already too far gone from just touching her, and I wanted her *now*. She was torturing me, and if she didn't stop, I thought I might black out.

I reached down and gently circled the wrist of the hand she had on my thigh, and I tugged her up. She glanced down at me, a confused expression on her face.

I just shook my head at whatever she was thinking.

"I can't…" I said, threading my fingers through hers and pulling her back toward me as a satisfied grin spread across her heart-shaped face. "But I *want* you. All of you."

I let go to graze the backs of her legs, from her calves to the curve of her perfectly round ass, and I swore to god, the little shiver she gave was like a drug.

"I want you too," she breathed.

She leaned down to press her lips to mine and shifted her weight until she was hovering above me. I swiftly rolled us over until she was laid out beneath me.

"Are you sure? Like out-of-your-mind sure?" I asked, grinning and hoping she had the same crystal-clear memory of our first time that I did.

"Out-of-my-mind sure. Yes," she agreed, smiling against my lips.

I reached for my nightstand to find a condom and rolled it on before taking full advantage of my position, raking my eyes over her body. She was so warm and soft, and I wanted to touch her everywhere and find out which places made her gasp or hold her breath.

There's time for that, I reasoned, warmth spreading through my chest at the truth of it. Her hands tangled in my hair, and I pressed my lips to her temple, her neck, her shoulder, and finally her lips as I pushed into her and groaned something unintelligible. Her heels locked around my back, and she guided me the rest of the way.

"I've wanted you for so long," I said, lightning bolts of sensation spreading to every inch of my body. I was trying not to sink my teeth into her like a teenager who didn't know better, but it was so tempting.

"Me too. For so long, Jesse."

Her whispered voice stumbled when she said my name, the *want* in her voice snapping something in my brain, so I gave in to everything. I reached for her thigh and guided it up, stretching until our limbs were tangled in entirely new ways, her calf on my shoulder and her taking me impossibly deeper.

"Oh *fuck*," she swore against my shoulder where her teeth currently resided.

"Do you like that?" I chuckled at her wide eyes and slow nod. "You feel so fucking good, Sam."

I wanted to forget where I ended, and she began. My body threatened to come apart, but I knew it was my heart too, because she was everything.

"Tell me what you need."

Because I was close. Too close.

"I need you to touch me."

I slid her arms above her head and held her wrists with one hand and reached between us and circled her clit with the other, adjusting pressure according to the whimper she let out, to make sure I took care of her before I lost myself.

I felt her break underneath me, letting the sound of my name from her mouth wash over me before I followed. I nearly collapsed next to her, unwinding our bodies to be able to hold her against me. I could feel her legs shaking around me, and I started rubbing circles on her calf and working my way upward.

"You're kind of hot," she murmured into my shoulder, huffing a laugh.

"Well, I've been reading a lot of romance novels," I replied, smiling as I trailed my fingers through her curls that had come free of her now-ruined braid.

"I'll keep supplying you with them. We've got a whole new shipment at the shop," she added with a deep contented sigh.

I finally left her to toss the condom, and to my horror, she was standing next to the bed attempting to get dressed, when I came back to the room.

"What are you doing?"

"I am putting clothing on my body. It's a whole new trend."

"No, no. I mean, if you want to put something on, of course, but I'll give you one of my shirts and a pair of shorts. For the record, though, I like you like this," I explained, crawling onto my bed, wrapping my arms around her from behind, and pulling her back to my chest.

"You want me to stay?"

"Did I not make it clear tonight that I'm kind of into you? Because if not, I am happy to show you again… just give me a few."

I relaxed when she did, and she let the skirt of her dress fall back to the floor.

"Okay, I'll stay. But yes to the t-shirt. I'll probably steal it, so make it one that's not your favorite." I pressed a kiss to her neck and pulled out a Mud Hens practice t-shirt, surprised that it didn't make me feel anything other than excited to see her in more of my clothes. There was not the familiar twinge of resentment when I saw the logo, and I thought that deserved another therapy gold-star.

I pulled the t-shirt over her head, being mindful of what was left of the flowers in the once-intricate braid around her head. Her curls were falling out of it around her face, and she looked beautiful.

"Thank you."

"Can I heat you up some food? I feel bad you didn't get to eat tacos. Or can I just bring you some water?"

"My exhaustion is only matched by how much I want tacos," she answered. "Can we eat on the couch and watch *Buffy*? That way, when I inevitably fall asleep, there will at least be pillows nearby."

"Done."

I grabbed some extra blankets from the closet before I threw the tacos in the oven to warm up. She found the episode she wanted to watch, and I stared at her from across my apartment, in awe that she was here and that we'd found each other at the right time and in the right place.

She did, in fact, fall asleep about twenty minutes into the episode, and I let her remain that way with her head in my lap until I couldn't stay awake any longer, either. I was able to coax her back to bed, and I learned that she was, surprisingly, a snuggler. Her leg intertwined with mine under the covers and her head tucked just under my chin. I fell asleep, happy in my new reality in a way I never believed I would be. It was nice to be proven wrong.

* * *

The sun was streaming in through my bedroom window at an angle that let me know it was later than normal. My phone read 8:45. The events of the previous night came rushing back in screaming color, and I turned over to find the other half of my bed empty. Frowning, I swung my legs over the side, testing my knee quickly before hopping up. I'd learned that one the hard way. It twinged, but I was able to walk without any real pain. I brushed my teeth and pulled on a hoodie and a pair of gray joggers before wandering out to my kitchen, really hoping she hadn't gone home without saying something.

I breathed in relief to find her at my counter, a notebook and pencil in hand.

"Good morning, beautiful," I said, making her jump slightly.

"Oh! Good morning. Sorry, I was in my own little world for a second."

"What's that?" I asked, referencing the notebook while I pulled out the coffee maker.

"A surprise."

I raised my eyebrows at her. "What kind of surprise?"

"One you'll like, don't worry."

She shot me a look, a confident smile on her face. She'd apparently been up long enough to re-do her hair into a much less complicated ponytail and start a project. I let her draw while I waited for the coffee to brew.

I pushed a mug to her across the island. She slid the notebook back at me. I looked at it for a long moment.

"Did you hand-draw a logo for the new rec program?"

She just nodded as she took a bite.

"To be fair, I would have probably had a full mockup by now, but I obviously didn't have my laptop with me. I looked on my phone at the logos for the parks and rec department in its entirety as well as the town so I could make something that would fit, and I think something like that will work well. I don't know if they're looking for a logo. They probably have their own designer. Anyway, this is my version of giving you flowers."

I looked at the design again. She had drawn the outline of part of a clover and worked in the first letters of Youth and Sports into the curves of it. Some of the letters had subtle patterns embedded into them that I realized were representative of various sports.

"If you flip to the next page, I made a sigil, which is kind of like a witch version of a logo, if I had to explain it. I would work it in digitally behind the logo image, and it's charged to offer welcoming energy, like a sense of belonging, for the kids who play there. I don't have to do that part, though, if you don't want," she added quickly.

"Why would I not want that? That's exactly what I hope for this program. This is... you're so talented. Is it weird that I didn't really know you could draw? I mean I know graphic design is an artsy sort of field… I just—"

"You've met my mother, no?" She laughed. "I took art lessons for many, many years. I just happen to be a mediocre artist. And I lost the joy in creating it long ago when I realized my mom expected me to make it into a career. Anyway, I usually stick to using software, but thank you."

"Well, I don't think you're mediocre at anything, but I understand your passion becoming your job. Coach Brown reminded me how it felt for the game to be fun. I think I'm genuinely excited about sports without the anxiety of letting everyone down for the first time since I played high school ball. Even if they can't use this logo, I'm having it printed on t-shirts and hoodies for myself. "

"Yeah? I'm glad you like it. And I'm glad you get to be excited about baseball again. You deserve it."

I knew the warm and fuzzy didn't necessarily come naturally for Sam, so her saying that meant even more.

"Will the *sigil* make it like a Care Bear Stare? Like walking around sending out good energy to everyone?"

She let out a surprised laugh. "You know? I don't know that I've ever heard it described better. Completely ridiculous image, of course, but yes. I've done sigil work in the past, but I've never combined it with my designs which seems like it should have been obvious. Anyway, you'll be my Care Bear Stare Design Test Subject."

Her eyes sparkled with amusement.

"Happy to be experimented on." I sipped my coffee and let the caffeine work its way through my body.

She looked thoughtful for a minute. "Jesse…"

"Sam…"

"Do we need to, like, talk about last night? Or about things?"

"We can. I'm fully prepared to embarrass myself by explaining how much I like you."

"I don't think you understand how this works, Garrett. You're supposed to look really torn and tell me how you *do* like me, but your job is just really monopolizing your time, and it's best if we keep things casual. Then you proceed to call me when you want to hook up, and I am forced to consider working some baneful magic as vengeance. It's all very straightforward. I'm sure it was in the handbook."

A flicker of anger surged through me that anyone had ever treated Sam like that, but I was also glad that each of our experiences led us here.

"Yeah, that sounds horrible. I'm going to stick with my way."

"God, I really need to run your whole birth chart to figure out how you got this way," she replied, shaking her head. "But fine, I like you too. Are we dating? Are you not into labels?"

"I'm *so* into labels. I'll happily wear whichever one you want. Boyfriend would probably be the most conventional, but maybe you have some sort of witchy version. Like a familiar? Is that what it's called? Are those only for pets? I have so many questions."

She was shaking with laughter now.

"Please, stop. You cannot be a familiar. But boyfriend would be fine."

Her eyes softened as she said it, and I wanted to kiss her. It took an embarrassingly long moment for me to realize that I *could* kiss her. Because apparently Sam was my girlfriend, and she was sitting in my house wearing my shirt.

"Can I kiss you, then? Because that seems like something a boyfriend would do when his girlfriend is sitting there looking adorable."

"I think we can do better than 'adorable.' You said something last night about 'so gorgeous.' I can't remember, exactly; I was very distracted." I made my way around the island to where she was perched on a barstool.

"You *are*. And allow me to distract you again."

Chapter 39: Sam

I realized my error as I stood at Lauren's door with my arms full. I'd read an entry of Christy's blog about making your own dessert platter, and I fully dove into that project and made two. However, I now faced the conundrum that Lauren had no doorbell, it was chilly, and I could not reach the silly little bee knocker. I settled for kicking the door lightly, knowing she'd kill me if I scuffed the paint with my boot.

"You could have just texted when you got here, and I would have come to help you," she said as she took in the comically large platters I balanced on my arms.

"Well… I didn't think of that. But can you take one now before my arm falls off?"

Lauren just shook her head and took one of the plates. "Oh! This one is like a rainbow!" she exclaimed, setting it down on her counter.

"Mhm! And this one is all black and white," I added, setting the other next to it.

"You do know it's *your* birthday weekend, right? Like you didn't have to make your own treats."

"Seeing your smiling face is treat enough for me, Laur," I said in a saccharine tone.

"I don't know what my brother has done to you, but I don't know if I like it," she replied, her face horrified at my corny line.

"Fine, fine. I hope you got me a kick-ass present since I brought all the sugar."

"Better. Still not quite sarcastic enough, but I believe in you."

She disappeared into her room and came back with a sparkly wrapped gift. I took it from her and almost toppled over because it was deceptively small for how heavy it was.

"Sorry. It's heavy." She shrugged.

"Thanks for that warning," I added, setting the box on the counter.

"Don't open the card! It's sappy, and I don't want to do sappy right now."

"No deal," I said as I ripped open the envelope. It was a Strawberry Shortcake card meant for a child, but it was adorable. It read "Have a Berry Special Birthday!" inside, but the entire left side of the card was filled with Lauren's handwriting.

Sam,

I am just so freaking happy you're back in Emberwood and that you're going to stay. I feel like I've been harsh over the past several months. Maybe that's what you needed, but I still feel kind of yucky about it. I don't think you're lost. I think you've found exactly where you're supposed to be.

And I can't tell you how my heart wants to explode seeing you and Jesse together. I know I don't let you tell me details, but I can see how happy you both are, and that's what both of you deserve. I love you like a sister… (and someday you might be one? Please? Can you two just get to it already?)

I know you'll have a wonderful birthday because you'll be with me. Okay, and Jesse and Zin, but mostly me. Wishing you all the good things for this year.

Love you always,
Laur

Big, fat tears had collected at the corners of my eyes and were slowly sinking down my cheeks.

"See? I warned you! Sappy!"

"I love you too, Laur."

I hugged her, and she hesitated for just a moment. I was not really a spontaneous hugger.

"And you weren't harsh. You were honest, and it was needed. I never felt like you were being mean."

"Okay. Just don't make me do it anymore."

"Promise. It's my turn to give you alllll of the tough love and advice now. Be prepared."

"Oof. I'll try. Now open!"

I redirected my attention to the gift and ripped open the paper. I lifted out a gorgeous crescent moon wreath. It was wrapped in black twine and covered in moss. There was an array of mushrooms in rainbow colors along the bottom curve of the moon, and tiny flowers crept up to the top.

"This is… where did you find it?"

"I went to a farmer's market over in Cloverdale a while back, and there was a lady selling these plus other, non-witchy wreaths."

"I must find her and carry these in the store!"

"Well, I'm glad you love it, but you're not allowed to think about work on your birthday."

"Okay. But you have her card, right?"

"Yes! Open more."

I reached further into the box and pulled out one hair product after another after another.

"It was time, Sam! Your hair is beautiful, and you need to be nicer to it."

I laughed, and my fingers hit a piece of paper at the bottom.

I pulled it out and laughed because it was a laminated coupon like we used to make for Mother's Day at school, promising eight hours of free decorating and style coaching.

"This is fantastic. Exactly what I wanted."

"I know," she said arrogantly, flipping her hair over her shoulder. "Plus, you make that big part-owner money now, so we can have fun with your wardrobe."

"Ha. I make that *little* part owner money now. But yes. New clothes would be good now that I can dress how I want and not for an office job."

I gave an exaggerated shudder at thinking of my black slacks and boring neutral cardigans from days of yore and Lauren scrunched up her face in agreement. "I also brought you a present."

"You *really* don't understand the concept of a birthday."

"Giving presents makes me happy too."

I shrugged. I dug into my purse and pulled out a small black velvet pouch. Lauren pulled it open and took out a small rainbow-colored dragon statue.

"Do I get my own car dragon?!"

"You do. This is Celestina. She's horrified by your driving and says you hit the parking blocks far too often, but she will try to help. Jesse's getting one too, but he's blue, and his name is Cerulean SeaWolf."

"Oh, I *love* her already. I will put you in my car today," she added, speaking directly to the dragon.

I just smiled and took out the second part of my gift.

"Now sit. Eat a marshmallow. You're cashing in on all the advice I owe you from the last four months of doing nothing but crawling through my quarter-life crisis."

I let my cards fly through my fingers and sent up my protection request. Lauren looked surprised and grumbled something to the effect of me needing to look up what a birthday was, but she sat anyway, and curiosity crept into her expression.

"So, about Jer…" I began.

Epilogue: Sam

Five months later: Spring

The sound of the packing tape gun was still annoying. However, I found it was maybe less tortuous than I had previously determined when I wasn't reeling from being fired and having a complete existential crisis. I carefully wrapped the altar table in what I had left of the bubble wrap and placed it in a box.

"Hey, I still have room in the truck for this load. Is this all that's left?" Jesse asked, looking around at the few boxes I'd just finished taping.

"Yeah, I think so. And it's not like I can't stop back by if I forgot something." I shrugged.

This little guest cottage had been a haven for me for the past almost-year, and I was going to miss it. Don't get me wrong, I was deliriously excited about the little two-bedroom rental home Jesse and I were in the process of moving into. It was not far from Zin's, and it was all one floor, a necessity for Jesse's knee, and it had its own little courtyard with a tree and room for some raised garden beds that I'd already gotten approved by the landlord. He owed Zin a favor. I didn't ask.

"Are you sad? To be leaving?"

"Nostalgic, but not sad. I can't wait to set up our office space and let Laur loose in the house to decorate."

"Yeah, can you rein her in a little bit?"

"Nope. I'm throwing away the reins. Lighting them on fire." I picked up a box and followed him out to the truck.

"The things I do for you, woman."

"You just love me," I quipped back. "In all seriousness, though, I promise that we can pick things for the house *together*. I'll stifle Lauren's creativity if I must."

"You just love me, too," he said, pushing the box he was carrying onto the truck and kissing me lightly before taking mine.

I stuck my tongue out at him in a very mature fashion.

"We *are* allowed to actually stay in the new house tonight, yes?"

"New moon is tonight, so yes."

"Of course. Obviously." He held my door open and helped me in before getting in on his side.

"Obviously," I continued when he opened his door. "Anyway, are you going to make it to the book signing tonight?"

"Yep! Game should be over by 6, and I'll change and head there. Are you excited to see your design on all those books at once?"

"I am! I feel like the book is mine, even though I had nothing to do with writing it. My mom texted a bit ago that she flew back from Hilton Head early and is riding down for the signing with my dad. So that's something."

My mom and dad had been on good terms for forever. Their divorce was as amicable as one could be, I supposed, they just weren't great as a couple. It was still a little odd that they would choose to road trip together, though.

"The book is still partly yours, Sam. You put your heart into that cover. And I'm glad your mom recognizes it too. Just... do I need to be ready to run interference?"

Months ago, I'd learned that one of our regular customers was a romance writer, and I fell in *love* with her books, no pun intended. She'd purchased some of the new notebooks in the shop that sported my original designs, and we became fast friends. She convinced me to try my hand at designing a book cover for her next title, and it was finally released today. I was hosting her book launch celebration at the shop tonight, and she was doing a short reading and a signing, and I was something close to giddy about it.

Giddy was never a word I would have used to describe myself, but there was no other way to convey the bubbly, giggly feeling I had at seeing my design on a romance cover.

"I guess it is a little bit mine," I agreed, unable to stop grinning. "And no. I think we've come a long way, and I'm not worried about it. I *am* still upset that the book release is the same night as the season opener. You know the littles are my favorite to watch."

"There will be a bajillion more games, I swear."

"I know, I know. Don't remind me that I have to share you almost every night from now until August."

In addition to working as the assistant director for the program, Jesse had elected to coach two youth teams during baseball season—one five-and-six-year-old team and the other middle-school-aged. I loved seeing the younger ones practice. They tried *so* hard and were so cute when they got a hit, but I knew Jesse was invested in the jr. high team. Those kids looked at him like he was their hero, and he was determined to make sure they had *fun* with the sport. I couldn't wait to see how their season went.

I had originally tried to talk him into only taking on one team, worrying that he might burn himself out or put too much stress on his knee, but the way he'd been coming home energized and genuinely *jolly* after working with his teams, I couldn't begrudge him the months of nights and weekends spent on the diamond. I'd even learned the rules of the game and everything.

"You're the most amazing, supportive girlfriend who ever lived."

He pulled my hand to his mouth and brushed a kiss over my knuckles. His openness with his compliments and affection still took me by surprise sometimes, but it settled around me like a warm hoodie.

* * *

I cleared the last surface of a cupcake wrapper as the evening wound down. The signing was a huge success— Gen sold out of the stock she brought and had a list of at least ten to sign and mail to people. The bookish cupcakes were adorable, and the colors matched the cover I'd designed.

Maybe cake decorating is my next endeavor. We could sell baked goods here at the shop.

I had to stop myself before my next hobby idea took hold. I was too busy as it was. Everyone had cleared out except for our families, plus Jer. I smirked at that.

"That was a wonderful event, Samantha. And you've outdone yourself with this cover. I can't wait to see Genevieve's book with your design on the NYT bestsellers list."

My mom gushed over the cover for the fourth time, and she was still pushing too hard. But she was trying, and I was practicing the art of letting things go.

"That would be an awesome accomplishment. I'm excited, though, because Gen mentioned me in some of her author groups on social media, and someone hired me to work on her next cover. It's a romantic suspense story, and it sounds amazing."

There was a light chorus of excitement and congratulations from my family and friends. I wanted to bottle this feeling and sell it as a potion. I thought back to my indecision from the past fall, worried that staying in Emberwood would be settling for a *small* life. In some ways, this life was small. Or perhaps it was slow. I felt like I got to enjoy my moments and do the things that made me happy without trying to follow someone else's rules. I was reminded every day that I'd made the right decision.

"Hey, Sam?" Jesse called from across the room.

"Yeah, babe?" I answered, making my way to him.

"Can you tell me what this tarot card means? I don't think I've seen this one before."

I felt a smile tug at my lips. I had been teaching Jesse to read tarot. He wasn't bad at reading intuitively, but he was trying to learn all the traditional meanings as well. Sometimes specific decks included their own little signature cards that weren't part of the traditional arcana, so I assumed that's what he had found. He'd been trying to find a deck he liked, and I'd seriously considered creating a baseball-themed deck for him. I let my hand rest on his bicep and leaned over to see what card he was looking at. He stepped back to give me a better view.

It was a hand-painted card, meaning it wasn't from a deck we sold in the store, but it was gorgeous. The image was of a girl with long, dark, curly hair wearing a pretty lace sundress, oddly similar to the one I was wearing. In front of her was a man with shaggy blond hair down on one knee. I took in the details of the card as my brain caught up with my eyes. The title of the card was labeled THE PROPOSAL.

"Jesse?" I murmured, turning to face where he'd been standing.

Only I didn't find him there because he was down on one knee, waiting for me to grasp what was happening.

"Sam, when you came back into my life, I was only just beginning to figure out who I was again, and I think you were right there with me. We've come so far, and I am so excited for everything that comes next. You give your all into everything that you do, and you continually surprise me with not only your talent and creativity, but with your unending loyalty and support for the people you love. I am so privileged that I get to be one of those people. It almost feels like I'm being greedy because I already get to live this amazing life with you, but I want you forever. Will you marry me?"

Epilogue: Jesse

I didn't expect my hands or my voice to shake as much as they were. I opened the ring box to show the amethyst and moss agate ring that both Zin and Lauren said was the perfect engagement ring for a witch, and they swore Sam would love it.

Her mouth dropped into a small "*o*" shape, and I waited patiently.

"How… what?"

She looked around the room at our best friends and families, and she started putting the pieces together that they hadn't all dropped everything tonight because of the book cover, though that accomplishment deserved to be celebrated.

"We're getting married?" she asked, tears welling up in her eyes.

"Well, normally, you'd say 'yes' first, but that would be the desired outcome." I grinned at her; glad my kneeling knee wasn't my bad one.

"Oh my god! Yes! Of course, yes!" she practically shouted at me.

I stood with some effort and took the ring out of the box to slide it onto her finger. Our friends and family burst into excited chatter, and there were plenty of happy tears in the mix, too.

"It's perfect. The ring. The *card…* where did you…" Her eyes floated over to her aunt before she finished the question. "You painted this? It's incredible."

"Naturally, dear. I *have* been taking art classes for the better part of a year. My technique has improved."

Sam gave a watery laugh at that, now staring at her ring again.

"You are too much. I'm going to design you the coolest wedding ring ever, and a coach's jersey that says *fiancé* on the back instead of *Garrett.*"

"*I* was thinking you could design my new tattoo. It could go around my ring finger, but I feel like I need one on the other forearm since you seem to like the skull so much. And this one could remind me of more than a drunken night in Florida."

Her eyes darkened predictably as she ran her nails over my bare forearm.

"You should take me home. To our new house. Right. Now."

She pressed her lips to mine and kissed me perhaps more insistently than she normally might in public, but she got her point across. I quickly thanked everyone for helping me pull off the proposal and tugged my fiancé out into the cool spring air. She seemed to be mesmerized by the ring on her finger, and I had to guide her around a trash can and a pole so that she didn't crash into them.

The only thing she claimed she had to do before making it to our room was to place the tarot card painting on the fireplace mantel.

"There. Now, it's ours."

"Now, it's home," I added, though I was looking at her and not the art.

This was what home would always be.

Prologue- Jeremy

Spring

My eyes were sweating. The spring air was warmer than it should have been when Lauren and I walked out of *Books and Broomsticks,* and this had to be the reason for the watery eyes.

"Do you need, like, a hanky or something, Jer?" Lauren asked, keeping up with me easily on the way to my car, though I had no idea how with the heels she was wearing.

"I have *allergies*, Garrett. It's a well-documented medical condition that—"

"That makes you cry when you see your best friend down on one knee, proposing to the woman of his dreams? You're allergic to commitment? Or love? Or—"

"All of the above, maybe. But fine, it was *nice*. They were both really happy, and..."

Jesus, I thought, my voice already tightening again thinking about Jesse's stupid proposal.

"It was just nice, Laur. I'm sorry I don't have a heart of stone like some people," I said pointedly as we reached my GTI.

Her lips quirked up, but it didn't light up her face like her smile usually did. Guilt tingled in my chest. I wasn't sure what I was guilty of—giving each other shit was what our entire friendship was based on. That, and the fact that her brother was my best friend.

"Thanks for the ride," she said as she slid into the passenger seat. "I really wasn't excited to get a ride home from the happy couple. Or my mother and her tears, though you're now making me think I didn't escape much of anything."

Her smile was a little bigger with that insult, and I just huffed dramatically and put the car in reverse. I opened my music app the moment silence settled around us and started a playlist that I thought she'd like. *Quiet* with Lauren and me was dangerous for too many reasons. I'd crossed the line from friendly to flirting more times than I cared to admit, and even if Jesse seemed to have calmed down somewhat about it, his disapproval was fine with me. I wasn't operating under the delusion that I was let-him-date-your-sister material.

"You can change the song if you want," I said, desperate for something benign to fill up the ride to her townhouse.

"It was nice."

"Hmm?"

"The proposal. It was kind of perfect. I did sound… negative, before. I'm not. My best friend is going to be my actual, legal sister. And they're so happy…"

"I know, Laur. I was just giving you a hard time. Sorry if it bothered you."

Things were getting far too serious, and we still had at least four minutes until I dropped her off. My hand gripped the gearshift to keep from reaching for hers, but I let my eyes drift to her pretty green ones. Her red hair was pulled away from her face but curled down her back. She looked gorgeous, and it killed me not to tell her that.

"No, I know. I just…whatever. I wanted to say it out loud I guess."

She bit her lip like she wanted to say more, but instead she rolled down her window and let her fingers glide over the night air. I sighed, wishing I had the right words or was the right guy to get her out of her head, but I didn't, and I wasn't.

I pulled into her complex and got out. I realized too late that I would never do that for a guy friend I was dropping off at home, and this looked like a date, but there was no turning back now.

"You're upholding the ideals of chivalry, Jer? It's like I don't even know you."

"I just don't want you to fall over in those heels and be held responsible for your concussion. It's a liability issue."

She rolled her eyes, linked her arm through mine, and leaned against me. Even in those shoes, she barely reached above my shoulder. Her hair tickled the back of my arm enough that I felt goosebumps rise in response.

"Your castle, milady," I said with a bow and a horrible British accent.

"Thank goodness you don't have an accent. That would be unfair in the grand scheme of things."

"Because I'm otherwise nearly god-like in my perfection?"

"I was going to say you were cute, but you really took it off the deep end, there."

"I'll take 'cute' coming from you anytime. You look gorgeous, tonight, Laur."

Fuck. This is not the plan.

I'd done so well keeping my mouth shut all night.

She fished her keys from her tiny bag and stepped closer to her door before stopping. Her eyes searched mine for an uncomfortably long moment.

"Do you wanna come in?"

She might as well have asked me to diffuse a bomb with how quickly my heartrate jumped. Every part of my body was screaming at me to already be inside her house with her back pressed against the door, finding out what she felt like under my fingers. But there would be no coming back from that, and we both knew it. It would put a definitive end to this game we played.

"Please don't ask me that," I got out, though it was barely above a whisper.

Hurt flashed across her face, and I hated it, but the hurt would be so much worse if I crossed the threshold—both literal and figurative.

"Fine, Jer. Have a great fucking night." And with that, she was inside, the door slammed and locked in an instant.
I stood there stupidly for several minutes, paralyzed with indecision about how I could make the last ten minutes disappear.

Instead, I shoved my hands in my pockets and made it my mission to kick any stray pebbled on the walkway back into the nearby landscaping. It was safe to say that I would *not* be having a great fucking night.

Chapter 1- Lauren

Three months later: Summer

A nagging sensation was wrapping its way around my spine as I got ready to tone my client's hair.

What am I forgetting?

She was talking to me about her high school reunion coming up next weekend over the Fourth of July, and I felt myself smiling and nodding about the dress she bought with the slit up to her hip as I started coating her newly lightened hair. Then it finally dawned on me that this was *not* the toner I should have been using.

Shit shit shit.

I tried not to let my racing heartbeat and the cold slimy feeling dripping down my back show on my face.

You can fix this, no big deal.

"Hey, Sarah? I think I have a better idea for a toner combo for you that will get us closer to the photo you brought. I forgot it even existed because we *just* started carrying this line, but if you're okay with it, I think I'm going to rinse you and go mix up the other. I honestly think you'll be so happy with it."

I was already pulling her out of the chair towards the sink as I spoke.

"Oh! Okay, yeah, that sounds fine. I trust you!"

Maybe you shouldn't, I thought.

My brain was not here. It wasn't even *there*, it was *everywhere*. My thoughts felt like the carnival that would be rolling into town next week—the lights the sounds the fireworks the smells of fried food—all of it happening at once, and I couldn't temper them. I rinsed Sarah as she changed topics, now chatting about her son and his handprint art that had come home from preschool.

Breathe in and out and fucking focus, Garrett.

I left her at the bowl and went to mix up the *correct* toner that was absolutely not a new brand, paying extra close attention this time. Christian eyed me suspiciously from his station when I came back with the new bottle, and I tried to convey to him what an idiot I was without speaking. He quirked a perfectly lined brow to let me know I'd have to spill it later, but he eased back into his conversation with his client.

My heartrate came down within a more normal range after I corrected my error. Sarah's hair ended up looking perfect, and she left me a hefty tip I didn't deserve. It was good that I had an hour break between appointments to get my shit together.

My iced coffee was sufficiently watery, but caffeine had the opposite effect on me as most, and I needed it. Christian floated gracefully into the chair next to me in the back room and picked up his own coffee, taking a long drink before facing me, his eyeliner still winged to perfection even after the four clients he'd seen today.

"Spill," he demanded.

"How does your eyeliner stay on your face after blow-drying? It's not fair."

"I'll teach you, grasshopper, after you tell me what you did." His chocolate eyes widened in impatience, his dark lashes and arched brows playing along.

"I mixed up a toner that would have been disastrous on her. Like I didn't even think about it, just threw it in the bottle and went on my merry way like an asshole. Thank god I realized it almost as soon as it touched her head, and I made something up about having a better idea from a new line. I need to get my brain together before I screw up something I can't fix."

"It happens to the best of us, darling. Don't beat yourself up."

"Oh yeah? When's the last time you almost had a client walking out of here a brassy blond?"

"Never, obviously. I wasn't referring to myself because my work is impeccable. But you know, everyone *else*." Another sip of iced coffee.

"You're a little bit of a bitch, you know?"

"Takes one to know one. Anyhow, I'm going to get a salad, you want anything?"

"Grilled cheeeeeese."

"You have the taste of a toddler." I just grinned and shook off what remained of my mistake so that I didn't make another one when my next client arrived.

* * *

This pattern of swinging from feeling like I could fall asleep standing up to being so awake I had no choice but to paint my guest bathroom at one in the morning had to stop. I *knew* there was a limit my brain would hit where I wouldn't be able to function, and my mistake at work only proved it.

I was *good* at my job. I didn't make careless errors like that, but lately it just seemed like I could not settle on a single train of thought. My brain was Grand Central, and all the trains were there at once. I dipped the paint roller back into the fuchsia color that resulted from me mixing all the red and pink paint I had left from my *I wanna paint hearts all over my wall* project. I compromised with myself that I'd only paint one wall, and then I'd force myself to lie in my bed and close my eyes and not open them until morning. I was going to kick insomnia's ass.

Interestingly, the thing about sleeping after weeks of *not*, was that I slept for fourteen hours straight. There were texts from my mom, Sam, Jesse, and Christian, and even two missed calls. Everyone knows not to call me unless they are dying.

Uuughhhh.

So much for accomplishing anything on my day off. I slid out of bed and at least threw in a load of laundry. *See? You can do things.*

I put a mini pizza into my toaster over and slumped over in one of my barstools.

235

SAM: Are you off today? I'm only working this morning and kinda wanna go look at dresses. There's a lady who hand makes these gorgeous gowns in Centerville.

LAUREN: Fuck, I just woke up. If you're still in a shopping mood I can be ready in 30 minutes

SAM: Eh, she closes at 5 and I got wrapped up designing invitations anyway. Happy hour at The Bar?

I felt guilt settle in my stomach. I was her maid of honor and should be taking more initiative on helping her with wedding planning.

Add it to the list of shit you should be doing. The pizza dinged, and I bit into it far too early, the sauce rendering my taste buds useless for at least three to five business days.

LAUREN: See you in an hour.

The thought of washing my hair was wholly overwhelming, but I made myself get in the shower to at least scrub off the rest of the fatigue still clinging to my body. I shot off a text to Christian, who'd only sent me a *Clueless* meme, letting him know he should meet us. He and Sam had met a few times, but I needed to make them *friends*.

LAUR: Will my brother be gracing us with his presence?

SAM: I know you're REALLY asking if Jeremy will be joining us to see if you need to have an excuse to bail at the ready, but no, Jesse is doing training for new coaches tonight.

I only validated her message with a middle finger emoji. She didn't appreciate how much creativity it took to avoid him in a town this small, especially when he was Jesse's best friend. I'd made up early appointments I didn't have, home projects that didn't exist, all in the name of making sure I'd only seen Jer in passing since the night he drew his line in the sand. He'd attempted to make two appointments through the salon website, and I'd canceled them and sent him a form message. Because I was petty.

After that disaster, I'd decided that if he had the balls to flirt with me for almost a year, then he should have had the balls to follow through. I ignored the simmer of mixed emotions in my stomach when I thought about what would have happened if he *had* agreed to come in that night.

Maybe you wouldn't *have flipped out and tried to pretend it never happened. It's just as possible you would have fallen in love and gotten married and lived happily ever after.*

My inner voice didn't even believe its own delusional words. But I wasn't prepared to admit that he might have made the right call. There were plenty of very cute tourists in town for the Fourth that would happily come in if I asked them.

Never mind that you have turned down the last two guys that've hit on you.

I frowned involuntarily.

I put my plate in the dishwasher and decided I should leave now and arrive early. That *never* happened, but the guilt about making Sam miss out on a day of dress shopping was weighing on me. I'd get a table and buy the first round of drinks. I checked my appearance briefly, satisfied with how my homemade halter top had turned out and headed to my garage and my little yellow Beetle.

I plopped down at a high top in the back and stirred my vodka soda, wondering if it was always boring being early. I liked arriving once things were in full swing.

"Hey, can I get you another?" a voice asked to my left. My gaze landed on a probably late-twenty-something guy wearing khakis and flip-flops.

Definitely a tourist.

Emberwood was such a random place to be a travel destination, but the town had done a good job over the last fifty years building up events and quaint lodging near Lake Eerie. For a relationship-failure such as myself, it was helpful to have a rotation of cute guys pass through. But tonight, I was going to hype up Sam about her wedding without distraction.

"Ah, thanks, but I'm actually waiting on someone." I shot him what I thought was an apologetic smile. He wasn't bad looking, I just wasn't going to make tonight about me.

"I don't see anyone yet…so what would one drink really hurt?" His grin widened and he leaned too far into my bubble, accomplishing the opposite of his goal, because now I was getting pissed off.

"Do you make it a point not to take no for an answer, Chad? Because it's not a great look."

"Hey, baby, sorry I'm late," a familiar voice murmured in my ear, though certainly loud enough for Chad or Brad or whoever this guy was to hear. Jer's arm wrapped around me from behind my barstool and made goosebumps erupt down my arms.

"Are you here to take our drink order, or should you be fucking off right about now?" Jer asked the guy, his voice as aggressive as I'd ever heard him.

The guy held up his hands like he was surrendering and scurried away back to a group of what I assumed was his flock of douchebags. Jeremy's hands left my body, and I sucked in a breath at the loss. I cleared my throat to hopefully cover it.

"You okay?" he asked, concern in his warm hazel eyes.

"Yeah. I'm good." He stood for a moment, clearly warring with whether or not he was going to walk away.

"Listen, I know you're avoiding me, and you're doing a stellar job, by the way, but do you want me to hang out until whoever you're waiting for gets here?"

"I'm not *avoiding* you. I've been busy."

"Right. You're a horrible liar. You can own it, it's fine. I can sit here while I wait for my takeout, though. I won't even try to engage you in conversation, so maybe you can still count this as another day we didn't talk or hang out." His tone was light, but the words held hurt anyway. *Join the club.*

"Well, I would hate not to check off today on my calendar, but I guess you did me a solid, so I'll figure out how to deal."

He shot me a smirk that made me dig my nails into my palm. I still hadn't recovered from his arms wrapped around me, and he shouldn't be allowed to look at me like that.

"How are you?"

Finding Recipes for Disaster is available for pre-order and will be available for purchase and on Kindle Unlimited on November 12, 2024.

Pre-Order beginning August 1, 2024

Novel available November 12, 2024

About the Author

Nicole resides in the PNW after thirty years in the desert and spends most of her free time with her laptop and an iced tea, enjoying the weather. A former English teacher, Nicole now stays at home with her awesome kids, home schooling and trying to visit every park in her city.

For infrequent and non-spammy updates, including ARC opportunities and the occasional free steamy novella, visit NicoleCampbellBooks.com and join Nicole's newsletter.

Acknowledgements

A huge thank you to everyone who

worked on this book with me:

My beta readers are incredible and made this book what it is.

There would be no book if not for the wonderful women who work the childcare at my gym. You all are all-stars for giving me time to write.

My editor K.F. Starfell for jumping in and giving such amazing feedback in addition to being a great supporter.

My cover designer, MargauxCreates for bringing theses characters to life and creating something I fell in love with.

My readers, new and old, for taking a chance on my book when I switched genres. So much love to all of you!

Last but never least: my friends, my husband, my kids, for being my biggest supporters even when I'm clearly being insane.